MISSION: REPAIR

RISE AGAIN WARRIOR SERIES, BOOK 3

STACY EATON

NITEWOLF NOVELS LLC

ACKNOWLEDGMENTS

The Rise Again Warrior series is so very important to me. Because of that, it gets some extra special tender loving care.

It is with a huge loving heart that I thank Lonnie Mitchell, my friend, my brother, and my fellow demon fighter, for taking time out of his crazy schedule to read over *Mission: Repair* for air force and military references to make sure they were accurate. You do not know how much I appreciate your daily check-ins and constant support.

To my father, who passed last September, but was helpful in helping me plot the story many months ago. I love you, Daddy, and I miss you every single day.

To my mother, who is forever encouraging me and always willing to let me vent, cry, or laugh.

Thank you to my editors and proofers, Kimberly Dawn, Dominque Agnew, and Lynn Mullan. I depend so much on all of you. Thank you for making my work shine.

To my husband, Jason. You are my heart, my soul, my forever hero, and I know that the love that we have for one another rivals that of Brady and Gracelyn. I can never be thankful enough for that—or for you.

And last but not least, to my readers, who have stuck by me through many months of turmoil, stress, pain, and grief. Thank you for your patience and support. It is for you that I write these stories.

AN IMPORTANT NOTE FROM THE AUTHOR:

This book deals with the sensitive subject of suicide. Details in this book could be a trigger to some.

The Rise Again Warrior Series is a series for entertainment purposes only. It is not to diagnose, counsel, or treat depression, suicidal tendencies, PTSD, or any other ailments and disorders mentioned in the books. The writer's words are fictional and based on her personal experiences and perceptions in her creative mind. The characters and situations in the books are fictional, and any resemblance to actual people or events is purely accidental.

If you or someone you know is suffering from suicidal thoughts, please reach out for help! Here are just TWO of hundreds of organizations that will help:

Veteran's Crisis Line: 1-800-273-8255 Press 1
National Suicide Prevention Lifeline: 1-800-273-8255

Military, veteran, or first responders looking for additional non-medical assistance can join the

Angels with Demons' facebook group

DEDICATION

This book is dedicated to the men and women who fight the demons daily and to those who have tragically lost the epic battle.

It is with heartfelt love and honor that I also dedicate it to the following people:

Sgt. Adam Kent Guinn, HSC 244th Engineer Battalion 7/16/80-4/07/20

SN Jack Perdue, Jr. USCG, 5/2/70 – 1/14/14

CHAPTER ONE

BRADY

"What's the first thing you are going to do when you get home?" Wiseman asked as he tossed a wrench onto the tool bench.

"Take a long shower," I said, glancing over my shoulder, "then hug my kids and make love to my wife after my belly is stuffed full of her enchiladas."

Wiseman laughed. "You're going to shower before you even hug your kids? That's wrong, man."

"Yeah, okay, fine. I'll hug my kids and wife, but I want a nice long, peaceful shower. It's going to take at least an hour to wash off all the grime." I stared out the hangar door where we housed the two V-22 Osprey choppers we had on the base. Pretty soon, there wouldn't be any on this base in Afghanistan, and that was quite alright with me. The dry winds outside blew the dust from the fields almost sideways. "I think the dirt from here is embedded in my skin. I'm definitely not going to miss it."

Wiseman glanced out the door. "Yeah, I'll be happy to put this place behind me once and for all. I can't believe we are finally closing this base. I thought maybe when they said they were that they might transfer us someplace else over here."

"I was thinking the same thing since we still had six weeks on our current orders, but I'm glad they changed them. It will be nice to get home early."

"What did your wife say when you told her?" Wiseman asked me.

I peered his way and grinned. "I didn't. I'm going to surprise her and the kids."

"Whoa! Man, I hope that goes over well. Ya know, Tuberlow did that to his old lady and found another guy living in his house."

I shook my head and laughed. "Nah, Gracelyn wouldn't do that."

Wiseman picked up another tool and shrugged as he turned back to the nacelle compartment where he was working on a tune-up of the transmission. "Tub didn't think his old lady would do that either, but she got lonely."

I frowned as I crossed my arms over my chest. "Gracelyn has our kids and her job to keep her busy."

At least, I hoped that was what had been keeping her busy. Tub's wife wasn't the first to find someone to warm her bed while her spouse was on deployment. We heard about it all the time. Some of the wives or girlfriends even hooked up with our friends.

I didn't think that Gracelyn would do that, but I hadn't thought that Tuberlow's wife would have either. They were like the perfect couple and had been together longer than Gracelyn and I had.

I'd met Gracelyn in high school my junior year. The minute she'd walked down the hallway, I'd fallen head over heels in love with her. Well, maybe not quite that quick, but I'd been knocked sideways by her bright smile and mischievous brown eyes. She'd been with two friends, and I'd had no doubt they were all freshmen by the naïve but excited looks on their faces.

That first week, I had searched the halls for her whenever I could. At the end of the week, I'd overheard her talking to a friend about going to the football game on Friday night, and suddenly, I had the urge to see the game myself—only I wasn't going to root for our team but try to get her number.

I found my opportunity to speak with her right before halftime as she stood near the concession stand with her friend. They were whispering to one another with their heads close together, their gazes directed toward a group of immature freshmen guys, not that junior guys weren't just as immature, but we *were* older. I had purchased my drink and then turned toward her, almost bumping into her on purpose. "Sorry, I didn't see you there."

Her friend rolled her eyes. "Yes, you did."

I grinned at her friend but then let my eyes drift to Gracelyn's face. For a few seconds, I couldn't think straight as I stared into her warm milk-chocolate eyes. Her skin was a golden brown from the summer sun, and her eyelashes were long and fluttered as she blinked a few times while staring back at me.

"Hi," I finally said, realizing that I'd been staring at her a lot longer than was appropriate.

Her friend bumped her arm, and she finally replied, "Hi."

"I'm Brady."

"Gracelyn."

"Gracelyn?" I laughed. "Sounds like the name of an angel."

She cocked her head. "Maybe I am an angel."

Right then, I knew that I wanted to be saved from all the evils of the world, and I knew that as long as Gracelyn was at my side, I would be.

We dated through high school, and the day she graduated, I asked her to marry me. I knew without question that she was my future, and when she said yes, it was the happiest day of my life.

Six weeks later, Gracelyn and I said "I do" in a quaint ceremony with our family and friends. Our honeymoon was at a small hotel an hour away near a park where we both liked to hike.

The week after our honeymoon, I left for BMT, our basic military training, with the U.S. Air Force at Lackland Air Force Base in San Antonio, Texas. I hated being away from her for those seven weeks, but when she jumped into my arms at the end of graduation, I thought my heart would burst.

BMT had been one of the hardest things I had ever accomplished. It wasn't because of the physical training—that was relatively easy. Not that it was easy-easy, but I'd always been athletic and had worked out since middle school. It was the mental training that I went through from the moment I arrived that had taken its toll on me.

It was as if once I stepped off the bus, I was in a different world. I had to stand tall, stare straight ahead. I had to listen to everything and keep my mind from wandering off—kind of like it was now. I chuckled to myself as I turned and glanced around the hangar at a few other mechanics working, cleaning, or packing.

Boot camp had prepared me for many things, but when I joined, I had never thought that I would have found the kind of family that I had now—not just Gracelyn, but my brothers- and sisters-in-arms. I would do anything for them—well, most of them. A few were total turds, but even that wouldn't keep me from having their backs if needed.

Back in boot camp, they taught us how to be soldiers—or airmen as we were considered. The mindset was the same, just different terms. We received our first instructions seconds after our feet hit the macadam, and those early few days were a blur. You had to think fast, pay attention to where you were going, and focus on not bringing attention to yourself.

Back in basic, the last thing you wanted was attention. If you were a show-off, you were pushed until you broke. If you struggled, you were pushed until you broke. If you spoke up for someone, you were pushed until you broke. Basically, the drill sergeants did everything they could to crush you.

Some shattered so hard that they left sniveling with their tails tucked between their legs. Some just plain gave up because they thought they were too big and bad to break. We eventually realized that they wanted to do that to us in order to rebuild us to their standards. Once we gave up our old selves, old habits, and bull-headed thinking, we could focus on the new men and women we were meant to become.

I broke in week four, and by the end of the sixth week, I found that I liked the new me that I was becoming. I'd also learned that I was a good leader. Back in high school, I'd been the class clown and had a ton of friends, but I wasn't sure any of them would have followed me onto a battlefield.

The people that I was with now, the ones that I had trained night and day with, well, they would follow me into hell and back.

I watched Wiseman as he sang to himself, pausing as he applied torque to the wrench and then taking the tune back up as if he hadn't missed a beat.

Master Sgt. Stuart Hoyer was heading toward us with Evan, an airman first class, and I turned to them, nodding respectfully. "Afternoon, Master Sergeant, Evan."

"Vanover, how are you today?" Sarge replied.

"Doing well, Sarge. Wiseman is almost done with the tune-up."

He nodded. "Good, glad to hear it." He grinned. "Can't believe we have one more week, and then we are out of here."

"We were just talking about that," Wiseman commented as he glanced over his shoulder. Both of his hands were wrist-deep in the nacelle.

"Thinking about what you're going to do when you get home?" Evan asked him.

"Damn straight," Wiseman replied with a smirk.

The three of them started talking about their plans when they returned, and I shifted off to the side, enjoying the conversation but not feeling the need to partake in it.

Instead, I thought about the day I graduated from BMT. My mother had come, along with my younger brother and, of course, my wife. I had never been prouder of myself. I was proud of the accomplishments I'd achieved and proud of my fellow airmen and airwomen who had been in my training squadron. There were two flights, or groups, in our squadron, and I respected every person in them.

The thirty-nine of us left of my flight had a bond that would last a lifetime. Even now, ten years later, I was in contact with many of them. Sadly, of the thirty-nine of us that graduated that day, seven were dead from training and wartime situations, and another one had committed suicide last year. That left thirty, plus me.

Seeing my brothers and sisters die in battle was difficult, but they had trained us on how to cope when we went through BMT—well, as much as they could anyway. All of us dealt with loss and grief differently.

Like Mackerel, who had been the life of the party in boot camp and had hid pain behind his jokes until he couldn't deal with it anymore, he had succumbed to his despair and put his service weapon to his brow last year.

That had been crushing news coming from another one of my original flight mates a few weeks before I deployed to the Middle East. This was my third deployment, and I was glad that it was almost over. I'd been lucky to be spared the anguish and torment to which so many others had fallen victim.

Just last week, one of the guys in our squadron had lost his mind, drunk as a skunk, and rightfully crying like a baby over a chopper crash that his biological brother had been in six months earlier. It was bad enough that he had died, but Cox had watched it happen when a rogue surface-to-air missile had been shot off by an insurgent hiding in the mountains to our north just after takeoff.

Twenty-two lives had been lost in that attack, and Cox had held it together as long as he could before the demons exploded and took him down. He was home now, despite protests to stay. Hopefully, the counseling he was going through would help—maybe—I hoped so.

"I'm going to head to chow," I told them as my stomach growled. "I'll see you guys there in a few."

As I began to walk across the tarmac, the other Osprey was powering up. A group of marines were gearing up to load.

The engines were loud, and I pressed my hands over my ears as I'd left my hearing protection in the hangar.

I loved the Ospreys and the versatility they had. They were designed to do both a vertical takeoff and landing, or a short takeoff and landing. It brought the conventional aspect of the helicopter and incorporated the long-range, high-speed cruise performance of a turboprop aircraft.

It was a beautiful machine.

I had always been one to love tinkering with engines and mechanisms, hence the reason why I went into Aircraft Electrical and Environmental Systems.

I lifted my eyes above the Osprey as something caught my eye in the distance. Because of the sound of the Osprey, I never heard the missile being shot toward us, but I didn't need anyone to tell me that was what it was. I had seen enough of them.

The world around me slowed as I began to run and wave my arms. I yelled, but my voice got lost in the engines, and it was too late for that anyway.

The Rocket Propelled Grenade clipped the working Osprey's tail and made a beeline straight into the hangar where it exploded into the second chopper where I had just been standing.

The blast launched me off my feet as projectiles spewed in

every direction, and I was slammed into a wall some feet behind me, my head striking so hard that I saw stars. My ears rang at a pitch I had never heard, and my right leg burned like crazy as I crashed to the ground several feet down. I managed to open my eyes once. The smoke was billowing into the blue sky, the flames playing peek-a-boo in the charcoal smoke. On the ground in front of me was a forearm, the name Monica scrolled in dark ink.

As my eyes closed, I had a feeling that I would never see my family again, and Gracelyn's angelic features came to me for only a moment before everything went blank.

CHAPTER TWO

GRACELYN

"*D*ane, go get your brother and get in the car. We are going to be late again!" I sure couldn't afford that. I was close to losing my job already.

"Mo-o-om," he whined in that voice that made me grind my teeth, "why do I always have to go get him?"

I gave him my best annoyed-mom look which wasn't hard these days. "Because Drew is your brother, and I am your mother, and I told you to do it."

"Man, I wish Dad were here," he muttered as he left the room.

Yeah, well, I wished his father were here too. Another month and a half, and he would be. I was counting the days for Brady to detach from his squadron and return home for new orders. I had to hope that, this time, his orders would be domestic-based, or at least on a safe international base, and not in a combat area where we would be required to stay behind.

In the ten years that I had been married to Brady, only three had been spent together for any lengthy period. The rest were pieced together with a month here, a few weeks there, and then he was off to another training class or flown to a base around the world to help repair something before he was deployed for six to nine months in a combat area.

Brady was great at what he did, and I was so proud of him for that. I just sometimes wished that he was not as good of a mechanic as he was. It would be nice if he weren't called to respond *all* the time. Someone else could go instead—really, I wouldn't mind.

Dane came back, dragging Drew by the arm. "Come on, idiot! You're making Mom grumpy."

"No, I'm not! You're making her grumpy."

"Enough! Don't call your brother names," I snapped as I shoved the last of the lunches into their bags. "You're both making me grumpy." I picked up their lunchboxes and gave the boys a final once-over. Both of my boys were miniatures of their father, with dirty blond hair and green eyes. "Dane, where are your shoes?"

"Upstairs."

I rolled my eyes. "Then go get them! Come on, guys. We were supposed to leave five minutes ago! Why would you not put your shoes on? Ugh!"

"I'm ready," Drew said eagerly as his older brother raced from the room.

I put my hand on his head. "Good! Now get your stuff and head out to the car."

Drew collected his backpack from the floor and snatched his lunchbox before spinning and dashing toward the door.

I followed, tapping the toe of my sandal as I stood at the front door and waited, calling up the stairs twice for Dane. Finally, he started down the stairs.

"Let's go, Dane! Get the lead out already! If you walk any slower, you're going to go backward."

He picked up his speed just a little bit, but once he reached me, he stopped and stared up at me with big, soulful, sad green eyes. "I miss Dad."

I sighed. "I know you do. I miss your dad, too, but we don't have time for this right now, Dane." I took him by the shoulder and pushed him out the door so that I could close and lock it. "It's a call night," I told him over my shoulder. "You'll get to see him on the video chat tonight, okay?"

Every Tuesday night, when Brady was able, we chatted via video for about fifteen minutes. Each boy got about five minutes alone with his father to talk about anything he wanted, and then I got the last few minutes. Sometimes, I didn't get as much as the boys did, but that was okay. I figured they needed his attention more than I did.

They were only nine and six, and they didn't understand all this traveling. They knew that their father was in a dangerous place, all their friends' fathers or mothers were, too, and sometimes they heard that a parent wasn't coming home again. That would always rock them hard, and they would miss him more and beg to speak to him. Brady and I emailed in between calls, and I kept him up to date on the good things and a few of the frustrations, but I had learned a long time ago not to write about the rough stuff.

There was nothing that Brady could do from the other side of the world, so there was no reason to bother him with the drama of raising two boys or how I despised my job, and I would be lucky to keep it much longer because I was constantly late or having to leave early.

If Brady knew, he would fret over all of it and feel guilty that he wasn't here to help. His fretting would lead to not concentrating on his job, which would put his life and the lives of the other people he worked with in jeopardy. I sure didn't want to be the cause of that because I was miserable right now.

I heard the phone ringing as I locked the door, but no one called at this time of the day unless it was a telemarketer. I sure wasn't going to lose my job because of one of them.

I rushed the kids into the car and was just about to close the rear door when I realized that I had forgotten Dane's lunch and had to run back into the house. As I did, I tripped over a shoe in the foyer and heard something hit the floor, but after a cursory look, I didn't see what had fallen.

I slipped into the kitchen just as the phone stopped ringing and snagged the blue superhero lunchbox from the counter before hustling back to the car.

I stretched the seatbelt over my soft belly and winced. Man, where had the time gone? I had told myself that I was going to lose weight while Brady was on this deployment. I'd had every intention of starting to work out again and of eating healthier. I had dreams of him coming home and being wowed by my new strength and curves.

When Brady left, I was twenty pounds heavier than I wanted to be, and now, I had added on at least another twenty. I had a whole bunch of new curves now, but not in places that I wanted them.

The problem was, the more Brady traveled, the more I found myself relying on food to comfort my lonely and stressed heart. I didn't blame Brady for my inability to stay away from chips, cookies, and carbs in general. No, that was my fault, but I wasn't sure how to get out of the rut.

Working as an administrative assistant to a rude and egotistical man who, oddly enough, didn't seem to have much respect for military personnel even though he did contract work for them, was taxing all on its own. Every morning, I woke up dreading the minute I would step into the office.

The man was a freaking slave driver, and I started packing my lunch shortly after I started there because I realized that the only way to get all the work done was to work right through lunch. I didn't get paid for that, but at least I had the satisfaction of having finished my work.

Of course, bringing lunch every day was a hassle, and even though I wished I had prepared a healthy salad or cut-up veggies to snack on, I ended up stuffing my mouth full of peanut butter and jelly or cheese sandwiches with crackers or chips. Afternoons always left me dragging, and it would be another cup of coffee and more snacks to give me the energy to muster on.

After work, I was rushing from the office to the after-school program to get the kids. Half the time, I was so exhausted that I hit the drive-through instead of having a home-cooked meal. If I did cook something, it was fish sticks or mac and cheese with tater tots and applesauce. We ate a lot of applesauce in our house since the kids didn't like other fruits and vegetables.

Well, Drew didn't. Dane was getting better at trying new foods. Maybe once Brady was home, and I had time to think straight, I might get a few minutes for myself each day. I could start walking or doing yoga, and I'd be able to plan healthier meals and go shopping without two kids whining about what they wanted and didn't want.

I did enjoy cooking, but it was hard to cook a proper meal for one person daily. Since the other two at the table were so damned picky, it was just easier to eat what I made them, and they barely consumed anything that wasn't on top of crust, had orange-colored cheese, or was breaded in some fashion.

I managed to get them to school without any more mishaps and got back on the road to my office. I reached for my phone that should have been in my slacks pocket and found it gone. Suddenly, I remembered the sound of something falling. I slammed my hand on the steering wheel, cursing softly as I realized that it must have been my phone.

I was lucky to find that my boss, Mark Taggart, wasn't in the office yet. Maybe something good would come out of today after all. I sank behind my desk, quickly waking up my computer and bringing up email while I listened to the messages that had been left.

I jotted down the messages and then grabbed my coffee cup

to fill it up with my first cup of the day. Usually, this would be my second, but I hadn't had time this morning to make one.

I was standing in the small kitchenette when someone stepped in behind me. "Morning, Gracelyn, how are you today?"

I glanced back at Doug, my boss's cousin and partner in the business. He was a kind man, in his mid-thirties and recently divorced. He always had a smile on his face. His hair was a little longer than I preferred and was parted on the side, feathering back toward the left. He also had a neatly-trimmed full beard the same reddish-brown as his hair and large expressive hazel eyes.

"Good morning, Doug. My day could be better. What about you?"

He chuckled as he set his coffee mug on the counter to add sugar to it. "Mine is fine, thank you. Kids giving you a rough time this morning?"

I rolled my eyes. "When are they not? I swear, when Brady comes back, I'm going to go stay at a hotel for a week just so that I can sleep and have peace."

He laughed. "I can imagine. I remember when my kids were that young. They have a lot of energy." He grinned at me. "I'm lucky if they even speak to me now. Teenagers are kind of scary."

I laughed. "I wish they were teenagers. I could use them not speaking to me for a little while."

I removed the coffee pot and filled my mug and then his.

"Is that what is on your mind today?" he asked.

"I was thinking that I can't wait for Brady to be home so I can start cooking real meals again and not eat grammar school food."

He looked at me quizzically. "Grammar school food?"

"Yeah, you know, pizza, mac and cheese, fish sticks, fruit cocktail, grilled cheese sandwiches. I'm tired of all that junk food. I need to start eating better so I can lose some of this weight. Brady is going to take one look at me and see nothing but a fat cow."

Doug put his hand on my arm. "Whoa, Gracelyn, you are not a fat cow. Don't talk like that about yourself. You are a beautiful woman, and I'm sure that Brady will be thrilled to see you no matter how you think you look. He's your husband. He's going to be happy to see you, and if he's not, you just tell me, and I'll make sure to set the record straight." He winked at me playfully.

I laughed as I looked away from him, feeling slightly uncomfortable with his compliment. I knew he was just being kind. There was no way he was serious. "Well, thank you," I told him as I focused my attention on stirring my coffee.

"Anytime, and if you need someone to cook for, I'm always looking for a free meal." He winked again, collected his mug, and left me staring after him.

What the heck was that? Was Doug kidding? Obviously, he was joking. He wouldn't be interested in me cooking him a meal. The idea was absurd.

I went back to my desk and was busy going through the emails when my desk phone started to ring. "Gracelyn Vanover," I said as I tucked the receiver into the crook of my neck.

"Gracelyn, you weren't answering your cellphone!"

I frowned as I tried to place the voice. "Vera? Is that you?"

"Yes," she said, her voice sounding raw. "There's been an accident."

My body went cold. My mind blanked momentarily. Were the kids okay? Of course, the kids were alright. I had just left them thirty minutes ago. Vera wouldn't call me about the kids anyway, her kids were in high school, so if she wasn't calling about our kids, that left only one person.

"Brady?" I squeaked his name out through suddenly dry lips. "Did something happen to Brady?"

"I don't know. I just know there was an accident on base, and men in uniform just showed up at Monica's door."

"What? Monica Wiseman had men in uniform at her door? What did they say? How do you know?"

"I was on the phone with her when they knocked. I heard them say there had been an accident, and then the phone was dropped and went dead."

"Oh, no! I'm at work, and my cellphone is at home, Vera! My house phone was ringing when I left in a rush for work today. What if something happened to Brady?"

"You need to get to your phone!" she said quickly and then began to cry. "No! No! No!" She sobbed in my ear. "Gracelyn, they just pulled up at my house. I can't answer the door, Gracelyn! What if Stuart is dead? I can't deal with this."

"Vera, answer the door. I'm going to head home and get my phone. I will call you as soon as I get there and then come over."

I was already logging off my computer as she agreed, and then I reached for my purse beside my desk.

I was turning to leave when Mark Taggart blocked my path. "Where the hell are you going?"

"Sir, I have to get home. Something happened to my husband and his squadron, but I left my phone at home. I have to get back to the house and find out what is happening."

"You have a job to do. I'm sure your husband is fine."

I lifted my chin. "Sir, I'm sorry, but I have to go. Fire me if you must, but I am leaving."

"If you leave, you will be fired."

I glared at him for about two seconds before I spun and grabbed my coffee mug and the two pictures off my desk. "Don't bother firing me. I quit! You're an ass, Mr. Taggart!"

I hustled around him as he gasped. I was out the door before I heard his reply, and I was shaking so badly when I got to my car that I dropped my keys twice.

A hand on my shoulder stopped me, and I spun to see Doug. "What's wrong?" he asked.

"I don't know, but I have to get home. There was an accident with my husband's squadron, and—" I stopped as bile rushed into my mouth, and I put my hand over it to hold it back as I fought to swallow it. The world around me began to spin.

Doug held on to my arms and leaned down, staring at me. "Don't think the worst, Gracelyn. Let me drive you home. You are in no condition to drive."

I nodded, and he took the keys out of my hand while I rushed around to the other side of the vehicle.

Strangely enough, while I was scared to find out that something had happened to Brady, I knew he was alright. He had to be okay! He had promised me he would be!

I gave Doug directions, and as soon as I arrived home, I bolted from the car and raced to the front door. I had to wait for Doug to catch up because he had my keys, but then I was shoving the key into the lock and pushing the door open.

I was on my knees right inside the door searching for my phone when I found it partially under a jacket that had fallen off the hook. I had six missed calls, and I called into my voicemail with quivering fingers.

When I finally got into my voicemail, I closed my eyes and prayed. "Mrs. Vanover, this is First Sergeant Leeward. Your husband, Technical Sgt. Brady Vanover, was part of a squadron involved in an accident earlier today. Your husband was transferred to Ramstein's Air Base in Germany. I will leave the number for the hospital. You can call them, and they can tell you his condition. I'm sorry for delivering this news over the phone and hope that your husband recovers quickly." He finished up the message with the phone number, and then I sank to the floor. It was only then that I realized I had tears pouring down my cheeks.

He was alive—Brady was alive.

CHAPTER THREE

BRADY

I'd woken up with a jolt to find someone over me. My ears rang, and the smell of burning fuel and flesh irritated my nasal passages. I turned my head at one point and watched people who were attempting to fight a fire in what should have been a hangar.

I should be helping them!

I tried to move, but the person over me pushed me back, and a scream escaped from my mouth. A needle pricked my arm a moment before the world faded away again.

The next time I woke, chopper blades whirled noisily over my head, and I was strapped to a gurney with an oxygen mask over my mouth. Someone was leaning over me again, a helmet obstructing my view of his face as he worked on my leg. At least I thought it was my leg. I couldn't feel much of anything.

My head rolled to the side, and I saw another gurney beside me. Next to it were two people I recognized from the hangar, but their names escaped me. Both of them were injured but not severe enough that they couldn't sit upright. My head rolled slowly to the other side, and I stared at the blur of scenery as we flew. A thought passed through my mind, I never expected my last view of this place to be from this position.

Suddenly, the medic working on my leg touched something, and the pain shot straight up my spine, and I screamed as if he were cutting my appendage off without knocking me out first.

"Hold on, Vanover; sorry about that." There was another prick in my arm, and the world ebbed to nothing.

The next time I opened my eyes, I was in another facility, and the lights and sounds were disorienting. I decided it was better to hide deep inside myself than to face what was happening around me. Part of me wanted to slip so deeply into the nothingness that I would never come back. I wasn't sure why that thought appealed to me. I just knew that it did.

I woke up a little more the next time to find myself on a plane. Around me were quite a few other injured people—some sitting, some lying. The leg didn't seem to hurt as much, and I wondered if I still had it. Maybe I couldn't feel the pain because they had cut it off.

I lifted my hand as a medic came by. "Where are we going?"

"Ramstein. Rest, and once you get there, they will finish repairing your leg. You'll be good as new in no time." He paused. "From what I heard, you were one of the lucky ones."

I frowned. "Lucky ones?" I asked as he shifted away. What was lucky about this? What had happened? I couldn't remember. I tried to bring back the memory, but as I did, it caused significant pain to radiate through my mind, and I ended up letting it go just as I began to see smoke in my mind. There must have been a fire. I sure hoped everyone was okay.

The next time I woke up, I could finally face the world for a little while. I was lying in a hospital bed, slightly upright, with a soft beeping noise beside me. I glanced around the light-blue room, blinking often as my eyes tried to focus. My head throbbed, and so did my leg.

I glanced down to see that my leg was still attached, but a

large section of my right quadricep was wrapped in gauze. My right arm had a few bandages, too, but they were small in comparison. I lifted my head from the pillow to look around, and the room spun. I put my head right back down with a groan.

"Hey, man, you're awake."

I forced my eyes back open and turned my head slightly as another wave of dizziness washed over me. "Yeah, I think I am."

The guy in the bed beside me had a large bandage over his chest and a few tubes sticking out the side. He nodded. "You look awake."

"Where are we?"

"Ramstein."

I blinked a few times. I was in Germany? How long had I been out? "What happened?"

He smirked slightly and then winced. "No idea. I was here when they brought you in. Where were you stationed?"

"Afghanistan." At least I thought I'd been in Afghanistan.

"Ah, I was in Kuwait."

I nodded, but the movement made me dizzy. "How long have I been here?"

"About a day. They brought you here after your surgery. I heard the doc say that you'd probably sleep for a while."

I was about to ask him another question, but a man in blue scrubs stepped into the room. "Hey, nice to see you awake. You got a good clock on the head, I heard. How are you feeling?"

I turned slowly. "Like I'm on one of those carnival rides that keeps going around and around, and I have cotton shoved in my mouth." My mouth was so dry that I thought sand would start spilling out of it.

He grinned and held a cup with a straw out to me. "Take a few sips."

Water had never tasted so fantastic. After I finished, he put the cup back on the tray a few feet in front of me. "That carnival ride feeling should subside soon. It is pretty normal with your concussion level."

"My level?"

"Yeah, you have a major concussion, a grade 3."

"What does that mean?"

"It means that you were unconscious and will probably be very symptomatic for a while."

"Is that why my ears are ringing?"

He pressed his lips together and shook his head. "No, that damage was caused by the blast."

"The blast?"

He studied me for a minute. "Do you remember anything?"

"No, I don't think so."

"Okay, let's start with this." He turned to the computer and began to log in. "What's your name and rank?"

"Technical Sgt. Brady Vanover."

"Okay, Brady, what do you do?"

"I work on aircraft electrical and environmental systems for the U.S. Air Force."

He nodded. "Where were you stationed?"

"Kuwait, no wait. Afghanistan." I pointed to my roommate. "He was in Kuwait."

The nurse nodded again after shooting a glance toward the other bed. "How old are you?"

I paused to think about that. "Thirty?"

"Are you asking or telling?"

"Um, telling. I'm thirty—I think."

"You are thirty. Married?"

"Yeah."

"Kids?"

"Two."

He grinned. "Boys or girls?"

"Two boys, Dane and Drew."

"You're wife's name?"

"Gracelyn."

He hiked a brow. "Pretty name."

"*She's* pretty."

He grinned at me. "I bet she is."

"So you are married with kids, and you were stationed in Afghanistan. What were you doing there?"

I hesitated. "I don't remember. I mean, I had orders to be there. Is that what you are asking?"

He shook his head. "What I'd like to know is the last thing you remember."

I tried to recall and winced as a pain shifted through my head. What *was* the last thing I remembered?

"I was talking to one of the guys I worked with, Chuck Wiseman. He was doing a tune-up on the transmission of our Z-22 Osprey."

The guy next to me spoke up, "You mean a V-22, right?"

I glanced his way, closing my eyes for a moment at the wave of nausea that filtered over me. "What did I say?"

"You said Z-22, but it's a V-22, right?"

"Yeah, a V-22." Why would I call it a Z-22? I knew better than that.

The nurse spoke reassuringly, "It's okay. Sometimes what we want to say and what we do say are not the right thing. It's part of the concussion healing process."

I frowned, perplexed. "Okay, I'll take your word for it."

He stared down at me for a moment. "Brady, do you remember an explosion?"

"No, was anyone hurt?"

"You were."

"I don't care about me; what about Wiseman, or—" I paused. Had there been anyone else with us?

The nurse was watching me as if he were waiting for me to fill in a blank. He would be waiting for a while because my mind was a dark jumbled mess. "Was anyone else hurt?" I finally asked.

"I know that several people were hurt, Brady, some killed. As to who or how many, I couldn't tell you that. Another three people were brought in with you. My understanding is that your location was targeted with an RPG, and one of the helicopters exploded."

"Who was brought in?"

He shook his head. "I don't know. They aren't on this floor. One of them is in serious condition up in the ICU. The other two are in general recovery."

"Can I talk to them?"

"I'll send a note down to general recovery to see if one of them is well enough to visit. I can't have you getting up just yet. We'll see how you feel in a few hours. Right now, I need you to rest."

I stared down at my leg. "What about my leg?"

"You had an eight-inch piece of shrapnel removed from your thigh. While your injury is not life-threatening, it's going to be a while before you are fit for duty again—" He looked away from me quickly, as if he had more to say, but held it back.

"What? What are you not saying?"

He shook his head and pushed the computer off to the side. "Don't worry about it. The doctors will talk to you about it later. Now, I have a message to get a call sent through for you. Your wife would like to hear your voice."

"Gracelyn knows that I was hurt?"

"Yes, Brady. They called her to advise her you were here."

"How long have I been here?"

"Almost two days."

"Two days?"

He nodded. "I'm Chris, by the way, and if you give me five minutes, I'll get that call placed for you."

"Thanks, Chris."

"You got it, Brady. I'll be back in a few."

As he left, I closed my eyes, wondering how freaked out Gracelyn and the boys were. How had they found out?

I must have dozed off, and I woke with a start when a hand landed on my arm.

"Brady, I have your wife on the line for you."

Chris held a phone out to me, and I took it, trying to shift to a more comfortable position. I winced at the pain throughout my entire body, especially up my spine.

"Gracey," I said into the phone.

A sob filtered back. "Brady, oh my God! I was so scared when I heard you were hurt. They said that you would be okay, but I had no clue when I got the message if you were alive or dead. I was going to fly over, but they said you would be coming home in a few days and not to bother doing that."

"I'm okay. Stay there with the boys. How are they? Do they know?"

"They know," she said softly. "The nurse said you don't remember it, but there were a few people who died, Brady. The boys heard about it through friends."

"Who died?"

"Brady," she paused, her voice lowering, "Chuck, Stuart, Evan, a few more, but I didn't know them that well."

"What? All three of them are dead?"

"Yes, Brady. Forty-one people died, six were injured. You were one of the lucky ones."

"Lucky?" I repeated the word. I was trying to recall what happened, but I couldn't imagine anything that might have caused an explosion. The nurse had mentioned an RPG. None of it made sense.

"How are you feeling?"

"I'm okay," I told her, although I was far from okay. My head and thigh were throbbing, my back ached, and my heart felt like someone was jabbing it with a pin. "But I'm tired. I'm going to rest. I'll talk to you again later, Gracelyn. Kiss the boys for me and tell them that I'll be home soon. I love you."

"I love you too, Brady. I'm so glad you are going to be alright. Call me soon. When you get back to the U.S., I'll fly to see you in Walter Reed before you get released."

"Yeah, okay," I said absently. I was still trying to process what Gracelyn had said. Forty-one were dead? Six injured? The whole thing was a blank in my mind, and I gritted my teeth as I leaned my head back and tried to recall what the hell had happened.

I slept on and off. Doctors came in, tests were ordered, and then I'd go back to sleep. My roommate was out of the room. Chris said he was in therapy, and I wasn't sure if that was mental or physical therapy.

I was sipping from my water glass when a nurse pushed a wheelchair into my room. "Turner!" I winced at the sound of my loud voice.

"Hey, Vanover," he said quietly as he tried to smile and get close enough to stick his hand out to me. I shook it and felt a quiver in his fingers.

"You okay, man?"

He shrugged as he glanced over his shoulder at the female nurse who said she'd be back in a few minutes to get him. After she left, he turned to me. "How you feeling, man?"

"I'm alright, I guess. What the hell happened?"

Will Turner studied me with a haunted expression in his eyes. "You really don't remember?"

"Nah, man, I don't remember shit before I woke up here. My wife told me that forty-one people died and six were injured, but I don't really remember anything after my sarge joined us and I said I was going to eat."

"I wish I couldn't remember," he said as he picked at his thumbnail. "I'd give anything for the whole scene to stop playing over and over again in my head."

"Will, tell me what happened, please. Maybe it will help me remember."

He nodded and seemed to brace himself. "I was coming out of the next hangar over, and I saw you leaving the Osprey hangar. The engines had just started up on the one outside, and a platoon of marines was on the tarmac. They were kitting up and preparing to load.

"You were walking toward me but paused, and then you threw up your arms and started to wave at them like you were trying to flag someone down. I glanced to the side just in time to see the RPG hit the first Osprey and go straight through the tail before it exploded against the one in the hangar.

"You went flying ass over teakettle about thirty feet in the air and landed not far from me." He swallowed. "All those marines on the tarmac died, man, and everyone inside the hangar, too."

He shook his head as he stared down at the bandage on his knee. "A minute later, and I would have been dead like them. I was heading over to your hangar to get something." He lifted haunted eyes to me. "A minute earlier, and you wouldn't have been here either."

We stared at one another for a long time.

Finally, he whispered, "Doesn't seem fair. You know?"

I wanted so badly to remember it, but it seemed to hover just outside of my reach. "No, it doesn't seem fair. I wish I could remember it, though."

He shook his head as tears filled his eyes and spilled down his cheeks. "No, man, you don't. You *don't* want to remember it. Be glad you can't, Vanover. I'd give anything not to be able to remember it. Trust me. That shit is going to haunt me for the rest of my life." He put his hand over his face and wept.

CHAPTER FOUR

GRACELYN

I was numb as I sat on the floor of my foyer and stared at my dirty wood planks. I needed to clean this floor. The random thought burst through my mind. Maybe it was because I didn't want to think of Brady injured, lying somewhere that I couldn't get to him. Germany was a world away.

I stared up at Doug, finally explaining what I'd learned. "Brady was hurt. That was a first sergeant calling to tell me that Brady was injured and taken to Ramstein Air Base in Germany. I have to call them to find out how he is. I don't even know how to call a foreign country."

Doug put his hand out. "Come on, let's get you off the floor, Gracelyn. I can help you. Why don't you play the message again, and then I will help you get in touch with your husband. I'm sure he's fine."

I took his hand and let him pull me up. He closed the front door and took me by the arm, gently leading me back to the kitchen. "Put the message on again."

For a moment, it seemed that I was outside of my body, watching the scene from the ceiling. My kitchen was a disaster, with breakfast dishes all over the counter. The dirty pans from dinner last night were still on the stove. The floors needed sweeping, the counters needed wiping down. When was the last time that I had cleaned out the fridge? I suddenly realized that I wasn't alone and shifted my eyes to Doug Taggart who was standing in my kitchen staring at me expectantly.

"What did you say?" I asked him, dazedly.

"Gracelyn, have a seat, and play your message again so I can listen to it." He directed me to a stool, and I sank to it, feeling numb. "Now, put the message on again."

I did as I was told, feeling as if I were on autopilot. What if the first sergeant had lied about his condition? What if Brady wasn't alive after all? What if he had died on the way to Germany or in surgery? What was I going to do then? What would I tell the boys?

I should do the dishes, clean the house up a little bit. Then I could make the call. I could find out if Brady was okay then. For some reason, the thought of hearing he was dead while staring at the dirt in my house didn't seem right. That wouldn't do. People would come over. People would see the mess.

I played the message again but didn't comprehend it as I realized my mother would be horrified at my house. I stared at my phone as it went to the following message, and Doug pushed a button to play it.

"Gracey! It's Vera! Something happened. Chuck Wiseman was killed. They said something about an accident and several people killed or injured. Call me back. I'm totally freaking out."

The next voicemail was nothing but a beep, and then the fourth one was Vera again. "Gracelyn! Why aren't you answering your phone? Oh, good Lord! Did you get a call? Did someone show up at your house? Have you heard from Brady? Please call me. I'm beside myself now."

The next phone call was a reminder for a doctor's appointment, and then Vera was the last one. "Gracelyn, you must be at work. I'm calling you at work. I have to talk to you. Maybe you don't know yet."

After that message, I lifted my eyes to Doug. He was frowning. "I'm sorry about all of this, Gracelyn. Do you want to call Vera back or the hospital?"

"The hospital. I need to know about Brady before I talk to anyone else."

He nodded and started dialing on my phone. He held the phone out to me, but I shook my head. "Can you do it, please, Doug?"

"Sure." He hit call and then waited for the line to connect internationally. "Hi, I'm trying to find out if a patient has been admitted there."

There was a pause. "Brady Vanover," he stated as he glanced at me.

He was quiet again. "This is a friend of the family. His wife, Gracelyn Vanover, is right beside me but asked me to make the call because she is rather emotional at the moment with the news."

He nodded. "Yes, I'll hold, thank you." He waited and then gave Brady's name and mine also. "Okay, and how long do you think that will be?"

He turned to me and gave me a slight smile. "Alright, we will call back then, thank you."

He hung up the phone and set it down. "Brady is there, and he is in surgery."

"Did they say what was wrong with him?"

He shook his head. "No, they didn't, but they said it wasn't a life-threatening injury, so that's a good thing, Gracelyn."

"He's going to be alright?" Dare I hope?

"Yeah, it sounds like it. The person on the phone told me to call back in about two hours, and they would let us know where Brady is and what's going on."

I put my hands over my face and started to cry. A moment

later, Doug put his arm around my shoulders. "Come here, Gracelyn. You can let it all out on my shoulder."

I got to my feet and curled against Doug's chest as the sobs broke out. Brady was going to be alright. I wasn't going to have to explain it to our sons. I wasn't going to have to inform Brady's mom or his brother. I wasn't going to have to live my life as a widow and raise two children alone. Brady was going to come back to me.

It was a while before I calmed down, and reality began to take over as I turned to Doug who was making me a cup of coffee. "Doug, I can't believe you did all of this for me. I'm fine. I swear I'm fine. I know you have so much to do at the office. You don't need to sit here with me anymore."

"You sure? I could wait till you call the hospital again."

I shook my head and stood. "No, really, I'm alright. The shock has worn off, and I know that Brady is going to be alright. I'm going to call them in another hour and then check on Vera and Monica."

"Alright." He wrote something down on the notepad on the counter. "Here is my phone number. If you or the boys need anything, you let me know."

"I appreciate it, Doug. You have no idea what it meant to have you here."

He cupped my cheek momentarily before he smiled and turned away. "I'm glad I could be, and don't worry about your job. If you still want it, I'll make sure you still have it."

I laughed slightly. "No, that's alright. To be honest, I hated working for your cousin."

He snickered. "Just between us, I kind of hate working with him, but believe it or not, I'm going to have an opening for an admin assistant in about three weeks."

"You are? Why? Is Bonnie leaving?"

"Yeah, her husband got new orders. She just told me yesterday."

Could my luck be that good? "You know what, Doug? I might take you up on that but give me a day. I need to figure out what's going on around here and when Brady will be getting home, but I sincerely appreciate the offer."

"You're welcome, Gracelyn. Again, give me a call if you need anything. I'm more than willing to help."

I walked him to the door, and as he turned, I stepped forward and hugged him again. This morning, if I had thought about hugging Doug, I would have laughed at myself. I barely knew the man, but he had been there for me when I needed someone, and I appreciated that more than he knew.

"Thank you, Doug." I opened the door and paused as I stared out. "Oh, crap! You drove me here."

"Don't worry about it. I'll call a car. You have enough on your mind."

"Thank you again, Doug."

"Glad he's going to be okay, Gracelyn. I'll talk to you later."

He took the three steps down, and then I closed the door and headed back to the kitchen. I bypassed it and went into the small family room where I stopped in front of a picture frame. It was from our honeymoon, and I lifted it, smiling as tears filled my eyes again.

"Come home to me, Brady. I don't care what might be wrong with you. No matter what, I will take care of you. Just come home to me."

For a long moment, I stared at the beautiful man who was the love of my life. Ever since I had known him, he'd had broad shoulders from working out—every muscle on his body lean and strong. How I wished I could run my hands over his short dirty-blond hair and caress the handsome face that smiled back at me from this picture. For another hour, I thought about my life with Brady and the ups and downs. I frowned at some of the fights we'd had and then realized how trivial they all were now.

The only thing that mattered was him coming home to the boys and me.

The boys! I glanced at the clock to see it was only eleven in the morning. I rubbed my temples. So much had happened in just a few hours that it felt as if it should be five in the afternoon.

Finally, it was time to call the hospital again, and I followed the directions that Doug had given me to make an international call. I asked for information on my husband and was transferred to a nurses' station.

"Hi, this is Gracelyn Vanover. I'm trying to find out the status of my husband, Brady Vanover. The last time I called, they told me he was in surgery."

"Hi, Mrs. Vanover, this is Chris, Brady's nurse. They just brought him up from recovery a few minutes ago, and I haven't had a chance to look at his chart yet, but let me see what it says."

"Thank you."

He asked me some other basic information about Brady to confirm that I was his wife, and then he told me to hold on a moment as he read the notes.

I tapped my toe on the floor as I waited and closed my eyes when he finally started talking. "Okay, so it looks like Brady had a piece of shrapnel removed from his leg. It doesn't look too serious, but he's going to need some physical therapy. The doctors also commented on a possible concussion, but until he is awake and can answer questions, I can't tell you much about that."

"Do you know what happened?"

"The only thing in the medical report was some kind of explosion trauma."

"Explosion? What exploded?"

"I can't tell you that, Mrs. Vanover. You'll have to wait until he's awake and can answer those questions himself."

"Okay, well, when do you think he'll be awake?"

"It's probably going to be a few hours. Your husband will be very groggy after the surgery, and depending on the damage to his brain, he might sleep for a day or two."

"A day or two? Do I need to fly over to be with him?"

"No, I don't think so. I have a feeling they will discharge him in a couple of days. It would not be worth the travel for you to come this far. You'd no sooner get here and then have to return. You'd be better off waiting until he got back to Walter Reed and then figure out his game plan."

"When do you think I can talk to him?"

"What I can do is put a note in the file to call you once he's awake long enough to hold a conversation. I have a feeling he's going to wake and doze on and off for a few hours, but he's out of the woods. His injury is not life-threatening, and he should be home to recover soon."

"Thank you. Please have someone call me when Brady is awake."

"I sure will, Mrs. Vanover."

I made sure he had my cellphone number, and then after I hung up from him, I sighed. I hadn't spoken to Brady, but at least he was going to survive and come home. That was the best that I could ask for now.

Now, what about Monica and Vera?

Suddenly, I needed to get to them, and I grabbed my purse, phone, and keys and rushed out of the door.

I drove to Vera's and found several cars parked there. I made my way to the front door and hesitated before opening it. I could hear voices on the other side, and I knocked twice before I opened the door. A woman turned to me, her eyes sad. She stepped forward. "Hi, are you a friend of Vera's?"

"Yes, our husbands were stationed in Bagram together."

Her eyes went wide. "Who is your husband?"

"Brady Vanover."

"Was he there?"

"He was. He's in Germany now."

She looked instantly relieved. "So he survived."

I nodded. "What about Stuart?"

She shook her head. "Charles and Evan didn't either. Vera was asking if anyone had heard anything about Brady."

"Where is Vera?"

"In the living room."

I thanked her and went to find Vera. On the couch in the living room, both Vera and Monica sat together holding hands. They were both staring off into space, lost in a different time and place. Monica saw me approach first, and she shifted her body forward.

"Brady?" Monica asked, and Vera's eyes lifted to mine. A knife stabbed me in my gut at the pain in her eyes. Vera and Stuart had been so close. They were like the perfect couple, and Brady and I had often commented on how we hoped that we were still as happy as they were when we reached our twentieth anniversary.

"He's alive. He's in Ramstein recovering from surgery. I haven't spoken to him yet."

Vera burst to her feet and threw her arms around me. "Oh, Gracelyn, I'm so glad he's alive. I couldn't bear the thought of all three of us losing our men."

I stared over her shoulder and wondered if Monica thought the same thing, but I was reasonably sure that she would have wished she could trade places with me in an instant.

CHAPTER FIVE

BRADY

$\mathcal{I}$t was six days later when they prepared me to fly back to the United States. I was anxious to get back on home soil. I knew that once I arrived, I would be at Walter Reed Hospital for a little while to continue my therapy and recover before they sent me back to Buckley Air Force Base in Denver where my family was waiting.

They weren't doing much exercise on my leg right now because the damage to the muscles was extensive, and they wanted it to have a few more days to heal before they pushed the therapy. It also didn't help that anytime I was upright, I was hit with vertigo so bad that I thought I'd be face-first on the floor within a second.

I could deal with the pain in my leg but hated the fogginess in my mind. I also wasn't a fan of the pain that spiked up and down my spine. The doctors kept saying that the pain in my spine would go away and had been caused by slamming into the wall when I'd gone airborne.

Of all the things happening in my body, my back seemed the most painful. After all this time, I would have thought that part of my injury would have started to heal. I asked them to do more tests, but they said they couldn't. If they did more tests, it would keep me from returning stateside.

One of my doctors told me to bring it up with my Walter Reed team and see what they said. I didn't want to be stuck here any longer than necessary, so I kept quiet. Instead of doing more tests, I greedily accepted the pain medication that they gave me. Before this incident, I wouldn't have even taken acetaminophen for a headache. That told me just how bad the pain was.

I still couldn't remember what had put me in this hospital bed, and several people told me that, eventually, the memory would return; however, as I remembered what Turner had told me and how he had melted down into a sobbing mess in front of me, I wasn't so sure that I wanted to know anymore—only I was determined to recall the incident. How could I mourn them or move on with my life if I didn't even know what happened to them?

Turner was one hell of a strong man, and I would never have imagined him crying like a child into his hands. That almost disturbed me more than the thought of what had happened.

I tried to picture Stuart, Chuck, and Evan dead, but I just couldn't seem to wrap my brain around it. Stuart and I had hung around at home together. Our families got along very well, and we always enjoyed our evenings around the grill. Chuck and Evan were close to me, too, but there was a divide between our ranks.

Stuart was our master sergeant, and the other two were senior airmen who reported to me, and then I reported up to Stuart. When the uniforms were off and the beers were pouring, we were all equal.

Our wives leaned on each other during our deployments, and I never worried about Gracelyn not having help with the boys. I did not doubt that Monica, Vera, and Shana were there to help if needed.

I began to wonder what was going on back home. All three of them were widows, all seven of their children were fatherless. What happened to them now? Where would they go? How would they deal with this blow? Gracelyn and I had never spoken of what would happen if I died. Had any of them?

I realized that there was a good chance that I wouldn't even make it back in time for their funerals, but then again, I had no idea where any of them would be laid to rest. None of them were from the Denver area. Stuart was from Ohio, Evan from Oregon, and Chuck from Arizona. There was no way I'd be able to attend any of their services, and that hurt.

On the flight back to the United States, I dozed and reminisced over good times with the men. The laughs, the moments of tension, the talks of wishes and dreams, and whispers of our fears. I tried so hard to push through the block in my mind, to remember our last moments together, but no matter what I did, I couldn't find it and would only cause myself to get an extreme pounding in my head.

One day I would remember, and I could mourn them then. Until then, I would fight to get back on my feet.

Three days after I arrived at Walter Reed, my wife finally arrived. As she rushed to my bedside and leaned down, I saw the anxiety, the tears, the sadness in her face, and I cried for the first time since the incident. I had put those feelings there in her heart and mind, and I was sorry.

She had no idea how wonderful it was to see her, and after a few emotional kisses and hugs, she leaned back and looked me over. "You have no idea how happy I am that you are back in the U.S."

I wiped the last of the moisture from my cheeks. "Yeah, well, if this hadn't happened, I would have already been home." She gave me an odd look, and I explained, "We were being sent home early."

"You didn't tell me that."

I grinned at her. "No, I was going to surprise you and the boys."

She squeezed my hand and chuckled. "I would have much preferred that surprise to this one, Brady."

"I'm sorry, Gracey. I would have too. How are the boys?"

"They are good. My mother is with them, and they can't wait to have you home. Do you know how much longer you're going to be here?" I shook my head and winced, causing her voice to shift into her soothing worried mom voice. "Oh, Brady, what's wrong? Are you in pain? What can I do?"

I laughed slightly. "No, the pain meds keep most of the pain at bay, but if I move my head too quickly sometimes, I get this incredible wave of vertigo that throws me for a loop."

"How long until that goes away?"

I shrugged as I leaned my head against the pillow. "I don't know. They tell me it could be a week or a month."

"Really? You would think that would have gotten better already." She returned my shrug. "You'll get through it, Brady. You always get through things."

I was glad she had so much faith in me. "Speaking of getting through things, did your boss give you a hard time for leaving?"

She bit her bottom lip, a trait that always told me the following words out of her mouth were not going to be good. "Um, about my job."

"What? Did they fire you?"

"No, I kind of quit, Brady."

"Gracelyn, why would you do that? I thought you liked your job, and we needed that money right now."

"I know we did, and I did like my job. I just despised my boss."

She hated her boss? "How long have you felt that way?"

"Since about a month after I started." She winced.

"Why didn't you tell me?"

"I didn't want to worry you. You were getting ready to be deployed, and you didn't need my stress. I tolerated Mark Taggart as long as possible, but I quit the day I found out that you were hurt. He told me if I left, he'd fire me. I decided to quit instead"—she put her hand up—"but don't worry. I have another job starting as soon as I get back."

I closed my eyes as my head started to thud a bit more. "Where are you going to be working now?"

"Do you want to rest, Brady?"

I shook my head, winced, and then peered at her from under hooded eyes. "No, keep talking. I get headaches if I have my eyes open too long, so don't mind me if I sit here with them closed."

"Oh, well, that is kinda yucky. Um, I'll be working at the same place, just for the other partner, Doug Taggart."

I barked out a soft laugh. "How did that happen?"

"The day that I quit, I was too upset to drive, so Doug brought me home, and he's the one that called the hospital to confirm you were alive and in surgery. I couldn't do it. I really couldn't do anything because I was too afraid to find out you were dead." She paused for a moment. "But then we found out that you were alive, and I fell apart, and Doug was nice enough to comfort me and then offered me a job. Bonnie, his admin assistant, is leaving this week. Her husband is being transferred to South Carolina."

I opened my eyes, keying in on one thing. "How did he comfort you?"

She blinked. "What do you mean, 'How did he comfort me'?"

"Did he pat you on the shoulder? Give you tissues?"

She frowned. "No, he let me cry on his shoulder." She gave me a stern look. "And Brady Lance Vanover, don't you *dare* say he was flirting with me. He was kind and helpful, and he was worried about the boys and me."

41

"So he comforts you and then gives you a job?"

"He knows I'm good at what I do, and he said he doesn't like his cousin any more than I do."

My head began to pound harder, and I closed my eyes again. "Fine, as long as he keeps his hands to himself."

"Seriously, Brady? Where is this coming from? The last thing you need to worry about is me cheating on you. I love you to death. I've been worried sick about you." I heard the tremor in her voice and opened my eyes to look at her.

"I'm sorry, Gracey. I'm not thinking straight. All these pain medications and the headaches wear me down and make me see things in an odd light."

She squeezed my hand. "It's okay. You just focus on getting better, honey. We are here for you every step of the way."

"Speaking of being there, how are Monica, Vera, and Shana doing?"

Her voice softened, and I could hear the pain in it. "Brady, they are all devastated. I tried to imagine what they were going through, but I just couldn't—thank God—and I think Monica is jealous that you are alive. She won't even talk to me."

"Are you serious?"

"Yeah, Shana has already packed the kids up and gone back to her parents. They are supposed to move her belongings in a few weeks. She couldn't even be near the base anymore. She fell apart every time she saw someone in uniform." She shook her head. "I saw Vera before I came here. She hugged me and told me to give you her love. She said Stuart thought so much of you, and she wanted you to know that she is praying for a quick recovery and for you to get back home soon. She's holding up really well. I honestly don't know how, but she is doing it. I haven't seen Monica since we found out."

"I wish I could attend their services."

"Yeah, I do too," she said softly as she ran her thumb over the back of my hand.

I pulled my hand back after a moment as I became strangely annoyed at her touch. "I'm going to rest a bit, okay?"

"Go ahead. I'm going down to the lounge to call your mom and your brother, and then I'll check on the boys and get a cup of coffee. I brought a book with me so I could read while you rested or were in therapy. I also brought you some of your favorite shorts and t-shirts and the boxers you wanted with your other shaving kit."

"Thanks," I mumbled as I slipped into sleep.

*W*hen I woke up again, Gracelyn was resting with her head back, her eyes closed, and her book closed in her lap. I studied her while I could. She looked tired, stressed, and her brown hair looked brushed in a hurry, but she was still beautiful even with the extra weight that she had gained.

What had she been doing while I was gone? Had she not been taking care of herself? Gracelyn had told me when I had left on deployment that she looked forward to losing the few pounds she had recently put on, but she looked like she'd gained a bunch more—not that I cared. I loved her for her heart and mind, not her body measurements.

As I reached for my water glass, I thought that the two of us could work together to get back in shape. Gracelyn could help me with my therapy exercises, and I could coach her into losing the extra weight. We would work as a team, and before we knew it, we'd be back to where we both wanted to be. I'd return to my job, and she'd be wearing those sexy skirts that I liked so much.

It was a good goal for us both, and I figured that I would tell her about it when she woke up, but an orderly arrived and helped me to transition from the bed to the wheelchair because it was time for therapy to begin.

Gracelyn woke up while I transitioned over to the chair. "Where are you going?"

"He has therapy now," the orderly said. "You can wait here or come back later, but he's going to be busy for several hours."

"Hours?" I asked as I looked up at him.

"Yeah, you have to go through testing, then meet with one of our physical therapists for final questions about how you are doing and what is hurting, and then you have an appointment with a staff psychiatrist before you go back for your first PT session."

"Why is he seeing a psychiatrist?" Gracelyn asked.

"It's normal procedure after an incident like Brady was involved in. They want to make sure he is doing well and doesn't have any issues from the traumatic experience."

"Well"—she stood—"I guess I'll go back to the hotel. Why don't you call me when you return to your room? I can come back then, and you can video chat with the boys."

"I can do that."

She leaned down and kissed me, squeezing my hand. "I'll see you later."

"Bye, Gracelyn."

She gathered her stuff as I left, and I looked forward to getting back and talking to the boys.

Only that's not what happened. By the time I returned to my room—four hours later—I was in so much pain that I couldn't keep my eyes open, and all I wanted to do was take my medication and pass out. Gracelyn and the boys would forgive me. I just needed a little bit more time to heal—just a little bit more time.

CHAPTER SIX

GRACELYN

*B*y day four, I had begun to realize it might be better if I returned home. It wasn't that I didn't want to be here for Brady, I did, but my mother told me that Dane was acting up more than usual. Drew was crying himself to sleep every night and having nightmares. I might have pushed to stay a little longer, but Brady didn't seem to want or need me around.

When I arrived in the morning, we would talk for a few minutes, but he always had therapy appointments or more tests which kept him busy almost all day. Once I was invited to the therapy gym and watched for a little while, but Brady told me to leave because he didn't want to bore me. I had a feeling that he didn't like me seeing him struggle.

I also was asked to attend part of a meeting with the psychiatrist. That hadn't lasted long. After he gave me a little information about traumatic brain injuries, he asked me to leave so he could continue his session with Brady.

Brady didn't seem to understand that I loved him enough to be there for him while he was struggling, whether it was physical or mental. I wanted to encourage him, push him harder, and be his biggest cheerleader. Unfortunately, he did not want me to do any of that. When I would broach the subject, he would say that I didn't understand what he was going through or that I didn't understand how hard this was for him.

I wanted to understand, but he refused to talk any more about it, and he never spoke about the incident at all. When he returned to his room late afternoon, he was always exhausted, cranky, and in a lot of pain. I would try to console him, brush my hand over his head like he used to enjoy, but he would push me away. He would send me back to the hotel before we even had dinner together.

Day five arrived, and I already had my stuff packed and was ready to head to the airport. I was able to change my flight, and I would be back in Denver by dinnertime.

Brady was sitting up in bed, glaring at the paper in front of him as he ate his breakfast when I entered, wheeling my suitcase with me.

"Morning, sweetheart. How was your night?" I asked him.

"Alright." He glanced at my bag. "Where are you going?"

"I need to head home."

"Why? I thought you were staying a couple more days."

"The boys are having a rough time with me being gone. I need to get back to them, and you're so busy that it doesn't make any sense for me to be here sitting around waiting for you when they need my attention."

"What about me? Don't I deserve your attention?"

I gaped at him, my lips parted slightly. "Brady, I've been here for four days, and you have barely spoken to me. You don't want me near your therapy sessions, and when you finally have time to talk to me in the afternoon, you are too tired or hurting too badly to do so. I think the boys need me a little more than you do. You need to focus on your therapy and rest. Then come home so we can get back to our life."

His voice was stern as he asked, "Am I holding you up from something?"

I stared, confused for a moment. "No, of course not. Brady, what's going on?"

"Nothing. You just seem to be in a hurry to get home all of a sudden."

"You know, if you had been more open to talking to me or sharing what was going on with you, I might have figured out a way to stay a few more days, especially if you had been able to talk to the boys in the evening. They think I'm lying about your progress."

"They think I'm not getting better?"

"They have no clue what you are doing. You haven't spoken to your sons since I've been here. You keep saying tonight, tonight, tonight, but then you are always asleep. I get that, but you don't seem to even want to talk to them."

"Fine, call them now."

"Brady, it's like six in the morning back home."

"So get them up. I'll talk to the boys now."

"Brady, that's not a good idea. My mother will be sleeping too. I don't want to disturb them."

"Fine, then don't complain that I don't talk to them."

Who was this grumpy man in front of me, and why was he snapping at me like this? I stepped closer to the bed.

"Brady, did you get some bad news that you aren't telling me?"

"Why would you think that?" His voice was little more than a growl.

"Because you are very testy with me, and I don't understand it. You're never like this."

"Yeah, well, whatever." He shrugged and pushed his breakfast away half-eaten.

"Aren't you going to finish your breakfast?"

He sneered at me. "No, I'm sure you want to though. Go ahead."

I jerked back. "What is that supposed to mean, Brady?"

He closed his eyes and shook his head. "Nothing, just go. I'll talk to you later." I went to the side of the bed and took his hand. He let me hold it for about two seconds before he pulled it away. "Go, Gracelyn. I need to rest before therapy."

I leaned forward and brushed my lips over his cheek. "I love you, Brady. You'll be home soon, and things will get back to normal."

His eyes snapped open so quickly that I jerked back slightly. "Normal?"

"Yeah, you'll be up and around and back home with the boys and me. You'll get back to work, and things will be normal."

He studied me, his green eyes looking slightly vacant. Was that because of the pain medication that he was on?

"Gracelyn, things will never be normal again. Just go home and take care of the kids. I'll be back as soon as I can."

I wanted to ask him what he meant about how things would never be normal again, but I didn't. He turned away and closed his eyes again. My heart ached because I couldn't think of how to help him.

After a few seconds, I left his room, pulling my bag behind me while leaving a piece of my heart floating aimlessly in the space around him.

---

*T*he boys were thrilled to have me home, and after an initial "When is Dad coming home?" they didn't mention him again. Sadly, they were used to him being gone and me being there to hold down the fort.

It wasn't until they were in bed that my mother and I sat

down on the sofa. She didn't need to say anything. I saw it in her eyes.

"He's going to pull through this, Mom. He's doing lots of therapy for his leg, and his head is starting to feel better. He doesn't have as many headaches."

"Did he talk to you about the explosion?"

I shook my head. "Not really. The only thing he said was that he didn't remember it and wished that he did. One of the therapists had me attend a session with Brady for a few minutes and explained that his brain suffered such an impact after the explosion that it damaged that memory area of his brain. He said that one day the entire thing might return to him, or it might never come back to him. Brady is very frustrated with that."

"I can imagine. You know that Brady always likes to be in control, and the man can remember everything."

"Yeah, his memory was always fantastic—almost photographic. I think it's going to be a long time before he gets back to where he was. He forgets words sometimes and seems confused when he tries to explain something in detail."

"If he's having such a hard time, why did you come home, Gracelyn? You know the boys were fine. Yeah, they were whiny because they missed you, but you could have stayed a few more days."

"No, I think Brady needed and wanted to do that part on his own. He barely spoke to me the entire time I was there, Mom. Most of the day, Brady spent out of his room in therapy and different appointments. He didn't want me hanging around for those, and when he got back at night, he was cranky and in pain. He barely ate dinner, and then he was asleep halfway through his meal most of the time."

"Aw, honey. Brady's body has just gone through a horrible trauma. He'll be better in no time."

"I hope so, Mom. I really hope so. I hate seeing him so

discouraged and angry. You know he got angry with me when I said I was coming home. I tried to reassure him that things would get better and get back to normal soon. He told me that things would never be normal again. What does that mean, Mom?"

"I don't know, sweetheart, but you are just going to need patience and be strong for him and the boys. I'm sure he was just disappointed that he wasn't coming home too."

"Yeah, maybe."

"Just be glad he's okay. Brady will bounce back before you know it, and you two will be busy running around with the kids, and this will all be a bad dream. Be thankful that he's alive, Gracelyn. You could be in the shoes of one of those other women."

"I know, Mom. I thank God every day that he didn't take Brady. I'm not sure what I would have done without him." I paused. "I can't imagine what Monica, Vera, and Shana are going through—or the other wives. I didn't know the other two wives from his squadron, but my heart just breaks for all of them. I don't know what to say to them—not that I have to worry about Shana—she's already gone—but I'm sure to run into Vera and Monica."

"If you see them, focus on how they are doing. Don't bring up Brady unless they ask—but let *them* ask. Don't brag about him being alive or home."

"I would never do that, Mom! It's just hard. I could have been in their shoes, and then what would I have done?"

My mom took my hand. "Then you would have come home, and your father and I would have helped you with the boys while you healed. You don't need to think about that, though, Gracelyn."

She was right. I shouldn't be thinking of that. I needed to focus on the positive and be ready for when Brady came home and needed my attention.

*T*hat didn't happen for another four weeks. Brady had told me that he was having trouble walking because his back hurt too much, and they finally did more tests and found that he had two cracks in his spine. He had to have surgery again, and a rod was placed against his spine to fuse it and correct the problem. It wasn't until he was finally able to stand for short periods that he could come home.

I had wanted to be there for his surgery, but he told me to stay home. Our conversations were shorter and shorter these days, but I knew that all of that would change once he got home.

Almost eight weeks after the injury, he finally arrived home. The journey was long and painful for him, but he was in a positive mood when he finally arrived—at least for a few minutes.

The boys were told repeatedly to be gentle with him, but the minute they saw him, they raced to his wheelchair and jumped into his lap. I could see the pain in Brady's eyes, and he was barely in the house before he said he needed to take more medicine and lie down.

For the next week, Brady spent a lot of time in bed, and when he was out, he was on the couch watching television or sleeping. If either the boys or I woke him up, he was testy and tense. Just last night, he had yelled at Dane for being too loud as he came in from outside and muttered that he should have stayed in the hospital where it was quieter.

After a few days of his temper and moodiness, the boys and I kept our distance and tiptoed around the house. He hadn't even gone to his therapy appointments since he'd been back, and I had tried to talk him into going, but Brady said he was in too much pain. After every conversation, Brady threw down a few more pills and gave me the cold shoulder as he rolled away.

After a week, I was tired of it. This was not the man I had married, and he needed to be thankful he was alive and get back to his life. "Brady, you need to get back to therapy. They keep calling to reschedule your appointments. You're never going to recover if you don't."

"Don't pretend to know what I need, Gracelyn," he snarled my way.

I stared at the back of his head as he once again lay in the dark bedroom. "Brady, what is going on? I'm only trying to help, but every time I do, you push me away. Tell me what I can do?"

"Nothing. I don't need your help."

"Well, you need something, Brady. Why aren't you going to therapy?"

"Because it only makes me hurt more."

"So you'd rather just lie here in pain and pop pills like they are candy instead of trying to fight past the pain? That's not like you, Brady! You've always pushed through the pain." My frustration at being shut out was making me almost as edgy as him.

"You have no idea what you are talking about, Gracelyn. Just shut up, alright?"

"Shut up? Since when do you talk to me like that? Brady, I know you are hurting, and you're depressed, but you need to stop this nonsense and talk to me or talk to someone if you don't want to talk to me."

He laughed and rolled to his back, glaring at me. "You think I can just stop hurting, stop being depressed? Just snap my fingers, and it will all be gone?" He laughed a bit cruelly. "Just like you could just lose weight, right? Snap your fingers if you want to, and the weight would be gone? Well, if that were the way that things worked, I wouldn't be hurting, and you wouldn't be fat."

I stepped back as if he'd physically slapped me. "Brady, what has gotten into you?"

"Nothing. Just go away," he snarled again, and I shuffled back slightly.

I blinked back tears, not wanting him to know how much those words had hurt me. Slowly, I turned as the first tear slipped out. I collected my keys and purse and was out the door before I could break down in sobs.

CHAPTER SEVEN

BRADY

*W*hen they found the cracks in my spine, I was glad—not that I was glad I had broken my back, but I was happy to know that I hadn't been making up the pain.

The problem was that after they put the rod in my spine, I was still in agony. The neurosurgeon told me that I was lucky the fracture hadn't paralyzed me because it had been very close to infringing on my spinal cord. As it was, several nerves were damaged, along with the discs above and below the fractures.

He didn't sugarcoat it when he told me that I would be in a lot of pain for a long time—maybe my entire life. He also expressed his concern with me returning to active duty. He said he wasn't calling it yet, but he did make a note in my chart. In my chart, he questioned my recovery. To my face, he said there was a ninety percent chance that I would be released from duty with a medical retirement.

That was the news he left me with hours before I was discharged from Walter Reed. Not, "Good luck, you got this!" or "Hope not to see you again here and have a long and rewarding career."

Nope.

"You're gonna be out of a job someday soon."

I came home in a funk.

Ever since he had said those words to me over a week ago, they had echoed in my mind, and the funk had continued to grow. What if I couldn't get back to my job? What was I going to do? I knew they had programs to help me, but the Veterans Administration could only do so much.

What would Gracelyn think when I told her that I wouldn't be able to do my job? Would she even want to stick around and be with a loser like me? Without my job, my career, the air force, what the hell was I?

Those were the questions that plagued me hour by hour the first week I was home. What also bothered me was that I couldn't even picture the damned event that caused all this mess in the first place. Maybe if I could, I would learn to accept it, perhaps even feel a little grateful that I was alive—maybe.

The docs and Turner had told me about the RPG and the explosion, but it just didn't compute because I couldn't put words to memories. The two pieces just wouldn't fit together. All I knew was something drastic had happened, and my entire life had changed. Nothing was the same, and nothing would ever be the same.

I was angry—so angry that sometimes I just wanted to scream and pound my fists, but the anger was stuck inside of me because it hurt to move. I was frustrated because I couldn't remember random details very long, and my once incredible memory felt like it was trying to hold sand in a colander.

Let's not even get me started on the depression. I'd never been depressed in my life. I might have been down or struggling at certain points in my life, but I'd never felt this unbearable weight pressing on my chest before, making it hard to breathe.

I didn't think that was a big deal. I mean, I did have the right to feel this way. A lot of good people had died, friends and co-workers. I was allowed to be angry about that and mourn them.

I had to think that the depression was because of their deaths—not my life—although part of me also thought that I was allowed to mourn my own life too. If what the doctors said was true, then I was done in the military, and instead of doing twenty-something and retiring, I was being led out to pasture barely halfway to that achievement. I hated that! It was like I was giving up, and I never gave up.

I couldn't even imagine telling Gracelyn that my career was over. What was she going to think of me? Would she be angry? Would she cry? Try to tell me that it would be alright—that we'd get through it together? I didn't want to see the pity in her eyes, and I sure as hell didn't want to hear her say that it was going to be alright and that I would find something else to do.

What the hell could I do if I wasn't able to do my job as a mechanic in the military? If I couldn't do it here, I wouldn't be able to do it in civilian life either, right?

A million questions raced through my mind, and when Gracelyn came into the bedroom and wanted to know why I hadn't gone to therapy, I lashed out.

"Brady, you need to get back to therapy. They keep calling to reschedule your appointments. You're never going to recover if you don't."

"Don't pretend to know what I need, Gracelyn."

"Brady, what is going on? I'm only trying to help, but every time I do, you push me away. Tell me what I can do."

"Nothing. I don't need your help." I wasn't ready to tell her the truth. Hell, I didn't even want to face it myself.

"Well, you need something, Brady. Why aren't you going to therapy?"

"Because it only makes me hurt more." It wasn't a lie. My back hurt constantly. The only time it didn't was when I was taking my pain medication.

"So you'd rather just lie here in pain and pop pills like they are candy instead of trying to fight past the pain? That's not like you, Brady! You've always pushed through the pain."

Didn't she think that I knew that? Didn't she realize that I knew that I wasn't the man I used to be? I just wanted her to go away. "You have no idea what you are talking about, Gracelyn. Just shut up, alright?"

I heard her gasp, and she couldn't see me, but I winced. In all my years, I had never said those words to her. In my right mind, I would never do that.

"Shut up? Since when do you talk to me like that? Brady, I know you are hurting, and you're depressed, but you need to stop this nonsense and talk to me or talk to someone if you don't want to talk to me."

She didn't know anything. "You think I can just stop hurting, stop being depressed? Just snap my fingers, and it will all be gone? Just like you could just lose weight, right? Snap your fingers if you want to, and the weight would be gone? Well, if that were the way that things worked, I wouldn't be hurting, and you wouldn't be fat."

I knew the moment those words left my mouth that they were wrong, but I just didn't care. I wanted to sleep, to hide from the pain, and I sent her away.

I hated myself for what I had said to her. I honestly did, but she didn't understand, and I couldn't explain it to her.

Moments later the front door closed, and the car started. I stared at the wall in our bedroom, wanting to run after her, knowing I couldn't.

We would have to get rid of the expensive minivan that she drove. I wouldn't be able to afford my truck. Where would we live? I knew we had a bit of money in savings, but that had been to buy a house in a couple of years. Now how could we afford one? How much of my salary did I get for disability?

A vortex of foggy questions spun through my mind, and I couldn't escape. I glanced at my watch and saw that it had been five and a half hours since my last pain pill. I was supposed to wait six, but what was thirty minutes? I popped one into my mouth and swallowed it dry. I was in too much pain to even walk to the bathroom to get a glass of water—or maybe I was just that damned lazy.

It was dark when I woke up, my sleep disrupted by rustling in the other room. I rolled to my back and used my palms to rub my eyes. I felt like I could roll back over and go back to sleep, but my stomach growled for the first time all day. I sat up, wincing as the pain in my back radiated up to my neck. Sitting upright was not comfortable, and I stood as soon as I had my vertigo under control. It didn't hurt quite as much if I stood, and my thigh was healing pretty well. It still ached, and I'd lost a lot of muscle strength in it, but I could get that back—maybe.

Of course, to get my leg strength back, I'd need to work out, and that would require me to leave the house. As I used the bathroom, I thought about what I'd said to Gracelyn earlier. I needed to apologize.

I washed my hands and then took my time making it into the living room. Dane and Drew were sitting right in front of the television, and I frowned at them. "Why are you sitting so close?"

They both stared at me, eyes wide as if they were waiting for something terrible to happen. "Um," Dane replied as he glanced toward the kitchen, "we didn't want to wake you, so we had the volume turned down."

"Yeah, we have to sit this close to hear," Drew added.

"Yeah, well, I'm awake now. You can turn it up a little bit and move back to the couch."

Drew grinned and went to get up, but Dane shook his head. "Nah, that's okay. We'll keep it low in case your head starts hurting again."

I brushed my hand over his dirty-blond hair as I walked past him toward the kitchen. Two pots were on the stove boiling, and Gracelyn was at the sink, staring out the back window into the darkness.

"Dinner almost ready? I'm suddenly starving."

Gracelyn practically jumped out of her skin as she spun, a knife in her hand. I glanced at it and hiked a brow.

She quickly set the knife down beside the carrot on the cutting board. "Sorry, you scared me. I was off in dreamland."

"What were you thinking about?"

"Nothing." She turned away from me and shifted to stand in front of the cutting board, putting her attention on cutting the carrot into small pieces.

I went to stand behind her, feeling responsible for her withdrawn mood. My hands rubbed up and down her shoulders, and I didn't miss the tension that held her stiff. "I'm sorry, Gracelyn. I should never have lashed out like that at you earlier. I know you were only trying to help."

She paused, setting the knife down and turning to face me. "Brady, all I want to do is help you, but you don't let me. I know that you hurt, and you're angry, but you need to get help. I can't make you go to therapy. You're not a child that I can force to do that. You have to do it yourself."

I nodded to her as I took her hands in mine. "I know. I just get so out of it sometimes that I can't think of what I need to do next."

"Maybe we could make a list," she suggested. "We could come up with a few things that you need to complete each day, and maybe that will help you."

It wasn't a horrible idea. "Okay, I can try to do that."

She stepped away from me and collected a notepad and a pen from the junk drawer. "I think the first thing that you need to do is try to get out of bed and eat breakfast."

"Is that what you think?"

"Yes." She nodded as she wrote it down. "Then I think you

need to call and make a therapy appointment, and then maybe take a shower before lunch."

I crossed my arms over my chest. "Planning my whole day now? What time do I get to lie down and rest? Should we put a bathroom break in there? Maybe what time I am supposed to pop those candy pills?"

She lifted her face to mine. "Why are you getting angry, Brady? I'm just trying to help."

"By putting down that I need to eat breakfast and take a shower? You act like I'm an idiot."

"I am not! I'm trying to think of things that will be easy to accomplish. Then when you finish them and cross them off, you'll feel like you did something."

I snorted. "Yeah, okay. I don't think crossing off that I took a shower will help me feel accomplished."

"Really?" She hiked a brow at me and crossed her arms over her chest. "When is the last time you took one?"

I looked away from her without replying. It had been a day or two—maybe three.

"I'm just trying to come up with baby steps, Brady. If you put too many things on your list, or they are too hard, you won't do them, or you'll feel bad because you couldn't do them."

I shook my head as I dropped my arms and started to walk out of the kitchen. "You know what? I'm not hungry. I'm going back to the bedroom."

"Brady!" she called out to me, but I was already out of the room. How she possibly thought that putting stupid things like that on a list would help me, I couldn't imagine.

In the bedroom, I glanced at my watch. I had at least another thirty minutes before I could take another pain pill. I grabbed a change of clothes and went into our small bathroom. I stood in front of the mirror and stared at my reflection. How did I have circles under my eyes when all I ever did was sleep?

I turned from the haunting image of myself and took a shower. By the time I finished, I was hurting pretty badly and took my medication early again. On a tray by the bed was a plate of spaghetti and meatballs, a salad, plus a piece of garlic bread.

I moved the tray to the floor near the door. I had no interest in food. All I wanted to do was sleep until the pain went away. I just needed a little more time, and then I would get back with the program.

CHAPTER EIGHT

GRACELYN

"*I* don't know what else to do, Doug. I've tried to talk to him. I've even pleaded with him, but I can't seem to get through to him. He just lies in the bedroom or on the couch and stares off in space or sleeps. He says he is in a lot of pain and is constantly taking more pills. I don't even think that he is waiting long enough between doses. It's like he just takes them to knock himself out."

Doug sipped from his straw as he listened to me. Since I had started working for him a couple of weeks ago, the two of us had become close friends. I had been stressed all day, and he had noticed and invited me out for lunch.

"Has he gone to therapy yet?"

"Not since he came home. This morning I left him a note to remind him to call for an appointment, but I don't know if he will or not."

"Maybe you just need to make it for him."

"But I can't make him go."

"You could if you gave him an ultimatum."

I stared at him, my eyes wide as I asked, "What, like I'll leave him if he doesn't go?"

He chuckled. "Nothing so drastic as that."

"I'm not sure what else I could threaten him with. Do you know that he called me fat yesterday?"

"He was joking, right?"

"No! He was comparing my weight issues to his inability to stop the pain. Said if we could just snap our fingers to make it all better, it would be great."

"Gracelyn, you have to let that go. If he's taking a bunch of medication, he's not in his right mind."

"Yeah." I set my fork down in my salad bowl. "I know that, Doug. I understand that's he's hurting and angry. Just because he is doesn't give him the right to attack me. Doesn't he know that I'm not happy with my weight? Man, what I wouldn't do to be forty pounds lighter."

Doug shrugged. "I can't imagine you losing that much. I think you would be too thin, but my opinion is beside the point. You have to be happy with yourself, and I understand wanting to change to make yourself better."

"It's not just making myself better. I wanted to be healthier and more active for the kids. I have two very athletic boys. Since Brady is always traveling, I'm the one who needs to throw a ball with Dane or kick a ball with Drew. It's exhausting."

"Well, the only way you are going to lose the weight is to stop complaining about it and do it. The same thing goes for Brady. He can wallow in his pain, or he can attempt to do something about it. You can't make him do it for himself. He has to want to."

I studied Doug for a moment. "You're right. I can't make Brady do it, but I can try to focus on myself. I noticed that I'm pretty cranky myself these days. I'm sure it's from worrying about him, but I need to figure out a way to calm myself."

"Maybe if you can do that, he will calm down too." He took a bite of his burger and then swallowed. "You know that you could go to counseling and talk to someone."

I laughed. "Why would I do that? I don't need to go to counseling. I'm not the one with any problems."

He shrugged. "Maybe a therapist could give you ideas on how to help Brady."

I sighed and dug around in my salad for a minute. "Maybe, but I don't want to talk to a stranger about our problems."

He chuckled. "You're talking to me about them. What's the difference?"

I rolled my eyes. "But you're not a stranger."

"No, you're right. I'm your boss *and* your friend." He winked, and I smiled at him. "But while I don't mind listening to you vent, you might be better off speaking to someone who could possibly help you."

"I'll think about it." He gave me a stern look, and I laughed. "I said I would think about it."

For the rest of lunch, we talked about work stuff, and as I sat at my desk later that day, I considered what Doug had said. Maybe I could find a support group to attend. I'm sure there were other women whose spouses had been injured and who were dealing with similar issues.

As the day went on, I thought more and more about it and made a mental note to look into it later tonight after I'd gotten home and put the kids to bed. I wished that I could have called Vera; this was one of those questions that she would have instantly had an answer for, but I didn't feel comfortable reaching out to her.

After work, I picked up the kids from after-school care and considered hitting the drive-through of a local fast-food restaurant, but I clenched my hands around the wheel and forced myself to drive past it. I knew that I had thawed chicken breasts in the fridge that needed to be cooked before they spoiled. Chicken breasts were a lot healthier than the fried chicken bucket I had just considered picking up.

Feeling proud of myself as I drove home, I listened to the

kids talk about their day while pondering what I could fix for dinner. I was almost home when I did a mental check and realized that I had all the fixings to make stir fry. That would be perfect. A healthy meal, and maybe the kids would even enjoy it. They did like the fried rice I made to go with it.

Feeling good about making a healthy decision, I was smiling as I approached the front door. As I stepped onto the porch, I heard an alarm, and smelled just the barest scent of smoke. Was that coming from our house? I unlocked the door with a shaking hand and threw it open to find smoke rolling along the ceiling toward the door.

I dropped my purse and keys on the front porch as I raced toward the kitchen. "Stay outside!" I yelled to the boys.

"Where is Dad?" Dane screamed in a panicked voice, but I didn't have time to reply. I was bewildered as to where Brady was. For all I knew, he was lying passed out on the kitchen floor. Inside the kitchen, I paused as I saw flames licking up the wall behind the stove. I searched the floor as I began to cough, but I didn't see Brady anywhere, so I turned and ran toward the stairs as I dialed 9-1-1.

In the bedroom, I found Brady lying on the bed—out cold. I shook him with vigor as someone answered the phone. "Brady, wake up! You have to get out of the house! It's on fire."

"Stop shouting, Gracelyn," he growled groggily at me.

I spoke to the dispatcher, telling him that my kitchen was on fire as I continued to shake Brady. Suddenly, he burst upright and wrapped his hand around my wrist so hard that I screamed.

He hissed at me, "I said stop shouting!"

I froze, my eyes bursting wide open as I stared into the pinprick pupils of his green eyes. Where was my husband? Was he even in there?

Like a light switch, Brady's demeanor flipped, and his face snapped toward the hall door. "Why is there smoke in the house?"

"Because it's on fire, Brady! You have to get out of the house!" I yanked out of his grasp and ran down the stairs. I was rushing out the front door, giving the man on the phone more information, and found the kids standing on the front porch crying. I snatched my purse from where I'd dropped it and corralled the kids off the porch and down toward the street.

The crackling of the fire was getting louder as I coughed, and the man said the fire department was on the way. When I turned around, I expected to see Brady behind me, but he wasn't.

"Brady!" I shouted and started to run back to the house, but Dane latched on to my arm and yanked me back.

"Mom! No! You can't go back in there!"

"Brady, your father is still in there."

"He's out!" Drew shouted and pointed at the door, and Brady was on the front step, coughing as smoke billowed out the open door behind him.

I shook out of Dane's grip and rushed to Brady, putting my arm around him to help him down the steps as he coughed harder. Sirens echoed in the distance as I leaned Brady against my vehicle. I stared at our house. The orange, yellow, and red flames were coming down the hall as if they were playfully taunting us to come back in.

I looked at Brady. He was staring at the house, his jaw hanging open. "What were you thinking, Brady?"

"What are you talking about? I was sleeping."

"Then who was cooking food in our kitchen? Did you start to cook something and then forget about it?" I rubbed my hands over my face. "Thank God that I came home when I did! I almost stopped to pick up dinner, and if I had, you would have still been inside the house, Brady."

"I would have gotten out," he said, but I saw in his eyes that he didn't quite believe that.

"No, you wouldn't have! Do you know how hard I had to

shake you to wake you up! You were so drugged out that you wouldn't respond, Brady!"

I was crying and shouting at him right there in the driveway and didn't realize that people were converging on us. Neighbors, people that knew us, people that thought we had the perfect relationship.

Well, weren't they in for a surprise now?

My next-door neighbor, Josie, put her hand on my arm. "Are you guys alright?"

"We're fine," I said and wiped at the tears on my cheeks and coughed again. "We are fine. That is all that matters."

I rubbed my hands over my face as the adrenaline of the situation continued to course through me. I went to the back of my minivan and popped the tailgate to have a seat. Josie and the boys followed me.

"Were you cooking? Did something catch on fire in the kitchen?"

"I don't know what happened," I told her. I didn't want to admit that my husband might have caused the fire. I was trying to convince myself that it was an accident, but was it?

Had he purposely gone into the kitchen, put something on the stove, and then gone into the bedroom to lie down? Had he wanted the house to burn down with him in it? My entire body grew cold as I turned to look at my husband through the window. Was my husband suicidal?

No. That couldn't even be possible! Brady was too strong for something like that. It had to be an accident.

The first fire truck pulled up to our house, and things went nuts as they busted out windows and dragged hoses through our front yard. All of my neighbors were outside watching now. All of them whispering to each other as they looked at us. What were they saying?

Did they think we had crappy luck? Maybe they did. Perhaps they were saying that the poor Vanover family couldn't catch a break. Brady gets hurt, and then their house almost burns down —bad things come in threes. Wonder what's next for them.

Brady came to sit at the minivan's rear, staring at the house as he did. A firefighter approached us. "I'm Fire Chief Wepner. Do you guys live here?"

"Yes," I replied as Brady nodded.

"What happened?" Chief Wepner asked.

I shrugged as I glanced toward Brady. "Ask him, I wasn't home."

Brady peered my way, but I didn't meet his eye. "I don't know. I was sleeping. She woke me up when she got home and found the fire."

"Ma'am, is that true?"

"Yes, I just got home with the boys. I could hear the fire alarm from outside, and when I opened the door, I could see the smoke back in the kitchen. I went to check it, worried that Brady might be on the floor. I saw flames going up the wall behind the stove, but Brady wasn't there, so I ran up the stairs and found him sleeping."

"Was there something on the stove?" he asked.

I shook my head. "I have no clue. You have to ask him if he was cooking something."

"Sir?"

He looked at me, then the house, and then finally at the fire chief. "I don't remember. Maybe I did start to cook something, but I get these sudden and horrifying headaches. When I get them, I can't remember what I was doing. I just have to lie down."

The chief nodded but didn't seem to believe him. "Should we get you looked at?"

"No, I'm fine."

"You are far from fine," I hissed toward him.

The fire chief looked between the two of us. "Anything I need to know?"

I shook my head. I didn't want Brady to get in trouble for anything, so it was better to keep my mouth shut.

After he walked away, I glared at Brady's profile. "You have to figure out what to do to get you off those pain pills, Brady."

He glanced at me with big sad eyes. "You should have just left me in the house."

His voice so soft I wasn't sure I had heard him correctly. I began to shake again. "What? What are you saying, Brady?"

He shook his head as he looked away, staring back at the house. "Nothing." He put his hand on my arm. "I'm sorry, Gracelyn. I'll call tomorrow and get back into therapy."

CHAPTER NINE

BRADY

I watched the smoke float into the evening sky. What the hell had I done?

When I woke up after everyone had left this morning, I found Gracelyn's note to call for therapy. I had crumpled it into a ball and thrown it in the trash can. Didn't she realize that I knew I had to call them? If I didn't, I was going to get in trouble with the air force. I was required to follow specific steps as I convalesced at home. It had just been a rough week. Not only was it a shock to my system to be home after months overseas, but my pain overshadowed everything else.

I hated the fogginess in my brain, despised the fact that my mind didn't want to operate the way it should. It was sluggish, and sometimes, words were difficult to retrieve. I could almost see them, but I couldn't reach them.

Although today had been a better day than most, I had felt pretty good for a while there. I had even thought that I would surprise Gracelyn by cooking dinner. I knew I hadn't told her this, but I realized how much she did for the kids and me. She was working, and running the kids everywhere, and making sure all of us had everything that we needed. The woman even left me labeled meals in the fridge, not that I was ever hungry. The pain pills destroyed my appetite—kind of like how that RPG had ruined my life.

For once, I didn't have a pounding headache and the need to hide in the dark. I looked through everything that we had in the fridge and found chicken breasts ready to cook. After checking a few more cabinets, I found the rest of the ingredients to make chicken parmesan. I set about breading the chicken and then turned on the frying pan, putting oil in it to begin frying the chicken.

Right after I put the chicken in, a sharp pain seared through my head. I'd gone to the bedroom to take a pill, and then what?

I frowned as I stared at a firefighter coming out of the front door, a smirk on his face and something in his hands. The fire was out now, and only residual smoke was escaping from the windows and door. Another two firefighters carried a large fan toward the house.

Had I taken the pill? Had I sat down on the side of the bed and accidentally dozed off? Had I forgotten about the food on the stove? How long had I been in the bedroom sleeping?

A sickening feeling slithered through my gut. What if Gracelyn hadn't come home? What if I had died in the fire? Would that have been so bad? No, it would have been easy for me. Gracelyn wouldn't have had to stress and worry over me anymore.

Drew leaned his head back against my chest, and I looked at my two sons. My sons would have grown up without a father. I wasn't okay with that.

The fire chief came over to talk to us, but I couldn't bear to admit this was my fault. The house needed some serious repair. Who knew how many of our possessions had survived the water and smoke damage?

Gracelyn was staring at me after the fire chief left us. "You have to figure out what to do to get off those pain pills, Brady."

I knew she would blame me. She had every right to blame me. "You should have just left me in the house." I hadn't meant to say that out loud, and the fact that I did scared me.

Her eyes widened. "What? What are you saying, Brady?"

"Nothing." I didn't want to die. I didn't want to leave my kids or my wife. I reached out to Gracelyn. "I'm sorry, Gracelyn. I'll call tomorrow and get back into therapy."

For a moment, the two of us stared at one another, and then her brown eyes began to mist up, and I put my arm around her and pulled her to me.

"Brady, I just want you to get better. I will do anything that I can to help you, but you have to help me too. You have to want to get better."

I kissed her brow. "I do, Gracelyn. I do."

By the time the fire department was done, I was lying in the cargo section of the minivan, with my arm slung over my eyes and my head pounding. It was apparent now that I hadn't gotten those pills down before I passed out. I needed my medication—badly—but they wouldn't let us into the house.

Finally, I heard someone say to her, "Here are the medication vials that we found beside the bed."

"Thank you," I heard Gracelyn say to them before she spoke to me. "Which one do you need right now?"

"All four of them."

"All four of them? That's a lot of pills at once, Brady. No wonder you sleep after taking them."

I ground my teeth in response. She didn't understand that they all worked together: a muscle relaxer for my back, a pill for the pain throughout my body, another tablet to calm my mind so I didn't overprocess things, and then the capsule to stop the migraines.

After a few moments, she handed me all the medication I asked for. "Hold on, I need to find you some water."

"I don't need water. I can take them dry."

"No, you can't."

"Watch me," I said as I threw them into my mouth and worked them to the back of my throat. Yeah, they tasted horrible, but at least they were in my mouth and starting to dissolve.

Fifteen minutes later, I began to feel the pills' effects, and my body and mind started to drift while the pain finally began to recede. The muscles that were clenched tightly began to ease bit by bit.

Maybe I should have cared that so many people were around, but I didn't. All I cared about was feeling nothing again after feeling so much for the last few hours.

That night, we went to a hotel. In the past, I would have taken care of everything, but not now. Now, I remained in the car with the boys as Gracelyn went into the hotel and got us a room. I had heard Gracelyn talking to a few neighbors who had loaned us some clothes and toiletries for the night. Dane carried that single bag of donated items and Gracelyn helped me to the elevator and up to the room.

The bright lights in the hallway made me feel ill, but thankfully the room was darker and quiet.

I was about to lie down on the bed, but Gracelyn pushed me toward the bathroom. "Nope, you take a shower and get the smoke off you. Then you can climb in bed and sleep."

"Mom, I'm starving," Dane whined.

"As soon as your dad takes his shower, I will go get us food."

"You can go. I'll watch the boys," I told her as I stood in the threshold of the bathroom door.

Gracelyn pursed her lips and raised one brow. Okay, so maybe that wasn't a good idea. She finally nodded, and I stepped in and closed the door.

After I got out of the shower, I found Dane and Drew sitting on the bed and Gracelyn staring out the dark window. I took a seat on the bed, and Gracelyn looked me over.

"I'm going to get us something to eat. Dane, I want you and Drew to take quick showers, five minutes each. Just rinse off."

"But we don't have any clean underwear," Dane stated.

"I know, you will have to wear the same ones. I'll buy us some new stuff in the morning."

Dane nodded and went into the bathroom, and Drew continued to watch the cartoon on the television.

She approached me, and I realized she had her phone clenched in her hand. Had she been talking to someone? "Are you going to be okay while I'm gone?"

"Yeah, I'll be fine." She stared at me for a long moment. "The boys will be fine too, Gracey."

She pursed her lips again and then collected her purse and keycard. "I'll be back in a few minutes."

After she left, I went to the window and peeled back the curtain. I saw Gracelyn step into the parking lot a few moments later, her phone to her ear. Who was she talking with? Had she called her mother? A friend? A lover?

I winced. Gracelyn wouldn't do that. Even though we hadn't been close since I had returned, I knew she would never cheat on me. She wasn't wired that way, but I still couldn't help but wonder.

She sat in her car for a while, and it was almost ten minutes before she finally started it and pulled away. I had nearly gone to check on her, but just as I had considered that, she left.

I went back to the bed and sat against the headboard, thinking about everything that had happened. Dane had finished his shower and snuggled up with me. It was the first time since I'd been home that we'd done this, and I frowned at myself. Man, I used to be so close to my kids and my wife. The last time I was home, I had hung out with the kids for hours, playing video games and watching television, and at night, I would make love to my wife for hours.

Since I'd been back, I hadn't even thought about having sex

with Gracelyn. How messed up was that? It wasn't that I wasn't attracted to her. I was. She was still beautiful, but I just didn't have the urge to do it. Was that from the pain medicine? The injury? Or maybe from the guilt?

Guilt—man, I seriously had something to feel guilty for now. I had caused the fire in our house. What if I'd been watching the boys and that had happened? What if I'd done that in the middle of the night with my entire family in the house?

I was still dwelling over my guilt when Gracelyn returned with two bags of food. One bag was filled with chicken nuggets and fries and another from a local convenience store. From that one, she pulled out a box of donuts and some juice boxes, along with a salad.

Drew came running from the bathroom, his hair still dripping wet.

"Go dry your hair, and then you can eat," Gracelyn ordered him as she spun him by the shoulders.

Dane sat at the small table near the window and dug into his food as if he hadn't eaten in a year. Drew was right behind him the minute he was back. Gracelyn set food beside the bed without saying a word, and I grabbed her hand before she could step away.

She looked at me, and I saw not only the pain in her eyes but sadness and evidence of crying.

"Gracelyn, I'm sorry."

"I know you are. If you want to make it up to me, you'll eat your dinner." She twisted her wrist away from me and collected her salad before she sat on the opposite bed and began to eat.

"Why did you get a salad?" I asked her as I peeled the paper off the straw to my soda.

"Because, as you were so clear to point out earlier, I should be watching my weight."

I winced. "Gracelyn, I'm sorry. That's not what I meant."

She turned and locked eyes with me. "That is precisely what

you meant. I get it, and it's okay. I do need to make better choices—about everything in life."

She turned her attention back to the television, and I wondered what that last part was about. Was there someone else in her life? Was she going to leave me now that I wasn't the same man I used to be? Maybe she had been involved with someone the entire time I'd been gone. Did I know him?

I didn't want to eat the food. In fact, the thought of putting anything into my mouth right now made me want to vomit, but I forced myself to. After a few bites, it became almost automatic, and I ended up eating the entire meal she'd purchased for me.

After she finished her salad, she began to clean up the mess and collected my wrappers. "Thank you for eating."

"Gracelyn, you don't have to thank me for eating." She studied me, her soft brown eyes still so sad-looking—and tired. "Why don't you go take a shower, and then we can all get some sleep. It's been a rough evening."

She nodded as she collected something that Josie had given her and disappeared into the bathroom. The lock on the door snapped a moment after she did. Was that to keep the kids out —or me?

CHAPTER TEN

GRACELYN

*B*rady was lying in the back of the minivan, and I was standing near the street, talking to Josie, when the fire chief came back to me. "Ma'am, we think we found the cause of the fire."

My eyes shot toward the minivan and then back to the fire chief. "What?" Oh, please do not tell me it was because of food on the stove! Let it be something faulty.

He sighed softly. "Looks like someone was cooking on the stove, with oil. Do you know what might have been there?"

"No," I replied as I sadly shook my head and crossed my arms over my chest. Josie put her hand on my back and rubbed in gentle circles. "Are you sure?"

"Yes, the pan that was on there is destroyed. Whatever was inside it is a charcoaled brick now, but there was evidence of oil in the area and melted plastic." He held out an odd chunk of something. "I'm going to hazard to say that the pan got hot, and the container of oil was close enough to the stove to start to melt and then catch on fire."

"Oh, good Lord," I muttered as I squeezed my eyes shut. Why

had he been in the kitchen at all? "How bad is the house? Can I go in?"

"It's not safe for you to go in tonight, and your kitchen is destroyed. The rest of the house has smoke damage, but you should be able to recover quite a bit after it is cleaned. We will have the house secured tonight, and then tomorrow after your insurance company comes through, they will let you go back inside and start the cleanup and recovery."

Luckily, we had renters' insurance. I gnawed on my bottom lip. "Is there any way you can get the medication bottles off the side table in the bedroom? My husband is going to need them."

He glanced at the minivan. "Has your husband ever done anything like this before?"

I shook my head. "No, he just got back from Afghanistan. He was injured in an explosion and cracked his spine. It also did a lot of damage to his thigh and he got a concussion on top of it. He forgets things sometimes, and he's always in a lot of pain."

"That's too bad," he commented with a shake of his head. "We will have someone grab the medication if we can find it. Do you know how many different ones there are?"

"I think there are four."

He nodded and walked away. Josie pulled me closer to her. "How scary that must have been for you."

"It was. I had no idea if Brady was alive when I stepped into the house."

"My husband had a concussion a few years ago," she said as she glanced around. "He had a tough time for a while, but then it slowly clicked back into place after about a year."

My face snapped toward her. "A year? It's going to take Brady a year to recover?"

"Oh, Gracelyn, yes. For some people, it can take up to eighteen months before they find a new normal."

"A new normal? What does that mean?"

"Well, in Jake's case, it meant that he had to write more

things down, especially numbers. He can't remember numbers very well. Concussions are pretty serious and life-altering for some people."

"You hear of people having them all the time, but then they are recovered. How could it possibly take over a year for someone to recover? That doesn't make sense."

"Trust me. It is possible, Gracelyn. Recovering from a concussion is very rough. Jake didn't work for almost a year, and when he went back to the office, he had to do half-days. It took him another four months until he could make it all day, and when he'd arrive home, he was exhausted."

"But he seems fine now."

"He is fine, but he still gets frustrated some days because he can't remember things that he should remember, and he's very jealous of those who get a concussion and recover very quickly. I hope that Brady recovers more quickly than Jake did."

"I do, too. I'm not sure Brady could deal with not being himself or it taking that long." I gnawed on my bottom lip as I dwelled over that. Would Brady recover and be himself again? Would the damage to his brain be too much for him to go back to who he was? What about his job?

Once the firemen packed it all up and the house was secured, we went to a hotel not too far away. I pushed Brady into the bathroom and then went to stand at the window, sending a text to Doug.

Had a fire at our house tonight. Staying in a hotel. I'm not going to make it to work tomorrow.

A minute later, my phone rang, and I put it to my ear.

"Are you alright? Are the kids okay?" His voice was rushed, concerned, and I appreciated it.

"Yes, we are all alright."

"What happened, Gracelyn?"

"There was a fire in the kitchen."

"What were you cooking, or was it an appliance?"

"I wasn't home yet. I came home to find the kitchen on fire and Brady in the bedroom asleep."

"Oh, Jesus, Gracelyn, please tell me the kids weren't there. Is Brady okay?"

I glanced at my wrist, remembering how hard Brady had grabbed it when I had woken him up. "Yeah, he's okay. I got him out. He didn't remember any of it."

Doug sighed. "Damn, Gracelyn. Is there anything I can do to help? Do you guys need a place to stay? You know you can come here. I have the room."

"I appreciate that, Doug, but we are at a hotel tonight. I have to figure this all out tomorrow. I'm so sorry I won't be there."

"Hey, don't even worry about it. Your family comes first." He paused. "Are you alright? I wish I were there to hug you."

I barked a short laugh. "Yeah, I do, too, but I'll be okay. I just wanted to let you know about tomorrow."

"Call me if you need to talk later."

"I will, thank you, Doug." I hung up and stared out the window, fighting the urge to fall to my knees and sob. Somehow, I kept hold of myself until I was leaving to get food. Then as I dialed my mother's phone number walking out of the hotel, the waterworks started.

"Hi, sweetie, what's going on?"

"Mom," I said in a strangled voice as I yanked open the door of my car.

"Gracelyn, what's wrong? Did something happen to the kids?"

"No, they are fine," I managed to get out. "We are fine, but my house—Mom, oh my God!—there was a fire at my house! Brady decided to cook something and left the stove on while he went into the bedroom and fell asleep."

"Oh, my word! Gracelyn, is he alright?"

"Yes, I came home before it was too late and woke him up. Mom, I was shaking him so hard, and he wouldn't move. I thought for a moment he might already be dead, and then he sprang up and yelled at me. The look in his face was like nothing I'd ever seen before." I hiccupped around the words as they all poured out. "He was like a man possessed, but then he snapped out of it, and we got outside before the fire blocked our path. Mom, those damn pills are destroying my husband!"

"Aw, Gracelyn, take a deep breath, sweetheart. All of you are alright. Be thankful that you all made it out okay."

"But he almost didn't! What if I had left the kids alone with him? What if they had been there and tried to put the fire out? What if something worse had happened, and I couldn't wake him up? I almost thought for a moment that maybe he started the fire on purpose to kill himself."

"Gracelyn! How could you think such a thing? Brady would never do something so stupid. I'm sure he got confused and just got momentarily distracted."

"He almost burned our house down during that momentary distraction, Mom! That's not being a little confused!" I shouted back at her as I wiped my nose. "I don't even know this man! He won't go to therapy! He won't talk to me! The boys and I tiptoe around the house so that we won't disturb him. If the kids even close the door too loud, he yells at them. My neighbor told me that her husband had a concussion and he couldn't work for a year! A year! The air force won't wait that long for Brady to recover! What if they kick him out? What are we going to do then?"

"Gracelyn, you are jumping ahead here. I think you need to calm down a little bit. Where are they now?"

"In a hotel room."

"Where are you?"

"In my car. I am going to get food. None of us have eaten."

"Okay, then you go get some food, and then you take a long shower and curl up in bed with those two adorable boys, and you get some rest. Tomorrow things will be better."

"What if they aren't?"

"They will be. I promise."

I guess they couldn't be much worse, could they? "Alright, I need to get food. I know the boys are starving."

"Call me tomorrow, honey. I love you."

"Thanks, Mom. I love you, too."

I wiped at my face, blew my nose, and then went to get food. Drew was just getting out of the shower when I returned, and Dane was watching television. Brady was surprisingly awake and watching me as I moved around the room. When I brought his food to him, he finally spoke.

"Gracelyn, I'm sorry."

"I know you are. If you want to make it up to me, you'll eat your dinner."

He would have to do a lot more than that, but eating would be a good start. He was looking sickly since he hadn't been eating much the last few weeks. I wished I could lose weight as quickly as he was doing now. I had to admit that I was a bit bitter as we conversed over my choice of a salad and his earlier words.

I ate in silence and then cleaned up the containers. Brady had eaten almost all of his food, and I was thankful for that. Drew was cuddled up to his side, and Brady suggested I go take a shower.

I was all about that. I stood under the water, crying again. I could not imagine what my house would look like tomorrow or what would happen next.

The last several weeks had been a nightmare with Brady getting hurt and then finally arriving home—not to mention changing jobs and dealing with my boys, who were very scared that something else would happen to their father. Now the fire, and who knew what tomorrow would bring.

For just a moment, I wished that I could take some of Brady's medication and disappear from the world as he did.

Wouldn't that be nice just to forget it all—to sleep without worrying?

After my shower, I dried my long hair and wished that I had my face wash. At least Josie had been nice enough to give us some cheap toothbrushes and a sample of paste.

After I finished, I told the boys to brush their teeth. I climbed into the opposite bed and pulled the covers up over my shoulder, my back to Brady.

When the boys finished brushing, they climbed into bed with me, one on either side, and I shifted to the middle of the bed to make room for them. When Brady had been gone, and they had been scared, we had done this quite often. It was probably as calming for me as it was for them.

As I lay there, I heard Brady turn the television off and use the restroom. When he came out of the bathroom, he stepped around the bed and kissed Drew's forehead, then he returned to the other side and kissed Dane's. I felt him standing there for a long moment. His sigh was deep and possibly filled with regret —or maybe annoyance. I didn't know anymore.

I listened to the sounds of him getting comfortable in bed, and a tear slipped out of my eye and dripped onto the pillow.

Tomorrow would be a better day—it had to be.

CHAPTER ELEVEN

BRADY

I was standing at the edge of the hangar, dust whipping past me from the wind. Inside the hangar, Stuart and Chuck were laughing at something, and Evan approached them. I smiled and considered returning to them, but flames burst out all around them almost as quickly as the thought occurred. Heavy, dense smoke billowed out of the hangar as I staggered backward as fast as I could.

As I watched—spellbound—the hangar morphed into my house, and I was backing away from the front door. In the front foyer, standing in the glow of the flames, were Gracelyn and the boys. The fire was coming dangerously close, and I waited for them to run out. Instead of leaving, Gracelyn gave me a sad look and then slowly closed the door.

"No!" I shouted and started to run toward them. I had to rescue my family! Just as I began to move forward, something exploded, and I was flying through the air. My voice was ringing in my ears as I fell to the ground with a thud.

I jerked upright and almost slammed right into someone.

"Brady! You are alright. It was just a nightmare. You're okay, Brady."

Gracelyn was in front of me, holding my face. I threw my arms around her and yanked her to me as I sobbed into her hair.

"You're okay, Brady. I'm here. You are alright, and the boys are safe too. We are okay."

"I think I remember."

"What?" she asked softly against my ear.

"What happened overseas."

Her hand stilled on my back, and then she squeezed me a little harder. "It's okay. You're safe now. You're home, Brady, and we are going to get through this together."

I pressed my face into her neck, breathing her in like she was my salvation. My body shook as the scene at the hangar returned, and while I couldn't remember the explosion or seeing the RPG, I remembered those moments before—or were they hours before? I wasn't sure.

"Do you want to tell me what you remember?"

I shook my head.

"Brady." She ran a hand over my head. "It might help to get it out of your head. Maybe if you told me what you remembered just now, you might be able to go back to sleep."

I pulled back, taking her face in my hands. "I don't know that I want to remember anymore."

She blinked, looking very confused and concerned.

I shook my head as I let go of her and lay back. "Come lie with me."

She nodded and climbed to the other side of the bed, where she slipped under the covers. I pulled her to me, and she laid her head on my chest. We had slept like this a hundred times, and just having her here right now comforted me.

"I remember a few moments before the explosion, at least I think it was a few moments before, but then there was fire around Stuart, Chuck, and Evan, but then suddenly I was at our house, and you and the boys were inside the house with the fire.

You closed the door instead of coming out. It was like you were saying goodbye to me or something."

"Oh, Brady!" She kissed my chest and squeezed me a little tighter. "I'm not going anywhere. We aren't going anywhere. We love you, honey."

I kissed the top of her head, and then suddenly, I needed my wife. I needed to make the physical connection with her that we hadn't made since I returned. I lifted her chin and kissed her, and then again. Each kiss became a bit deeper, a bit more passionate.

I rolled to my side, wrapping my hand around her neck and holding her mouth to mine so I could kiss her as she deserved. She moaned slightly as her hands drifted over my back, then she whispered, "I missed you so much, Brady. Love me. Please love me."

Being as quiet as we could so as not to disturb our boys in the next bed, I made love to my wife. It was the first time since I had come home that I had felt almost normal—almost.

After we were finished, she curled up against me.

"I love you, Gracelyn. I'm so sorry about everything."

"Shh," she said softly as she put her fingers over my lips. "I love you too."

The two of us drifted off to sleep as we had done a hundred other times, and I had to believe that things would be okay. We'd get through this—I would get through this.

---

*T*hings always look different in the light of day, and today, they didn't look all that great. The boys were whining that they had to go to school, but Gracelyn told them it would be a lot more fun than digging around in the house. They didn't think so, and I finally snapped at them to stop arguing with their mother.

I had never been one to snap, but recently, I just couldn't help it. These kids didn't know how good they had it. I had been around the globe and seen the devastation and poverty in which many children lived. My kids had no right to whine about anything, especially not about going to school or wearing borrowed clothing.

After we dropped them off at school, we headed toward our house to meet with the insurance adjuster who just happened to be out our way today. I was in pain today but trying not to take my medication. Not taking it made me irritable and tense, but I knew that I needed to be clearheaded to help Gracelyn. I couldn't leave everything to her. She already did so much for our family.

We were sitting in the driveway waiting for the adjuster when her phone rang. She looked at the screen and quickly answered it. "Hey, Doug."

I watched her from the corner of my eye which was difficult because it caused my vertigo to kick in.

"We are doing alright, thank you. I dropped the kids off at school a few minutes ago." She was quiet, and then she glanced my way. "He's with me right now."

I turned to her, and she gave me a weak smile and looked away. She leaned her head back against the headrest and closed her eyes. I frowned as I looked away.

"I appreciate that, Doug, but we are alright. We are meeting with the insurance company in a few minutes. I'll see what they say."

What was he offering to do?

"Okay, yeah." She laughed. "No, that file is in a pile on the right side of your desk. I put it there yesterday afternoon before I left."

A moment later, she was saying goodbye to him and smiling as she hung up the phone.

"What did he want?"

"To check on us and see how we are doing."

"You mean to check on you, right?" I glared at her. "Are you sleeping with the guy?"

Her face snapped toward mine, and her jaw dropped to her chest. "Are you serious? No! I am most certainly not sleeping with him! How dare you even ask that, Brady!"

"What? Your boss calls you and wants to help you out, and you hang up the phone smiling. You haven't smiled all day, but whatever he said made you smile."

"What he said was that he was going to give me a raise because I was an awesome assistant, and with how things are going, getting a raise is a damn good thing right about now."

"What's that supposed to mean?"

She pursed her lips and looked away. "Nothing."

"Grace, what did you mean by that?"

A car pulled up in front of our house, and she reached for the door handle. "Nothing, Brady. It meant nothing. Just forget I said it."

Like hell, I would. I climbed out of her vehicle and grabbed her arm before she could get too far away. "Are you having an affair with that guy?"

She yanked her arm out of my grasp and leaned forward, hissing, "I am going to pretend that you did not just ask that question of me a second time! The answer hasn't changed in the last minute, Brady!" She shifted back and glared at me as the car door opened in the street. "Just because he is kind and he is a male, it does not mean he is trying to get me in bed. Some men just want to be friendly."

"No, they don't."

"Are you saying that you want to sleep with all the women that you are friends with?"

"No."

She rolled her eyes. "Yeah, okay, Brady." She spun from me and smiled at the insurance guy as he approached us.

"Mr. and Mrs. Vanover? I'm Mike Vito, sorry about the fire. Do you know how it started?"

Gracelyn looked toward me, and I shifted a little uncomfortably.

"I was cooking and stepped away from the stove for a few moments."

Gracelyn added quickly, "I guess my husband left an oil bottle too close to the burner, and it melted and caught on fire."

"Ah, I've seen that happen before. Anyone get hurt?"

"No," I replied.

He nodded. "Okay, good. Let me take pictures outside, and then we will step inside and go through the house. Have you been in since last night?"

Gracelyn shook her head. "No, they told us to wait for you."

"Alright, give me a few minutes, and then we can take a look inside."

He walked away, and Gracelyn watched him go, her arms crossed over her chest.

"How did you know about the oil?"

"The fire chief told me last night. They found the oil bottle melted on the stove."

"Damn."

She looked at me but didn't say anything. Instead, she went toward the front door and unlocked it. "Oh, man, it smells horrible in there!"

I stood on the front step, staring into the charred front hallway and smelling the smoke and ash. I swayed, and the heavy scent of chopper fuel filled my nostrils, along with the smell of burnt flesh. I startled back, losing my balance on the top step and falling toward the grass. At the last second, I snatched the handrail and kept myself from slamming into the ground. Muscles in my back spasmed, and a flash of something had me clenching my eyes as I shook my head to clear my mind. An RPG was coming toward us! Duck! We had to get down!

"Duck!"

"Brady! What's wrong?"

I shoved at the hand touching me, and I stumbled back, feeling the pain burst from my leg up to my spine and into my skull where it started to throb painfully. My legs lost their ability to hold me upright, and I sagged to the ground as a high-pitched scream rent the air. "Brady!"

I was sucking in the air, trying to calm myself, trying to stop the pain, as someone pulled on me. It took all my energy as I struck out against the insurgents coming after me. I would not let them take me prisoner!

Suddenly they were gone, and I was alone, and I curled in on myself, holding my head with both hands. "Stop! Just stop!" I said, rocking back and forth as my head throbbed to the fast rhythm of my heart. "God, please stop!"

"Brady." The soft sound of my name was spoken on a sob. I wanted to push it away, but part of me wanted to embrace it also. "Brady, it's Gracelyn. It's Gracey, your wife. You are safe now, Brady. You're safe." She brushed her hand over my head to sooth me.

"Is he okay?" a man's voice asked.

"Yeah, he'll be okay. Can you help me get him off the ground? I'm going to take him back to the car. He can rest in there while we look at the house."

I heard the footsteps approaching, but I was stumped on who it was.

"Brady, stay calm. We are just going to help you to your feet so you can sit in the car. I have your medicine. You can take some."

"Oh, Mrs. Vanover, you're bleeding!" a voice said.

I wanted to open my eyes and see what had happened to Gracelyn. How had she gotten hurt? My brain wouldn't connect with my muscles, and my eyelids remained closed.

"I'm okay. Let's just get him off the ground." She sniffled as she put her arm around my back. "Brady, I need you to help me. We need to get you off the ground."

"Mr. Vanover, I'm going to pull on your arm." His voice sounded cautious, as if he thought I would hurt him. How could I hurt him when I couldn't even deal with the pain in my head?

I didn't fight either of them as my stomach rolled with the altitude change. I leaned on them both as they led me someplace. Then a door opened, and Gracelyn was putting me into a seat. She began to lower my seat back as she spoke. "You stay here where it is safe, and you rest. What medication do you want?"

"Nothing," I muttered as I rolled slightly to my side. I heard a sigh, and then the door closed.

"I'm sorry about that," I heard my wife say to someone.

"There is nothing to be sorry about. You need some ice for your face."

"I'll be okay. It's not that bad."

"Mrs. Vanover, I don't mean to pry, but does he do that often?"

Their voices got a little lower as if they had moved away from the vehicle; however, my hearing was so attuned to noise that everything was amplified.

"Do what? Punch me? Or fall to the ground and clench his head in pain?"

I froze. Had I hit Gracelyn? No! There is no way that I could have hit my wife.

"Hit you—well, to be honest, Mrs. Vanover, either."

Gracelyn was quiet for a moment. "He was injured overseas several weeks ago. He's still recovering. He's starting to remember what happened to him over there. The fire in the house has brought the memories back, and he's not dealing with them well. He'll get better, and no, he has never hit me before. That wasn't him. That was the monster called PTSD."

She thought I was a monster. I was. Holy shit! I had hurt my wife. I should have died in that explosion. I should have died.

CHAPTER TWELVE

GRACELYN

I had a headache, and my left eye hurt, but I attempted to play it off as no big deal. When Brady came out of this and realized what he had done, he would be overwhelmed. I knew that he would never do anything to hurt me physically —ever!

I should have left him at the hotel. After telling me that the fire had brought back some of the memories, I should have suggested he stay there. He was the one who had said he wanted to join me, and he'd be alright. He was anything but.

When Brady yelled "Duck!" I knew that he was back in Afghanistan or some other war zone. I didn't think as I went to him, and I never considered him fighting my assistance.

I touched the side of my face and winced as Mr. Vito and I headed inside the house. Once I was done with this, I needed to call our landlord and let him know the extent of the damage. I had sent him an email this morning and told him I would contact him as soon as I learned more. He was a nice man and said he might have another property we could stay in while this one was being repaired. He rented to a lot of military folks and was retired from the air force himself. I appreciated him more than he knew.

The walls down the hallway were dark from soot, and the odor was very pungent and almost overwhelming. Mr. Vito made notes and took a few pictures as he went. At the kitchen entrance, I paused and stared at the destruction. A couple of the cabinet doors had been torn down, and many of the dishes were broken.

"Did the fire break the dishes?"

Mr. Vito paused next to me. "No, that was probably the force of the water from the hose."

"Oh," I commented, not having considered that.

"Well, the entire kitchen is going to need to be gutted and replaced. There is no doubt about that. We will also have to check the floor in the room above. Flames might have damaged the supports." He made more notes, took some measurements, and then took more pictures.

As he moved to the family room area, I snapped a couple of pictures and sent them to my mom and Doug.

Mr. Vito said that the family room and dining area, which were open to the kitchen, would need to be gutted and done again. There were burn marks up the drywall, and the once light-beige walls were now a dingy charcoal-gray. The dark walls sucked the light out of the air, and it seemed almost suffocating in the room. I shivered and glanced back at the front door where the sun was shining on the porch.

I followed Mr. Vito around as he talked about what would need to be done for the rest of the house. He explained the processes for cleaning and replacing. He said that while some of our clothing might be ruined, most of it could be cleaned and would survive, especially if it had been inside the closed drawers of the dressers and not in the closet.

All the carpet would need to be replaced, and of course, everything would need painting. He anticipated it taking two months to make all the repairs. Before he left, he handed me a check for five thousand. "This will allow you to get the bare necessities like clothing, toiletries, essentials, and help get you set up in a temporary place. You will need to start going through your house and mark down what will be destroyed and what can be repaired or cleaned. I'll tell you right now, you might as well start shopping for new mattresses because you will never be able to clean the ones you have after the amount of smoke damage that I saw in there." He thumbed back over his shoulder toward the small two-story we rented.

"Thank you, Mr. Vito."

"My email is on my card, send me over the lists as you get them, and you can start getting the quotes, or having your landlord start getting the quotes to have it repaired. As the quotes come in, we'll start issuing checks for the work."

He paused before he left me and glanced at my vehicle. "I hope that things get better for your husband."

"Thank you."

"Make sure to put some ice on your eye when you have a chance." I gave him a kind smile and shook his hand before he turned to leave. I realized that while this whole process was rather daunting, he had been a pleasure to work with. I knew that if I had questions, he would be willing to assist.

Brady was still lying back in the seat, but his door was open now, and his arm was slung over his face.

"How are you feeling?" I asked him.

"How bad is the house?"

"Well, it's bad, but not horrible. The kitchen, family room, and dining room will have to be completely redone, but there is hope for the rest of the house. I need to go in and try to salvage some of the clothing to get it washed. Are you going to be alright out here?"

"I want to see the damage."

"Brady, I don't think that's a good idea. I think you need to stay out here in the car and wait for me to be done."

He pulled his arm away and opened his eyes. He blinked a few times as he squinted from the sun, and then he frowned. "What happened to your eye?"

I sighed. "You hit me by accident, Brady. It's no big deal."

He jerked forward, thrusting his hands toward my face, and I flinched back. His face paled with his hands frozen in midair. "Gracelyn, I'm sorry. You know I would never hurt you."

I took hold of one of his hands that were still hanging in the air between us and felt a quiver in it. "I know, Brady. As I said, it was an accident. Look, why don't you stay out here, and let me do this really quick, then we can get some food and go back to the hotel. I need to make a few more calls."

As I spoke, my phone began to ring, but I quickly shifted it to voicemail when I saw it was Doug. I didn't need Brady getting upset again. "My mom," I told him. "I'll call her back later. I sent her some pictures of the kitchen."

He nodded and leaned back in the seat again.

"I'll be as quick as I can be."

It ended up taking me about thirty minutes to dig through the bedroom drawers, stuff clothes into trash bags and hampers, and then carry them all out to the car. I made sure to grab my detergent and a few other things that we would need that could easily be cleaned.

The car smelled almost as bad as the house when I climbed inside. I opened the windows as I backed out of the driveway. "We can pick up food, and then I can take these to the laundromat and start cleaning them. It's going to take a while to get them all done, but at least I can do a couple of loads at a time."

"Do you want me to help?"

"No, I can do it. You should rest. Besides, Rebecca said she would pick up the boys today and bring them to the hotel, so they will need someone there when they get dropped off."

"Okay."

On the way back to the hotel, we stopped for fast food, and for just a moment, I thought about ordering a salad, but after all the labor I was doing today, I deserved something more than a salad. Thankfully, Brady stayed quiet about it. When we got back to the hotel, I went into the bathroom to wash my hands and came up short when I saw my face. Holy cow! No wonder the guy at the take-out window had done a double take!

My left eye was swollen, and there was a small cut at my brow, with dried blood coating my temple. Plus, my fair skin was already bruising. I took a picture of my face and then washed the blood away and cleaned my hands.

Brady was lying on the bed, and I paused when I stepped out. He seemed to be sleeping already, and his food sat on the bedside table untouched.

I collected mine and ate in silence on the other side of the room as I stared out the window. When I was done, I gathered my things, placed his medication vials beside his food, and left him to rest.

Hopefully, he would be awake by the time the kids arrived later today. At least here in the hotel, they couldn't get into that much trouble. At least I could hope.

I went by the bank to deposit the check and made sure to get several rolls of quarters. I had no idea how much those machines cost these days, but with three rolls, I thought I might have enough.

I was lucky that the place was relatively quiet, and I lugged in half the bags and split them up between three massive washers. After those were done, I retrieved the rest of the clothes and sorted those between another four washers: two large ones and two small ones. Then I sank into a chair and closed my eyes, sighing.

My phone buzzed, and I saw a message from Doug. *Wow, that's pretty bad. How are things going?*

Okay. I am at the laundromat doing seven loads of laundry at once.

Where? You alone?

Happy to be Clean, and yeah. Kids at school. Brady is sleeping at the hotel.

Need anything? I'm about to run out and get lunch.

Thank you, but no. I brought a book with me, and I'm going to sit here and pretend the outside world doesn't exist.

He sent me a laughing emoticon and said he would talk to me later. I set my phone to the side and collected my book. I was only four pages into it when I saw two feet pause in front of me. I lifted my eyes and was surprised to see Doug.

"What are you doing here?" I set my book down and stood.

His brow furrowed. "What the hell happened to your face, Gracelyn?"

I put my fingers to my brow. "Oh, it's nothing, a little misunderstanding."

Doug stepped closer, lifting my chin to inspect the injury. "This is way more than a misunderstanding. Did Brady do this to you?"

I shifted away from his touch. "Doug, it's no big deal. Brady was in the middle of a flashback, and he didn't know what he was doing."

"I don't care what kind of mindset he is in. He should not have hit you. If that's the frame of mind that he is in, you should not be with him. Wasn't the fire his fault? He's dangerous to you and the boys."

"No, he's not. I know it might seem that way, but he's not, and I'm not leaving my husband when he needs me the most."

"It's kind of obvious that he needs some dire help, Gracelyn. Is he in therapy yet?"

I didn't want to admit it, but I did. "No, he was supposed to call them, but then all this happened."

He stared down at me, his face stormy. "Yeah, well, if he

touches you again like that, I'm going to have a little chat with him."

"Doug, that's not a good idea. Brady already thinks that we are sleeping together."

He jerked back. "What?"

"I know! I told him we weren't, but because we talk, he thinks there is more going on between us than there is."

"He doesn't believe you?"

"I don't know what he thinks right now. I just know that he has asked me about you twice, and both times I told him we were just friends."

"That is what we are."

"I know."

Doug stepped forward. "As a friend, can I hug you? You look like you could use one."

I laughed slightly. "I could use one."

Doug put his arms around me, and it reminded me of the day that I found out Brady had been in an accident. Doug had comforted me that day, and here he was doing it again. Maybe it was wrong to seek this comfort in another man's arms, but it didn't mean anything to me, not like Brady thought. Doug was just my friend and my boss.

Doug stepped back, holding me at arm's length. "You going to be okay?"

"Yeah, I am."

"Want some company for a little while?"

"I'm sure you have better things to do."

"Oh, trust me, the mountain of paperwork that I have to get done will still be there in another thirty minutes."

"Okay, then have a seat."

For the next few minutes, I told Doug about the house and what had happened. I made light of Brady's part in all of it and forced myself to sound more upbeat about the process. Doug, in turn, made me laugh, and for the first time in almost a day, I relaxed a little bit.

When he was getting ready to go, I stood with him, and he hugged me again. As he pulled back, the two of us paused, our faces only inches apart, and I couldn't help but wonder for just a moment what it would be like to kiss him. I jerked back. That thought was so very wrong.

"Thanks for stopping by, Doug. I really appreciate it."

He winked, said goodbye, and told me to let him know when I was ready to come back to work.

After he left, I shifted the laundry from the washers to the dryers and thought about what had just happened. Maybe I shouldn't be spending time with Doug alone. Perhaps he did want to get me in bed. That wasn't what I wanted, though.

Maybe I had briefly wondered what it would be like to kiss him, but if I were honest with myself, I had imagined kissing other men before. I hadn't really ever wanted to do it, but I had been with Brady since I was in high school. He had been my one and only boyfriend. He was the only man I had ever kissed romantically.

I frowned as I sat down. Was it normal to wonder such things when you had been with someone for so long? I hated myself for even asking and shoved the whole thing out of my mind and returned to my book.

CHAPTER THIRTEEN

BRADY

*I*t had been three days since the fire. The kids continued with school, and Gracelyn went to work. After work, she brought back dinner, helped the kids with their homework, made phone calls to deal with the housing issue, and then passed out.

I lay in bed, glaring at the ceiling, or the wall, or the window. Once in a while, I'd stare at the television, but usually, I would listen to it as I zoned out. The only food I ate was what Gracelyn brought at night. I could have walked next door to the convenience store and gotten a sandwich or something else, but that required me to get out of bed for more than five minutes.

It was on the fourth day that I finally picked up the phone—not to call a buddy or Gracelyn, but to make an appointment for therapy. As luck would have it, the shrink that I was assigned to for my mental health was available the next day. The physical therapist couldn't fit me in until Monday.

Things with Gracelyn had been iffy this week, and I knew that this would make her happy to hear. Even though we had intimately connected the night of the fire, we hadn't spoken very much since.

I missed the days when I would come home from work, and she would ask, "How was your day?" and then I'd fill her in on all the serious and silly things that had happened while she cooked dinner or while we ate. The kids would share, too, and then after dinner, I'd play with the kids or snuggle on the couch with my wife.

Now, we were all quiet and withdrawn, and we needed things to change. Gracelyn was right. We had to find our new normal again—even if that meant me not being in the air force anymore.

I hadn't told her about that yet. I was hoping that, miraculously, things would change, but even I knew that things would never change with me sitting on my ass all day doing nothing.

I looked forward to telling her when she got back to the hotel tonight, but when she arrived in a flurry, she dropped off food and the kids and said she had to head out to see the temporary housing that we were getting from our current landlord. If it fit our needs, we could move in this weekend.

After she left, I fretted. I hadn't even known she had a lead on the house. Why hadn't she told me? What else wasn't she telling me?

The boys ate their dinner, did their homework, and were getting ready for bed when she finally returned.

"That took you a long time."

"Yeah, well, it was on the other side of town, and the traffic was hectic. I had to wait for our landlord to arrive, and then I needed to look at the place, plus I hadn't eaten, so I stopped to get something after I saw the place, and then went by the store to get a few more things."

I remained quiet as she spoke with the boys. While explaining what she had been doing this evening, she hadn't looked at me once. Gracelyn was huge on eye contact. She never wanted to have a conversation with someone if they weren't looking at her. Why wouldn't she look at me?

She gathered the clothes she had been sleeping in and said she was taking a shower. Gracelyn wasn't one to take showers at night, so why was she doing so tonight?

Had Gracelyn lied to me? Had she been with someone? With her boss? I dwelled over that while she was in the bathroom and started giving myself a headache. Before she came out, I popped one of my migraine pills to keep from getting one and closed my eyes. I had every intention of asking her when she got out of the bathroom. As I started to drift, I could have sworn I heard someone weeping, but I was just too tired to care.

I woke up gasping with a spasm in my lower back and the room dark. Gracelyn shifted on the other bed but didn't seem to have woken up. I slipped out of bed as quietly as I could and stretched my back to ease the spasm. I glanced at her phone that was on the nightstand between us. It said it was two-thirteen.

I collected my prescription vials and went into the bathroom where I could turn on the light. I blinked a few times as my eyes adjusted, and then I stared at my reflection. My face was thinner, and there were circles under my eyes, although my beard growth hid my shallow cheeks. I'd lost muscle mass on my chest, arms, and stomach. There were two small scars in the final stages of healing on my arms. Nothing that I could see said that I should be in this much pain.

I stepped back from the mirror and lifted the edge of my sleep shorts, pulling them up to show the scar on my leg. It was still healing, and the flesh was thick and pink, but even it didn't look painful. It looked like it would hurt if I pushed on it or stretched the muscle too far.

If anyone were to look at me, they wouldn't see the amount of pain that I was in. They couldn't see the nerve damage to my spine. They wouldn't be able to tell that my brain thudded painfully or that I was confused about random things. They would have no way of knowing that I forgot names or places that I had been to or that memories were sometimes jumbled like a tangled string. They wouldn't understand that numbers didn't add up correctly or time didn't make sense as it once had to me.

My wife and children weren't even aware of this. Dane had asked me to help him with a math problem, and I had stared at it for too long before I told him to wait for his mother to come home because I had a headache.

I hadn't had a headache. I just wasn't sure how to do the problem, and I had felt like an idiot. I was over thirty years old! I knew how to do simple fifth-grade math. I had excelled in calculus in high school, and here I had blanked on dividing with fractions? I was a loser.

I stared at the man in the reflection again. What did people see when they looked at me?

That was easy. They would see a drug addict with pale skin, withdrawn eyes, pinprick pupils, and jumpy reflexes. They would see someone who hides inside and has become unsocial.

They wouldn't know that I hid because I was embarrassed. I hated that I got confused or collapsed in on myself when the pain struck. I used to be strong—able to take on the world.

I stared at the bottles in front of me. Would I ever be able to live without those? Would I ever be able to take on the world again? I lifted my chin and stared into my bloodshot green eyes to see the answer.

I would never be the man I used to be—I knew that—but I had yet to accept it.

What did my sons think of me when they looked at me? Did they pity me? Miss me? Wish I had never come home?

And Gracelyn—what did she think? Did she still love me? I was pretty sure that she did love me, but did she love me *enough*? Did she think I was less of a man because I didn't want to face life? Did she wish that I had never come back, that she was free of my issues?

I knew she didn't want me dead—at least I hoped she didn't

—but wouldn't it have been easier if I had died than for her to have to deal with all of this?

I opened one of my prescription bottles and poured the topiramate pills on the counter, counting them. There were twenty. I opened the bottle of oxy and dumped those on the counter, too—another eighteen pills. If I took all of those, just those thirty-eight pills, I would drift off to sleep and never wake back up, right?

I wouldn't be in pain anymore.

I wouldn't cause any more problems for anyone.

Gracelyn and the boys could move on.

They would do better without me.

Gracelyn could handle it—she was already doing just fine without me. She could move closer to her mother, get help with the boys. She could find another man to love.

Someone else would be a father to my sons. My heart ached, and I lifted my face to see tears rolling down my cheeks. I watched as one slithered from my eye to my chin and then dropped to the floor.

I didn't want Gracelyn to fall in love with someone else, and I didn't want to miss out on my boys growing up. I put my hands to my face and sat on the edge of the tub, fighting the urge to scream.

Tomorrow, I would get help.

Tomorrow, I would begin to fight back.

I had an appointment, and the shrink would help me get through this. I didn't want to think about killing myself. I wanted my life back! I wanted my wife and children smiling at me again.

I moved two pills to the side, collected two more pills from the other bottles, and then put the rest from the counter back in their respective containers. I swallowed all four dry even though I was right next to the sink. Then I wiped the salty tears from my face and went back to bed.

I stared at the ceiling, thinking over the fact that Stuart, Chuck, and Evan hadn't been given a chance to fight for life. They'd been blown to smithereens. Jesus, did they even have anything left to return to their families?

Haunting and grotesque images filled my mind, and I couldn't get them to go away. I welcomed the drug-induced sleep that finally took me away.

Sadly, the images didn't disappear completely, and I kept waking up as different versions of the same scene came back to me. All four of us in the hangar, laughing, making plans for the future, and then an explosion. Sometimes I was right there in the thick of it; sometimes I was on the sidelines, and I watched.

Every single time ended with the same image before I would burst awake. An arm from fingers to just above the elbow, and the name Monica staring back at me from the tattoo on Chuck's arm.

I was sitting on the floor of the bathroom when Gracelyn's alarm went off. A moment later, I heard her walking around and then a soft knock on the door before she pushed it open.

"What are you doing in here, Brady?" she asked as she blinked against the bright light.

I shrugged.

She came to stand in front of me and then put the lid down on the toilet before she sat. "Did you have a bad dream?"

I rubbed my face. "Yeah."

She put her hand on my knee. "Aw, I'm so sorry. Do you want to tell me what it was?"

I shook my head. "No."

"You know that you can. I'd be okay with that."

"Gracelyn, I don't want to put words to the pictures in my mind."

She leaned away and sighed softly. "Well, you should tell someone."

"I will." I paused. "I have an appointment with my shrink today."

She looked happily startled, and it irritated me that making her just the slightest bit happy made me feel better too. "You do? When did you make that appointment?"

"Yesterday."

"Why didn't you tell me?"

"You were a little busy last night."

"Oh, I'm sorry. You should have told me. What time is it? I'll need to let my boss know that I have to be gone for a while."

"No, you don't."

She frowned at me. "How are you going to get there, Brady? You can't drive yet."

"I'll call for a Lyft, or Uber, or whatever they have here."

"Brady, I'm sure that Doug wouldn't mind me taking the time off to take you."

The last thing I wanted was for her boss to know I was in therapy. It was none of his damned business. "Thanks, but no thanks. I need to do this on my own."

She seemed slightly disappointed, but then she smiled. "Okay, well, that's good. If you find that you need me to come to get you, all you have to do is call me. I'll come right over."

"I think I can get to and from the medical complex." I knew I sounded irritated; I didn't mean to, but that just seemed like my normal now.

"I'm not saying that you can't, Brady. I'm just saying that if you get worn out or if you get a horrible headache, I'll come get you. No reason for you to suffer on your own."

She squeezed my knee and then said she needed to use the restroom so she could get ready for work.

My back ached as I got off the floor, and I shuffled a little bit as I returned to the main part of the room and went to the window where I gazed out into the early pinking of the morning sky.

I should be leaving right now to get to the base. Usually, I walked out the door at five minutes after six each morning to grab my coffee and breakfast before I met with my flight.

I had taken all of that for granted before. I had taken so much for granted.

CHAPTER FOURTEEN

GRACELYN

*I*t had been four weeks since Brady had started therapy. He saw a psychiatrist once a week and had physical therapy two days a week for his back and leg.

On Tuesday mornings, he would start his day with mental therapy and then move on to physical. Those mornings he was always positive, almost energetic, and he would say, "I got this" with a grin. Monday mornings were usually the best times of the week. It was almost like it used to be, with shared laughter, smiles, and a few jokes between him and the boys. I'd even get tender touches, a hug or two, and maybe a kiss—all of which were rare these days.

But come Monday night, everything would change. He growled at us and was often nasty and bitter. He barely ate dinner and typically went to bed early in a lot of pain. I had tried to help him with suggestions of massage, hot baths, heating pads, but he had always told me to leave him alone.

The day after wasn't any better. His back would ache terribly, and his leg would throb from the exercise of the previous day. Plus, he still had vertigo issues and headaches constantly, and loud sounds made him ill.

I knew that he was supposed to be doing exercises every day at home, but Brady only did them when he went to therapy. Unless he did them when we weren't home—but I doubted that happened. Perhaps if he did them daily, he would regain his strength and get past the pain faster. Of course, I couldn't tell him that. I had no idea what I was talking about—at least that was what he told me.

On Wednesdays, Brady was a little more tolerable, but he was usually quiet and kept to himself. I was thankful that my life was busy with taking the kids to school and sports and working. It was almost as if he were on deployment, except he wasn't.

I had once wondered what it would have been like if he hadn't come home. We would have all been devastated, but life would have gone on eventually. After I'd had that thought, I'd felt horribly guilty and refused to think such things again.

Thursday mornings, Brady would be in a decent mood and be optimistic once again about physical therapy, and the evenings would revert to Mondays. Fridays resembled Tuesdays, but luckily, on Saturday and Sunday, he was slightly better when the kids and I were home.

He even went to a baseball game of Dane's and watched part of a soccer game for Drew, although halfway through, he had to rest in the minivan when his vertigo hit, and a migraine broke through.

No matter how the days were, the nights were worse. We were living in a small two-bedroom ranch house while contractors repaired our house. I sure missed the two-story home that we had rented. It wasn't that it was all that much bigger, but it was laid out differently.

Brady had nightmares almost every night. They were always worse on Monday and Tuesday nights, but they could happen anytime he was sleeping. He would thrash in bed, groan, scream, and kick. I tried to help him a few times, but I got punched in the face again, and after that, I started slipping out of bed and sitting on the floor or going into the boys' bedroom and climbing into bed with them.

Many nights, Brady would get up and pace. If we had been in our two-story, it wouldn't have been a big deal. We weren't able to hear someone walking around downstairs, but here—we heard everything.

He was like a caged tiger some nights, and he would talk to himself as he walked from the kitchen to the living room down the small hallway and then back to the living room and kitchen. Just last night, he had been like that. He had been highly agitated in bed, thrashing around for almost thirty minutes before I gave up sleeping and climbed out of bed to join Dane in his.

After I climbed into my son's bed, Brady had gotten up and started his circles around the house. He was in the hallway outside the bedroom door when I heard him say, "I'm a loser."

I winced and remained still. On another turn down the hallway, I heard Brady mutter, "I should have died."

I clenched my eyes, hating to hear the pain in his voice. Dane must have been awake because he turned toward me and whispered, "Why does he want to be dead?"

I brushed the hair off his brow. "Oh, honey. He doesn't want to be dead. He is just feeling guilty that his friends are dead. Your father is dealing with a lot, but he'll get better."

"You promise?"

I smiled at him in the darkness, the soft glow of the nightlight shining off his eyes. "I promise. Your dad will get better soon. Now close your eyes and go back to sleep."

He snuggled against me, and I rested my cheek on his soft hair. I sure hoped that I was able to keep that promise. I wanted my husband back. I missed him, and I hated seeing this person he was becoming.

*B*rady led me through the medical complex. He was wearing a baseball cap, and his head was down as if he were focusing on each step he made. He didn't look anyone in the eye, and that bothered me. Brady had always been the type of person to meet everyone's gaze with a smile, nod, or a pleasant word.

By the time we reached the waiting room, Brady was a different person. No longer smiling or pleasant, he had turned in on himself and spoke in single words. He checked in and took a seat. I slipped into a chair beside him, glancing around the sizeable utilitarian waiting room. The chairs were blue, the walls white. The lights were fluorescent and overwhelmingly bright. Posters about rights and rules lined the walls. Computer monitors hung from different places with last names listed. As I watched, the top name Martin began to blink, and the number six showed up beside it. A man two rows over got up and went down a hallway as another man limped slowly past him.

A poster off to the side near us said, "Don't be a statistic. Ask for help." What kind of a statistic was it talking about? I frowned as I scanned the room again and counted the twenty-six occupants. There were a few women here, but primarily men sitting alone. Some stared into space, and others played on their phones. Two sat with their eyes closed. One made eye contact with me and gave me a single abrupt nod.

About thirty minutes later, Brady's name flashed with the number twelve next to it. He glanced at me but didn't say anything as he stood. I followed him again, assuming that was what I was supposed to do.

We passed another man in the hallway, his head down. The corridor was filled with doors—all closed, except for room twelve. That door was open, and Brady stepped in, and I heard him say, "Doc," as I turned the corner.

"Brady, good to see you. Mrs. Vanover." The doctor stood,

held his hand out to me, and smiled kindly. "I'm Doctor Felcroft. I've been working with Brady since he joined us here. Come on in and have a seat."

"Thank you, Dr. Felcroft. It's a pleasure to meet you. Please call me Gracelyn."

I sat in a chair slightly off to the side from where Brady was. The doctor sat beside a desk filled with papers and files. His salt-and-pepper hair was in slight disarray as if he had been running his hands through it. His brown eyes were bright, and his mustache was a little too bushy for my taste, but he seemed like a nice enough man.

"How are you doing today, Brady?"

"Fine," Brady responded.

I tried not to frown. So Brady talked like this to his therapist, too, huh? Here I thought we were the only lucky ones.

"Just 'fine'? How are the nightmares? Did you have any this week?"

Brady shrugged slightly. "A couple."

"A couple!" I barked out in astonishment

Dr. Felcroft turned to me, a brow lifted. "Mrs. Vanover, you seem to think it's more than just a couple."

I nodded. "Brady has nightmares every night. Sometimes more than once, and some nights, he is up pacing for hours and doesn't sleep at all."

The doctor turned to Brady. "Is that true?"

"She's making it seem worse than it is," he replied as he glanced at a bookshelf and avoided both of us.

"How can you say that, Brady? You wake me up every single night thrashing and crying, and then you get up and walk around the house for hours."

"Sorry to bother you," he muttered.

"Brady, stop that! You know it's not a bother."

He laughed and finally looked at me. "Really? Do you like

117

being woken up every single night with me striking out at you? You like sleeping in our sons' room?"

"Of course I don't like it, Brady. I'm worried about you. I worry all the time about you. I wish that you could sleep better, and the nightmares would go away."

"Why? Because they bother you?"

"No!" I jerked to the edge of my seat. "Because they bother *you*! I want *you* to get better, not for the boys or me, but for *you*!"

He frowned at me and then growled, "You don't want me to get better for you? Or our sons? I thought that was why I was trying to get better, for you all so that we could have a normal fucking life again."

"Brady, don't use that nasty language with me."

"Why? Because it might offend you? Like my nightmares offend you? Like me having to go lie down in the middle of Drew's soccer game offended you?"

I gaped at him, my mouth opening and closing for a moment. "What are you talking about?"

The doctor put his hands up. "Okay, let's calm this situation down a little bit. Brady, it's obvious that your wife thinks your nightmares are an issue. Be honest with me, do you have nightmares every night?"

He sighed and rubbed the side of his face. "Yeah, or else I can't sleep."

"We can give you medicine for that. Are the dreams the same, or are they different?"

"They are all the same with slight differences."

"What are they about?"

Brady glanced at me. "I'd rather not say in front of Gracelyn."

I pursed my lips as the doctor flicked a glance my way and asked Brady, "Why? Because you think it will *offend* her?"

"No, because I don't want her to know the shit I've seen."

"Gracelyn, what do you think? Do you want to hear it?"

"Of course, I want to hear it. Maybe if I know what Brady is dreaming about, I might be able to help him."

"Come on, Gracelyn. You just got offended by me using the F word. Trust me, hearing about what I went through and saw overseas would put you over the edge."

"Brady, you have no idea what will put me over the edge. I'm your wife. I vowed to be there for you through good and bad, sickness and health. If this isn't sickness and bad, I don't know what the heck is. I'm here for you. I want to help. I want to know what you went through."

"Be careful what you wish for, Gracey," he said as he looked away.

"Okay, maybe another time we can venture into him telling you what he dreams about. Right now, I'd like to know how you two are doing as a couple."

"What does that have to do with anything?" Brady asked, looking disgusted at the question.

"Well, having a stable home life is essential, Brady. Knowing you have people there to support you is important for your recovery." The doctor turned to me. "Are you willing to support him, Gracelyn?"

"Of course! You don't even have to ask that. I want to help Brady with anything he needs."

"Alright, then let me ask you two this: Are you both communicating with one another?"

I gnawed on my bottom lip for a moment. Brady glanced my way as I responded, "Well, I am trying to communicate with him, but he never wants to talk to me. I have no idea what he does when he comes here, and he never talks about anything other than what his pain level is or tells us to be quiet because he's trying to rest."

"That's not true," Brady hissed toward me. "You never try to talk to me."

My brows popped high. "You're kidding, right? Brady, I try to talk to you all the time, but you ignore me."

"No, you talk to Doug all the time, not me," he snapped.

I blinked rapidly for a moment and then explained to the doctor, "He's my boss."

Brady turned to me, and his green eyes looked sad. "If he's just your boss, then you should leave your relationship with him at the office. There is no reason for him to be calling you at home."

"How many times do I have to tell you, Brady, that Doug is my boss and my friend, and nothing is going on with us."

The doctor put his hand up. "Brady, are you suggesting that your wife is having an affair?"

"I'm not suggesting it. I know it."

I laughed. "That's funny! You know it! Well, I sure wish someone had told me because I guess I'm missing out on something that I'm supposed to be enjoying."

The doctor looked like he was going to laugh but shook himself out of it after a moment. "Gracelyn, you are telling your husband that you have not been unfaithful, correct?"

"That is correct! I have not, nor will I *ever* sleep with my boss. He is a friend who has been there for our family during a rough time. That's it! He gave me a job when Brady got hurt, and it has been a lifesaver since his salary was adjusted and he lost his hazardous duty and family separation pay."

"Brady, you don't believe her?"

"It's kind of hard to believe her when she is always sneaking around and talking to him."

"Holy cow, Brady! I do not sneak around and talk to Doug!"

"Brady," the doctor started, "do you know of any time that Gracelyn has lied to you before?"

He shook his head.

"Is your ability not to trust her something new?"

"Well, yeah. I never had a reason not to trust her."

I was exasperated. "Do you want me to quit my job, Brady? Are you asking me to do that? If you want me to quit, I will. Just say the word." I was willing to do anything, including removing the only person from my life who had been someone I could lean on.

"No, I don't want you to quit your job," Brady said sullenly as he hung his head.

"It's probably a good idea not to do that right now until you have a good nest egg. It will make transitioning easier."

"Transitioning?" I asked, confused. Brady tensed and clenched his hands.

"Yeah." The doctor looked almost as confused as I did. "Did Brady not tell you that he was being medically discharged from the air force?"

My jaw dropped, and I stared at the side of Brady's head. "And you tell me that I'm not communicating."

CHAPTER FIFTEEN

BRADY

I was getting a headache, and I knew it was because my blood pressure was going up. No, I had not told Gracelyn about being released from duty. Felcroft and I had just started to discuss it last week, and I had sort of put it out of my mind so that I wouldn't stress over it.

I hadn't thought that Felcroft would say anything about it in this session. I also hadn't wanted Gracelyn to come, but he had said it was necessary for my recovery. He wanted to make sure that she was on board with the changes and help I needed. It was a joke. How did they know what I would need as they processed my paperwork to release me from duty?

It could take two months, it could take a year, but sometime in the next twelve months, they would hand me a packet of paperwork on how to deal with my disability as a retired service member. It sucked!

My physical therapist explained that due to the amount of damage done to my spine, I would probably be on pain medication for the rest of my life. They couldn't keep me on active duty if that were the case. My therapist had also said that if they had found the cracks in my spine in Germany and had done surgery right away, I probably would have made a full recovery and would have been close to returning to active duty now.

I hated hearing that. I had known that something was going on when I was in Ramstein, but they told me to wait and have it dealt with at Reed. I wished I could go back and force them to look into it. I would have stayed another week—a month—just to skip all of this torture.

I also hadn't told Gracelyn about that. I didn't want to see the pity in her eyes or hear the questions of why I hadn't pushed the issue. As it was, her staring at the side of my head was making me want to throw up my breakfast. I didn't want to disappoint her, but that seemed to be all I could do these days. My head started to throb with the beating of my heart.

"Brady, why didn't you tell your wife about that?"

I shrugged a shoulder. "I guess I forgot."

"You forgot?" Her voice got a little shrill. "How could you forget that you were losing your job, your career? That is a big deal, Brady. I can't believe you didn't tell me."

"You know what?" I stood. "I don't need this shit today." I rushed to the door while both of them protested and yanked it open, disappearing into the hallway. My physical therapist would have been impressed by my speed, but my adrenaline was surging and blocking the pain.

Gracelyn called my name from the waiting room, but I was already bursting through the double doors into the main hallway. I couldn't talk to her right now. I couldn't see the disappointment in her face, the betrayal that I couldn't take care of her anymore. I had sworn to do that, and now I couldn't.

I was a failure!

I was a loser!

I wanted to slam my fist into the wall, wanted to tear my hair out as I screamed at the top of my lungs. Instead, I hit the stairs and rushed down three flights. On the ground floor, I pushed through the exit into the courtyard and walked as quickly as I could away from the medical building. I didn't care where I was going. I just needed to get away from the demons descending on me.

I walked off the campus into the town outside the base, and I kept walking. I had pushed myself pretty hard earlier, and now I was limping slightly, but I kept moving.

Images flashed through my mind over and over again—pushing against one another for attention. Accusations from Gracelyn at not having told her, anger, pain, disappointment—it all tore at my soul. Then I'd see the faces of my friends, of the men I had worked with in Afghanistan, and my heart would ache more. I should have died with them. I should have saved them. I should have done something other than stand there and watch it happen.

I kept on walking, and somewhere after the fourth phone call from Gracelyn, I turned off my phone. I almost tossed it into a trash receptacle, but I shoved it into my pocket instead.

I had been walking for a while when I started to hurt—a lot. I decided to take a break and slipped into a small café. I found an empty booth near the back and ordered a sandwich and iced tea. What I wouldn't do for an ice-cold beer or a couple of shots of whiskey. I hadn't had a drop of alcohol since I was overseas, and suddenly, I was dying to pour something down my throat.

I retrieved my pills from a small pill container in my pocket under the table and then tossed them back when the tea arrived.

As I sat there, I tried not to think about the confusion and accusation I had seen in Gracelyn's eyes. I should have told her. Why hadn't I? Maybe because I knew that as soon as she realized that I wasn't going to recover fully, and I wouldn't be the man she married, she would leave. She'd run off with Doug or someone else.

It didn't matter who it was. I'm sure they would be better than I was for her—for the kids. I hung my head, fighting to block the emotional pain. Once they discharged me, I'd be nothing, just a has-been—an afterthought.

Maybe a few guys would say, "Hey, you remember Vanover? He was a good guy. What happened to him?"

Someone else would say, "I heard he got discharged. He missed getting blown into bits and pieces by a hundred yards but got injured enough to mess him up. They couldn't fix him, so they let him go."

The other guy would go, "Huh, that's too bad. You ready for chow?"

Just like that, I'd be gone, and they would all move on.

The waitress set my burger in front of me, and I stared at it. What the hell did I have now? I couldn't go back to civilian life from ten years ago, and I couldn't hang with all these military guys anymore. I didn't belong.

I pushed the plate back, dropped some cash on the table, and walked out. Down the street, I came across a small, dark bar called Purgatory. Yeah, that seemed fitting. The sign said it was open, so I slipped in and grabbed a stool at the bar.

The bartender was a tall, mean-looking guy with a burn scar from his right eye down his throat and under his shirt. His voice was gravelly as he spoke. "What can I get you?"

"I'll take a draft and a shot of whiskey."

He nodded and worked on my order. I couldn't help it, but I watched him. The skin was roughly puckered on his face and neck. Damn, that must have been a hell of a recovery.

He set the beer down in front of me and then poured me a shot. "You want me to start you a tab?"

"Nah," I said. I dropped a twenty on the scarred surface of the bar.

He gave me his back as he went to the ancient register and

rang me out. He set the change on the bar and turned away without another word. He went back to wiping down bottles behind the bar.

Maybe I could be a bartender—seemed like an easy enough job. Serve drinks, polish glass, listen to guys talk about the woes of their lives. Yeah, maybe not. I lifted the shot and stared at it.

I was not supposed to drink when taking this medicine, but I just didn't care. I needed something else to numb the pain. Maybe drinking the alcohol would kill me, and then I wouldn't have to decide to do it myself.

After I threw back the shot, I sipped my beer. God, that was good, so damned good. I set my glass down and glanced around. I was the only person in here besides the bartender. "This your place?"

He glanced at me. "Yeah."

"Why did you name it Purgatory?"

He smirked, but it looked funny since the one side of his face didn't move like the other side did. "Seemed fitting after this." He pointed to the scar. "I'm living in my own hellfire."

"What happened?"

"Jumped into a bad situation and couldn't get out."

"Jumped?"

He studied me, and I saw it in his eyes. He was former military. "Airborne."

"Damn, man."

"Yeah, so when I discharged out and got my head straight, I opened this place."

"They are starting the process with me—discharging out."

"Medical?"

"Yeah," I nodded.

"What'd you do?"

"Walked away," I said, and he gave me an odd look. "I was walking out of our hangar when a rogue RPG took out two

Ospreys and a lot of people. I got thrown against a wall, cracked my spine, among other things."

"I heard about that, heard that unit was attached here." He shook his head, and for a second, I felt like someone understood me, but then he frowned. "That wasn't that long ago, was it?"

"Couple months ago."

"You still on narcs?" He raised a brow and nodded his chin at my glasses.

"Yeah, so?" I shrugged.

He put both his hands on the bar in front of me. "I don't know jack about you, man, and you don't know jack about me, but what I do know is that coming in here just as I open to try and hide from your pain—or your life—is not what you should be doing, and you should not be drinking if you are taking any medical cocktails."

I started to get pissed. Why did everyone have to give me their damned advice?

He pushed back, putting his hands in the air in front of him. "But you do you, man. Just know, I'm not serving you any more of the hard stuff, not right now. Just one shot is going to make you wish you'd died all over again."

"I wish that every day already. Maybe it will finish the job."

He eyed me with a slanted gaze. "You telling me you wish you'd kicked it? Wish you'd been blown the hell up with your squadron?"

"Yeah, sometimes."

He shook his head. "Man, you have a lot of healing to do, but hiding behind booze or painkillers is not going to help you. Trust me, I know. You need to surround yourself with other people and get help."

"I don't need that."

He laughed. "You don't? Boy, you're in Purgatory at two in the afternoon. Of course, you need help." He sighed. "You just find out you're being released?"

"Last week, but my wife found out today."

He nodded and then shook his head as if he understood what I was going through. "She sticking by you?"

"I don't know. I didn't hang around to find out. She was angry that I didn't tell her."

"Why didn't you?"

"Because I wasn't ready."

"You love your wife?"

"Yeah."

"Then you need to talk to her. Women are a lot stronger than we give them credit for. I almost lost my old lady because I didn't open up to her. Mind you, she doesn't know *everything*, but she knows enough that she gets me and my moods. If you don't tell your lady what's going on inside your head, you are just going to push her out the door and into someone else's arms."

"It might already be too late," I told him as my shoulders dropped, and I wrapped both hands around my beer. The shot that I'd thrown back was sloshing around in my stomach, and I felt a bit off.

He shook his head again. "Then you need to get your head squared away fast. If you want to keep your wife, you need to get with the program."

He turned around and fished in a drawer for something. "Look, I talked to this one guy once as he was coming through town. Here is his card. They do some pretty good work, and they have a number to call if you are in crisis."

I glanced at the card. "Yeah, I don't think I need that."

"You might not think so, man, but from where I'm sitting, you do. I've been where you are. I know the signs. Take the card and call the number. It might just save your life."

The phone behind the bar began to ring, and he went to answer it. I picked up the card and looked at it: Rise Again Warrior, Services for Servicemembers in Need.

The name on the card was Nate Hardy. I tapped the card on the counter twice before I guzzled my beer and then slipped the card in my pocket as I climbed off the stool. Before the bartender was off the line, I was out the door. The leftover foam slowly ran toward the bottom of the empty glass, the only sign I had ever been there.

CHAPTER SIXTEEN

GRACELYN

*B*rady was gone before I could even think to stop him. I rushed out after him, but he was moving too quickly for me to reach him. Well, at least he could move fast when he wanted to. I returned to room twelve.

Dr. Felcroft gave me a sad smile and held his hand out to the chair Brady had been sitting in.

"How long has he known?"

"We talked about it last week."

"And it's official? They are discharging him?"

He nodded. "Yeah, the paperwork has already been started."

"How long?"

"It could take a couple of months to a year. While that is happening, Brady will continue his treatments here. Then we will transfer his records to a VA center of his choice to continue if he wants to."

I felt the anger building deep inside of me. "So Brady gives ten years of service, risks his life, fights for freedom, and now they are just going to push him out the door and tell him if he wants help, he can get it? It's like they just gave up on him!"

"I understand your frustration, Gracelyn. There are thousands of service members in that same position, but what are they supposed to do? When one falls, he is replaced. Why do you think we run so many basic training classes? Because people are either injured, killed, step away after an enlistment period, or retire. The military can't hold on to everyone. That's why we have the VA system, to help those who have moved on."

"But what if he doesn't want to move on? What if he wants to stay?"

He sighed. "I'm sure Brady wants to stay, just like all the other guys in his shoes, but Brady has damage to his spine that will never heal completely. He will be reliant on pain medication for the rest of his life. They can't allow him to remain active duty while doing that. It would be one thing if they thought eventually he would be off the medications, but doctors have already stated it's permanent."

"Permanent? He's going to be in this much pain for the rest of his life?"

"Probably."

"What am I supposed to do? How do I even begin to deal with this, Dr. Felcroft?"

"Are you in therapy?"

"No."

"Well, I suggest you find some support groups. That way, you'll be able to vent your stress when you need to." He paused and shrugged. "Or you could leave him."

My jaw dropped. "How could you say that? I vowed to be there with him for the rest of my life. I will not just walk away."

"You would not be the first to do that. It's hard dealing with someone with PTSD along with a compounded TBI and a dependency on narcotics. Most women would leave."

I stood and glared at him. "I am not most women." I started to walk away, and he called out to me.

"Gracelyn." He smiled and held something out to me. "I know you're not. Brady is a lucky guy. Give him time, find a support group for yourself, and just keep moving forward. It will either work, or it won't."

I took the paper he held out to me. "What is this?"

"It will help him sleep at night." He smiled and then looked away, dropping a folder onto a stack of at least ten more. "You can leave the door open," he said as he pushed a button on his desk. The screens in the waiting room were now blinking with another name and the number twelve.

"Thank you for your time," I said as I slipped into the hallway and fought the tears. I tried to call Brady, but he didn't answer. I tried again when I got to my car, and then I drove around the complex looking for him. Maybe he'd gone to physical therapy and had put his phone down. I tried him a few more times, but eventually, it went directly to voicemail.

Fine, he could find his own way home. He had no right to be angry with me. I wasn't the one who had withheld important information. What were we going to do now? What was Brady going to do without the air force? For as long as I had known him, he had talked about joining. I'd been surprised that he hadn't joined straight out of high school, but he'd told me that he'd wanted us to be married first, and then we would start our journey together.

I had known from the beginning that it was going to be hard, but I was strong enough to handle it. I wasn't afraid to do things on my own, and Brady had taught me enough about fixing stuff that, while he was gone, I had been able to repair the hose on the dishwasher and a gasket on the sink. I also mowed and did the weed eater on our lawn; however, I had been looking forward to Dane taking over that job soon since he was almost ten.

Since this morning, I had planned to be at the medical complex for a while longer, and then we were going to go pick up the boys together and get dinner, but now I had hours to kill.

I decided to stop for a cup of coffee, and then I pulled into the park and picked up my phone. There were only two people in this world that I wanted to reach out to when I was upset. One was Brady, and that wasn't happening. The other was my mother.

"Hey, sweetie, how are you? How did the appointment go today?"

The minute she asked, the tears started. "Oh, Mom! It was horrible."

"Horrible?"

"Mom, first Brady accused me of not talking to him, and then of having an affair with my boss, then I found out that Brady's being discharged!"

"What?"

"Yeah, and he has known about it at least a week and never told me. Mom, I have no clue what is going on inside his mind. Why would he hide that from me? Why not tell me so that we can start talking and planning? I don't get him anymore. I keep trying to be there for him, but he just keeps driving this wedge deeper between us, and I don't know how to stop this."

"Okay, well, you are going to have to find a good time and place to talk to him about this in a way that he won't get defensive."

"He's always defensive."

She sighed. "Now, what was this about him thinking you are having an affair with your boss?"

"Yeah, he says that because Doug and I talk when we aren't at the office, he thinks we are having an affair."

"Are you?"

"What?"

"You do know that there are other ways to have an affair with someone, right? You don't necessarily have to sleep with him."

"What are you talking about, Mom?"

"Well, maybe you are involved with him, and you don't even

realize it, Gracelyn. Perhaps you have been leaning on Doug when you should have been leaning on Brady."

"Mom, Brady does not *want* me to lean on him."

"Have you asked him that?"

"No."

"Well, then maybe you should."

"I'm so confused right now." I rubbed my brow with the heel of my hand. "What does me not leaning on Brady have to do with having an affair with my boss?"

"Gracelyn, you can have an emotional affair with someone where you get attached to them, learn to care for them, depend on them, seek them out for comfort or to help you relieve stress, and not sleep with them."

I chewed on that for a moment. Was that what I was doing?

"Sometimes having an emotional affair is worse than a sexual one. With sex, it's physical, but when you put your emotions into it, then it changes you and the way you see things."

"Oh, my Lord. Have I been cheating on my husband, and I didn't even realize it?"

"Honey, don't be too hard on yourself. Brady isn't the only one who has been suffering. You and the kids have been, too, and you opened yourself up to someone who was there for you. It's natural to do that, but now that you are aware, you might want to distance yourself from your boss."

"Well, that might not be hard since Brady is being discharged. I mean, I'm sure we will move. I just have no idea where we will go."

"You are always welcome to come home."

I laughed. "Oh, you don't want us there, not right now. Brady is constantly altering his moods, and it would wreak havoc on you and Dad."

"Well, that might be the case, but you know our door is always open for you all."

"Thanks, Mom."

"When is this going to happen?"

"The doctor said it could be only a couple months, or a year. We have no idea."

"What is Brady going to do?"

"I don't know, Mom. I have a feeling he doesn't either. That might be why he didn't tell me about this."

"That's possible. What are you going to do now?"

"I don't know, either. Right now, I just wish I knew where Brady was. He walked out of the session, and he's not answering his phone."

"Are you home?"

"No, not yet. I decided to wait a little longer before I went home, in case Brady calls me from someplace and wants me to pick him up, but I think I might go home now."

"He might already be there," she suggested.

"Yeah, he might."

"Well, perhaps now that you know, he'll talk to you about it."

"I doubt it, but we'll see."

"I love you, honey, and we love Brady too. You let him know that we are there for you all with whatever you need. It's going to be rough for a while."

"Mom, it's been rough for months now. I think we are getting used to that."

"How are the boys doing with all of this?"

"Alright, I guess. Dane is worried about Brady. He heard him say something the other night about wishing he were dead."

"What? Is Brady talking about committing suicide? You have got to be kidding me, Gracelyn. You need to talk some sense into him. Killing himself is not the way to go about things."

"Mom, he wouldn't do that. He loves us too much. He was just in one of his moods and up pacing the house in the middle of the night. He was talking to himself, and Dane overheard it. I had to promise Dane that Brady wouldn't do anything to hurt himself."

"Of course, Brady would never do something to hurt himself. Suicide is very selfish, and he would never be that selfish."

"Yeah, well, anyway, the boys are okay." I sighed. "Look, Mom, I'm going to go. I just got a text message. Maybe it's Brady. I'll talk to you later."

"Okay, love you, sweetie."

"Love you too, Mom."

I hung up the phone and looked at my screen, hoping that Brady had reached out to me, but the message was from Doug.

I frowned at it. Was my mother correct? Had I been leaning enough on Doug that I had formed a more profound attachment to him than I should have? Maybe, but Doug knew that I loved my husband. He knew that I was there for my husband, no matter what. I was sure I was just leaning on him as a friend and not as more.

I called him instead of texting back. "Hey," I said after he answered.

"I didn't expect to hear from you. How are things going?"

"Not so great. Brady walked out of his session when he got upset."

"Why?"

I gnawed on my bottom lip. Should I tell him why? Was that too personal? No, it would eventually affect my employment, so maybe letting him know ahead of time was better.

"Brady is being medically discharged."

"Oh, damn. I'm sorry to hear that, Gracelyn. I can imagine how hard that is on Brady."

"Yes, I'm sure it is."

"What does he say about it?"

"I don't know. He walked out of his session today. He has known about this for at least a week and didn't tell me."

"He should have told you."

"Yes, he should have." I paused. "He also told his doctor that he thinks we are having an affair."

He laughed. "But you told him we aren't, right?"

"Right, but Doug, do you think that our relationship is inappropriate? I mean, we do talk quite often, and not just about work. We talk about our kids, and you talk about your ex-wife, and I talk about Brady. Is that inappropriate?"

"No, I don't think so. That's what friends talk about, and I consider you a good friend, Gracelyn. I won't deny that I care about you, but I am aware that you are a married woman and committed to that relationship."

"Are you saying that if I weren't married or committed to my husband, things would be different for you?"

He paused before answering. "Gracelyn, I don't think this is a conversation that we should be having, especially over the phone. Look, we'll talk about it later. Right now, tell me what you're doing."

"Getting ready to head home."

"Okay, well, you do that, and we'll take this conversation up again another time."

"Alright. I'll see you at work tomorrow."

"You got it. Have a good afternoon, Gracelyn."

On the way home, I stopped by the store and then the pharmacy. While I did those things, I thought over the conversations with my mother and Doug. Maybe I was looking too deeply into all of it. I needed to put my attention on my husband and what our future was going to hold.

That's what my plan was when I arrived home. As I stepped through the kitchen door from the garage, I paused. My eyes raked over the three empty beer cans lying haphazardly on the counter.

I set my bags down and slowly walked into the living room where the television was playing. Brady was passed out on the couch, a beer can in his hand tipped to the side, and the carpet under it was wet. I stared at him for a long moment, my heart jumping into my throat. Was he breathing? Was he alive?

My hand went to my throat as I stared at his chest, looking for movement, and then I saw the slow rise and fall of it before he shifted his body and dropped the can altogether. He rolled to his side and curled up against the pillow. I dropped my face into my hands as I shifted back into the kitchen, stifling a sob until I was far enough away that he wouldn't hear.

He was alive.

CHAPTER SEVENTEEN

BRADY

*O*n the way home, I sat in the back seat of the car that I'd hired and thought briefly over how I felt. After a few minutes, the nausea had gone away, and I liked the floating feeling I now had going on. It had been a long time since I'd had a buzz, and it was kind of cool that I got one with one shot and a beer. I used to have to down quite a few to get this feeling.

Around the corner from the house, there was a small store that sold beer. I told my driver that I'd give him a ten-dollar tip if he stopped. He did, and I popped in and came out carrying a case.

In the driveway, I punched in the tip and then carried my beer into the house. I was a little surprised that Gracelyn wasn't home, but that was good. I knew she would get on my case for leaving—and probably for drinking too. I wasn't in the mood to hear it or to argue about it.

I let myself inside the house and went right to the kitchen where I tore into the box and pulled out two cans. I stuffed the rest of the box into the fridge, and I pulled back the ring to enjoy that fresh, crisp snap as the tab broke the seal. A moment later, I was guzzling the beer. I drank almost half of it before I took a break and burped. Damn, that was good.

As I took a seat on the couch, I wondered where my wife was. Maybe she'd decided to hang out with the doc for a while, maybe whine on his shoulder about how much of a loser I was for not telling her, or perhaps she had left the medical complex and went to cry on Doug's shoulder. That was more probable.

I finished the rest of that beer and popped open the top to the next one. I was halfway through that when I felt the buzz building again. My stomach felt off, but that didn't stop me from continuing. Now that the buzz was back in full force, I really liked it.

My mind drifted, and even though I was not too fond of all the thoughts wandering through it, I was able to divert them quickly enough. After the third beer, my footsteps were even more unsteady, and my eyelids weighed pounds, but I didn't care. By the fourth or fifth one, my head was rolling on my shoulders, and my stomach was right there with it. My vertigo was back, but I was blaming it on being drunk.

I didn't know what beer I was on when I couldn't keep my eyes open anymore, and I welcomed the silent darkness that beckoned.

I woke to find it dark in the room and the house silent. My bladder was screaming for release, and as I stood, I stepped onto a wet spot on the rug. What the heck was that from?

I used the restroom and wandered into the kitchen, bouncing off a couple of walls as the alcohol and sleep hadn't completely left my system. In the kitchen, I turned on the lights and blinked. My eyes went to the digital clock on the microwave. Holy crap, it was two in the morning.

What time had I fallen asleep? Three? Maybe four? I had slept at least eight hours. I couldn't remember the last time I had slept that long. That was pretty good, although the banging headache that I had and the pain radiating up my spine were something less than desired. I poured a glass of water and found my pill bottles on the table beside the couch.

After I took them, I debated going to bed, but I felt wide awake and knew that I probably wouldn't fall asleep anytime soon. I walked back to the bedroom and quietly opened the door. Gracelyn had her back to me, and I tiptoed around the bed and stared down at her.

She had both hands tucked under her cheek, and her lips were parted slightly. Her face was hidden in shadow, but I could see just enough that my heart clenched in my chest. I didn't want to lose her. Gracelyn and the boys were my world, but what could I give them now? What kind of a life was I going to be able to provide for them on a disability pension?

I knew Gracelyn well enough to know that she would want to take on the burden and would work harder to provide for us, but she shouldn't have to. I didn't have a problem with my wife being a breadwinner—not at all—but I didn't want her to have to do *all* the work!

Anxiety started to creep up my spine, and I left the bedroom. I paced in the living room and felt like the ceiling was beginning to crash down on top of me.

I went back to the kitchen and opened the fridge. I hadn't eaten since yesterday's breakfast, but nothing looked good—except the silver cans of beer. I snagged one, then went to close the door, opened it again, and grabbed another.

As I went back to the living room, I began to walk in circles again, my thoughts going in a million directions. What was I going to do with myself? What would I ever possibly be able to do if I was in this much pain all the time? I guzzled half the beer as I tried to contemplate an answer.

I would never be able to keep Gracelyn happy. I should let her go, but then I'd lose my boys. I didn't want to lose my boys, but I didn't want them to have a loser father either. I took another big gulp.

I should have died in Afghanistan. Evan should have lived, or Stuart. Stuart should have taken my place. Why hadn't I suggested that we all go to eat? That wouldn't have worked because Chuck had been in the middle of a job. He'd never leave something half finished. What if I had helped him? What if I had done it? Would it have gotten done faster? Could I have gotten them all out? Could I have saved them?

I poured the rest of the brew down my throat and dropped the can on the counter, popping open the next one as I rounded the island and began to do my circles again. The walking hurt, but I needed to move. I couldn't sit still. If I sat still, the demons would tackle me and take me down. I could try to outwalk them this way.

Was Gracelyn cheating on me? Was she falling in love with Doug? Who the hell was Doug even? I'd never met the guy. Was he a nice guy? A total douche? Had he ever served in the military? Did he like kids? If I weren't here, would he be good to my kids?

I tried to imagine Dane playing ball with another man or Drew kicking to someone other than his mom, but I couldn't. Yet I couldn't picture myself out there doing it either. What kind of a father would I be if I couldn't go out and play ball with my kids? Bending over to tie my shoes was excruciating. What about repeatedly bending over to pick up a ball?

The doctors had already told me I'd be on pain medications for the rest of my life which meant I would hurt for the rest of my life. What kind of a life was that?

I had finished my second beer and went back to get two more. Halfway through the second, my stomach rolled, but I didn't care. Maybe I'd puke myself to death. Perhaps I should toss back a couple more pills with the beer, numb myself completely.

Could I numb myself so thoroughly that I didn't feel anything? I was pretty sure I could, but would I survive it? Did I care if I died? No, not now. I wished I were dead. I stared at the pill bottles on the table as I took another drink, my gaze getting a little fuzzy.

If I were dead, then no one would have to worry about me; I couldn't disappoint anyone. Gracelyn would smile again, be happy, and the boys could have someone to play ball with them. They didn't need me.

I picked up one of the bottles and poured it on the table as I sank to the couch cushion. I stared at the pills as I took another drink. If I took all of those, everything would go away—the pain in my back, the pain in my head, the constant ache in my heart. It would all be gone.

I opened another bottle, poured those out, then the third one, and finally the fourth one. I twirled my finger through the pills, mixing them up, blending them into a kaleidoscope. If I drank enough and took them all, I'd fall asleep and be gone— just like that—not quite as fast as Stuart had died, not quite as messily as Chuck's death, and not quite as dramatic as Evan's. I wouldn't be a hero to anyone—I wasn't a hero anyway—I was a loser. I began to sob as I raked a hand through my hair and grabbed a handful of it, pulling it hard enough to send prickles of pain through my scalp and down my neck.

A sound to my side captured my attention, and it took me a moment before I realized it was my phone. I picked it up, and something fell into my lap. The card that the bartender had given me earlier stared at me.

The word *crisis* was the only one that I could seem to focus on for more than a moment. Was this a crisis? Was I in crisis? What the hell *was* a crisis? I tossed the card to the table and finished the beer.

I went to get another one and remembered that I already had one on the cushion beside me when I returned. That was okay. I'd drink them both.

I stared at the pills. I wanted to take them all and make this all go away. My eyes crept to the card beside the pile. What if I called? What would happen? Would they report it? Would they even answer? Nah, it was two in the morning—okay, probably after three now. No one was going to answer the phone.

What if I tried, though? What if I dialed and let it ring? What if I didn't, and I took all these pills?

I set the beer down and reached for the card and didn't even realize I was crying until I blinked and felt a tear run down my cheek. I stared at the small piece of paper. Nate Hardy. Would he answer if I called, or would it be some random person who answers phones at night? Maybe a recording. Would he call me a loser? Tell me to suck it up and deal with it?

My hands shook as I lifted my phone. Was I going to call this guy? I didn't even know if I wanted to talk to him. I banged my fist against my forehead for a moment, sobbing slightly as I contemplated what I should do.

I could put it down, and I could curl up and sleep—or I could take all those pills and swallow them down. It would be fast.

My wife would find me—or maybe my boys. Oh, my god! My kids would see me. I rocked back and forth, but then they would know the pain was gone. I'd be gone, but so would the pain—for me at least.

I sobbed once more and reread the card. A voice in my mind urged, *Call Nate.* Who was Nate? Why should I call him? *Call Nate.*

I had to focus hard on the numbers as I plugged them into my phone, and I double-checked them three times to make sure I had the correct number. Then I stared at it, rocking back and forth as I did. *Call Nate. Call Nate. Call Nate.* The words kept echoing through my muddled brain, and finally, I pushed the call button and put the phone to my ear with a shaking hand.

It rang once, then a second time, and I was about to hang up on the third ring when a deep voice answered, "Hardy here."

Hardy? Oh, yeah, Nate Hardy. "Um, hey."

"What's up, brother?"

Brother? I squeezed my eyes closed.

"You having a rough night?"

"Um, yeah." I cleared my throat and wiped a tear from my cheek.

"I'm glad you called. I've had lots of those bad nights. Do you want to tell me what your name is?"

"Are you going to call my command?"

"Nope, not unless you want me to."

"No, I don't."

"Alright, then this call is between you and me. What do I call you? Batman? Thor? Shadow?"

I actually smiled a little bit. "No, I'm Brady."

"Brady, what branch?"

"Air force."

"Ah, man, a flyboy. That's okay. I won't hold it against you." Nate snickered slightly, and a small smile lifted my cheeks. "I'm a former jarhead."

"How long you been out?"

"Some days, it feels like I never left."

"Yeah, I get that."

"So you want to tell me what's going on?"

"Before I say anything, let me ask you a few questions first. You a shrink?"

He laughed heartily, and I could hear something ticking in the background. "Not in the slightest. I leave that to my good friend Lauren. I'm just a man who looked down the barrel of his handgun a few too many times and finally got help. You looking down your own barrel?"

"Nah, I don't own a gun. My wife doesn't like them in the house with our kids."

"Okay, what you looking at then? What is your bullet, Brady?"

"My pills."

"You have them in front of you?"

"Yeah, all poured out."

"How many are there?"

"Probably sixty or so."

"What are they for?"

"Pain, migraines, nerves, shit like that."

"You been drinking?"

"Yeah, I had a couple of beers."

"You got one now?" I heard the blinker again.

"You in your car?"

"Yep, heading to pick up breakfast."

"I can let you go."

"No, I'm good. You didn't answer my question. You have a beer in your hand now?"

"Yeah."

"Okay, Brady, I'm going to ask you a tough question. Is that alright?"

"Yeah."

"Why did you call me?"

"What?"

"Why did you pick this phone number, at this moment, to call me? I need to know where your mind is right now."

"I don't know."

"Yes, you do. What were you thinking about before you dialed my number?"

I swallowed. Could I say the words out loud? Would he think I was a loser for thinking them?

"I think—" I paused and cleared my throat again. "I think I'm in crisis, except I'm not exactly sure what that is."

"Brady, you thinking that the world would be a better place if you weren't in it?"

"Yeah."

"You thinking that the pain will be gone if you kill yourself?"

"Yeah."

"You thinking the guilt will end when you're gone?"

"Yes," I whispered as tears rolled down my cheeks. "I just want it all gone."

"Then listen here, Brady. You are one hundred percent in crisis, my brother, and I'm going to help you figure out how to get out of it. Is that okay with you?"

"You can do that over the phone?"

"Nah, man." He chuckled. "I'm going to do it face-to-face. What's your address, Brady? I'm going to send someone to hang with you until I get there."

"Are you serious?"

"As a heart attack, brother. I'm going to come to you as soon as you tell me where you are."

"But I'm in Denver."

"Then I guess I'm gonna be in Denver in a couple of hours. I'm going to conference someone in with us on this call. Is that okay? He is a close friend of mine, and he is going to make my travel arrangements and help me get someone over to you while I travel. Is that okay?"

I leaned back. "Are you really going to come here?"

He chuckled. "Yeah, I'm really going to come to you, Brady. Now hold on while I get Derek on the line with us."

CHAPTER EIGHTEEN

GRACELYN

$\mathscr{W}$ hen I woke up, I heard voices in the living room. At first, I didn't think much of it, but then I heard someone speak, and I knew without a doubt that it was not my husband or one of my sons. I listened more carefully, wondering if Brady had the television on loud, but that didn't seem to be it either.

I threw the covers back and grabbed my robe, confused as to why someone else would be in our home at—what time was it? I glanced at the fitness tracker on my wrist and saw it was just after four-thirty in the morning.

I opened the door carefully and paused as I listened. A deep rough voice spoke. "I think we should make some coffee. You okay with that, Brady?"

"Yeah," I heard my husband respond.

"No, you just keep sitting right there. I'll find everything we need."

Who was in my house, and why was he going to be digging through my kitchen? I yanked open the door and strode to the living room just in time to see a large man with a ponytail disappear around the corner into my kitchen. Brady was on the couch, his head back, his eyes glued to the ceiling. In front of him on the dark wood coffee table were all his pills spilled all over the place.

"Brady? What the hell is going on, and who is that man in our kitchen?" I didn't mean to sound angry—okay, maybe I did mean to sound that way—but I was in a bit of shock at having a houseguest at this time of the morning and not being awake yet.

He lifted his head slowly, as if it weighed a ton, and stared at me with eyes that were not focusing as he blinked and squinted. "Gracey, did I wake you?"

"No, but that strange man in my kitchen did. Why do you have pills all over the table? What are you doing?" My confused and addled brain was making my voice rise. It was apparent that my husband was intoxicated again. I had hoped he would have slept it off and that, by morning, he would have been fine. Obviously, he had woken up and continued to drink.

"Ma'am." A deep voice behind me had me spinning as I pulled my robe closed tighter over my chest. "I'm Will. I'm a friend of Brady's."

I looked him over. I thought I knew all of Brady's friends, but I had never seen this man before. I would remember him if I had. He was taller than most of Brady's friends, and his shoulders were broad. He had a scar down his face that was very pronounced with his dark hair pulled back. I shuddered as I looked into the solemn eyes of the man. He looked like a violent biker and not someone with whom my husband would be friends. I shuffled back a step, wondering how I was going to protect my family from this man.

"I do not know you, and I want to know what is going on. Why are you in my house?"

"Relax, Gracelyn, his name is Will. He owns Purgatory."

I jerked back. Purgatory? Was he an evil biker? "Excuse me?" I squeaked.

He stepped forward. "My name is Will Burke. I own a bar in

town called Purgatory, but I'm also on an emergency response team for veterans and service members in crisis."

"Crisis?" I barked out the word. "What are you talking about?"

Will looked over my shoulder toward my husband briefly. "Why don't you have a seat, and I'll explain what is going on."

"No! I will not have a seat until you tell me what the hell is going on!" I was getting anxious and confused, and I never swore unless I was feeling that way. What did he mean by crisis?

He stepped back, putting more space between us. "Ma'am, Brady made a call earlier tonight to a friend of mine that helps veterans and service members when they become suicidal."

I gasped as I turned to look at Brady. "Brady would never do that!"

Brady was staring at the ceiling again, and my eyes drifted to the table. Oh, my Lord! Had Brady thought of taking all of those? Was this because he thought I was having an affair? Did he want to kill himself because of a misunderstanding? No!

"Brady! What are you thinking!" I rushed toward him. "Please tell me you were not going to take all of those just because you think I'm sleeping with my boss!"

He closed his eyes, and his head rolled to the side away from me. "Is that why you were going to take those?" I bent down with tears in my eyes and started to scoop them up in my hands. My hands were shaking as I tried to gather them together, and tears dripped down onto the table and the pills.

"Gracelyn, stop," he said, but I was incensed and kept trying to get them all into my hands and away from him. They kept falling out of my hands, and I couldn't see straight. I was so mad, so hurt, and so confused. I loved him! How could he want to kill himself because he thought I was cheating on him? Suddenly, Brady grabbed my wrist. "Stop! Gracelyn, Stop! Leave them alone. Leave them right there."

I stared at the man in front of me. His breath smelled like a brewery, and his eyes were pinpricks, the whites of his eyes more red than white. His skin was pale, and he looked almost ten years older suddenly.

"Just leave them there," he said as he let go of me and sat back again, hanging his head. I opened my hands, letting the pills fall back to the table, the rat-a-tat-tat as they landed on the wood the only sound in the room. I stared at them and then sobbed as I put my hand to my mouth.

"How could you do that? How could you even think that? You can't kill yourself!" I hissed the last part at him.

Suddenly, there was a hand on my arm, and I shied away from it, staring at Will as if I'd just seen him for the first time. "How are you here? Why are you here?"

"Gracelyn, help me make coffee, and I'll explain more of what is going on."

I turned back to Brady, his gaze locked back on the stupid ceiling. I looked up. What was so damned interesting on the ceiling?

"Come on, let's go in the kitchen." He held his hand out, and I nodded and began to walk into the kitchen. I was vaguely aware that the house was a mess again and briefly considered that I should be ashamed of that with a guest in the home, but he looked like a biker, so what did he care?

"Do you want to make it, or would you like me to?" he asked once we were in there.

I frowned. Will had excellent manners for a scary-looking man. "The coffee and filters are in the cupboard above the coffeemaker."

He gave me a smile that was such a contrast to his scar that his eyes seemed more friendly, and I sank into a chair at the table.

"Can you please tell me what's going on?"

"I met your husband earlier today when he came into my bar outside the base. We talked for a few minutes, and I saw some things in him that I recognized all too well, so I gave him a card and told him to use it if he were ever in crisis."

"What does crisis mean?"

He finished putting the coffee grounds into the maker and removed the carafe before he turned to me. "It means you are at your wit's end and not sure you want to continue."

"You mean suicidal?"

"Yes, among other things," he replied and then began to fill the carafe as I rubbed my temples.

Why would Brady want to do that? It didn't make sense. He had a great life, two fantastic kids, and our marriage was something to be proud of—well, usually.

"How are you here now?"

He poured the water and glanced my way. "Because Brady called the number."

"The number to who? You?"

"No, a buddy of mine that works for a place called Rise Again Warrior. They help veterans and other servicemembers get back on their feet, physically and mentally."

"Did Brady tell you that he is being released?"

"He did."

"Is that why he wants to kill himself?"

"I can't tell you what's in his mind or why he wanted to do anything. Even if I could, I wouldn't tell you. He deserves to tell you in his own words when he's ready to talk about it."

"When is that going to be?"

He shrugged and then held up his finger. "Let me check on him."

I nodded and waited as he stepped out of the kitchen. Indistinguishable murmurs filtered back to me for a few moments, and then Will was back. "He's going to try and sleep a little bit—which is a good idea now."

"Why now?"

"Because the alcohol is coming out of his system. He took his medication and then drank quite a few beers. I wanted the alcohol to be wearing off before he went to sleep."

"So what happens now? Do you call his doctor and talk to him about what he's going through?"

"No." He shook his head and pointed to the seat across from me. "Do you mind if I sit with you?"

"Please." I felt like a horrible host and suddenly remembered that I was in my robe and that my hair was probably a total mess and my face bare. My mother would have a Southern fit.

After he was seated, he laced his fingers on the table. "His appointed shrink is too busy to give him much help. Right now, he's only putting a bandage on the problem. There are too many people who need help and not enough doctors or time to help them all."

"So why aren't you helping them?"

"Because they haven't asked us to help. Brady did." He smiled, and it lit up his eyes, making the blue a little lighter and his face not so scary. "When Brady called, he spoke to a good friend of mine named Nate Hardy. Nate works for Rise Again Warrior. He's on his way here now." He glanced at his wrist. "Should be here in another four hours or so."

"Why is he coming here?"

"Because Brady called and asked for help. When someone calls, we respond. Because Nate needed to hang up to get on a plane, I was asked to sit with Brady until Nate gets here."

"Like a babysitter?"

He shrugged. "We call it a buddy watch. We didn't want Brady to do anything to hurt himself while we were getting to him."

"What is going to happen when this other guy, Nate, gets here?"

"Well, Nate and Brady will have some serious heart-to-heart, and he'll see where Brady is. He'll decide if Brady needs to go inpatient immediately—"

I jerked back. "Inpatient? You mean like in an institution?"

He laughed slightly. "Not a rubber room with padded walls, but rather a place that is specifically for servicemembers who are at that point in their lives. Think more of rehab."

I massaged my forehead with my fingertips. I could not imagine Brady in any type of rehab. It seemed ridiculous. "Okay, so if he doesn't need that, then what?"

"Then Nate will see if he fits the criteria for coming to Rise Again Warrior. If that's the case, they will get a medical transfer for him, and he will head in for treatment."

"What treatment do they have for someone who is"—I hesitated—"feeling like Brady?"

He smiled kindly. "It's not about being suicidal, Gracelyn. It's about fixing the problems underneath that and helping him realize that he is worth it. We need to make him see that even though he might be disabled or have emotional issues, he can make it and have a great life. His life is not over just because he doesn't muster every day anymore."

I thought about what he said. "Where is this place?"

"South of Knoxville, Tennessee."

"How long will he have to be there?"

"Well, that all depends on how he does with treatment. He could be home in six months or a year."

My jaw dropped. "He would be stuck there for a year?"

"Not 'stuck there', Gracelyn, but recovering and learning how to deal with the demons he has in his head and on his shoulders. He needs to learn to accept himself as a different person and learn to adapt to what is different. He also needs to learn how to communicate better, not only with himself but with you and your children."

Was it possible that this place could help Brady? "Will, do you really think that Brady would kill himself?"

His eyes looked suddenly sad. "Yes. It might not have been tonight or even this week or next. It could be six months down the line after he has destroyed his marriage and his body and mind, when he falls so far down into the hole that there is no chance that anyone can reach him."

"And he's not too far? You can help him?"

"I do not doubt that RAW"—I frowned, and he chuckled—"Rise Again Warrior, that's what we call it, RAW—I do not doubt that they can help Brady. I was where he is. I even tried to kill myself twice, and they helped me. Now I help back."

I studied him for a moment, and now that I had a chance to look at him, he didn't seem all that scary. Yes, his appearance was rough, but he was kind and sensitive, and the fact that he wanted to help made him an angel in my eyes. I reached over the table and put my hand on his wrist. "Then help my husband, Will. Please help me get my husband back."

CHAPTER NINETEEN

BRADY

*A*nother man got on the phone with us and said hello, and then the three of us talked about where I lived. The other man that Nate called Derek said that he'd make the arrangements and ended the conversation with me, saying that he'd see me soon.

After he hung up, I asked Nate, "Is he coming with you?"

"No, Derek has a few other things going on. What he is doing right now is contacting our pilot and reaching out to someone in your area to sit with you while I get on a plane and head your way."

"I don't need a babysitter," I grunted.

"You still have pills lying in front of you?"

"Yeah."

"Then you need a buddy to watch your six."

I stared at the pills thoughtfully. "I could still take the pills while I'm on the phone with you."

His voice grew a bit deeper as he said, "You could, but you won't."

"What makes you think I won't?" I challenged.

"Because you called me, Brady, and because you want help

out of this pit of despair and pain. Man, I wanted it all over with too. I hated the guilt that weighed down on my shoulders all the time."

"How did you get it to stop?"

"I learned to accept the guilt for what it was, and then I let it go."

"I can't do that."

"Not now, but one day you will."

"What makes you so sure?"

"Because we are going to give you the help that you need. Before you know it, you are going to be able to look in the mirror and like the guy staring back at you."

I barked out a laugh. Yeah, right, I thought to myself.

For the next few minutes, Nate asked me questions about myself and my family. He didn't say anything about my service or what I was upset over. Instead, he focused my mind someplace else.

"Hey, I want you to go to your front door and open it. I have a buddy out there that is going to hang with you until I arrive."

"How do you know someone is here?"

Nate chuckled. "Because I just got a message from Will that he's in front of your house but doesn't want to knock and wake anyone up. Go let him in."

I staggered to the front door and opened it, expecting no one to be there, and was momentarily shocked to see the bartender standing on the front step.

"Hey, Brady, I'm Will. Glad you made the call, brother. Can I come in?"

I stepped back to let him in, and he pointed to the phone. "You still got Hardy on the line?"

"Yeah."

"Let me speak to him. Let's go sit down."

I handed him the phone and stumbled as I turned. Will was right there to stand me up straight and kept his hand on my arm. My head was spinning, and my stomach wasn't far behind.

"Hey, Hardy, I got him. Have a safe trip, and we'll see you in a few hours." He was quiet as he helped me to the couch. "Yeah, he's got a nice selection all over his coffee table. I'll shoot you a photo after we get off."

I could hear Hardy talking as I leaned my head back. I stared at the ceiling. If I closed my eyes, the room spun too much.

"Will do. I'll let him know."

He set the phone down on the table, and I lifted my head to look at him as he pulled his phone out and pointed it at my table.

"What are you doing?"

"Sending some pictures to Nate." He took a couple more shots, including one of me and a few of the prescription bottles. I was having too much trouble trying to keep from puking to care.

"How you feeling?"

"A little sick."

"Let me grab a trash can for you in case you puke."

I grunted as my stomach revolted against the abuse I had thrown at it. A noise in the kitchen distracted me, and then Will was back with a big bowl. "Here, hold this."

No sooner did he hand it to me than I leaned over and used it. The taste of beer and bitter prescription drugs burning their way back up made me gag over and over. He shoved some paper towels into my hands, and I blew my nose and wiped my face once I was done. He disappeared for a moment, and I heard the toilet flush before he was back, pushing the bowl back in front of me.

He was quiet as I sat there staring at the ceiling. "You didn't just talk to this guy in your bar, did you?"

"You mean Hardy? Nah, he saved my life."

Before I could speak again, I went through another bout of

retching, and then I felt slightly better. Will brought me a glass of water and emptied the bowl again. I bet he hadn't expected to be doing this when he had arrived.

He asked a few questions about what I'd done since I'd last seen him and how much I'd had to drink, and then he suggested he make coffee. As he went into the kitchen, I received a reminder that we weren't alone.

Gracelyn was none too happy to find me on the couch in my current condition, and I knew she was probably freaking out about Will, but I didn't have the strength to deal with it.

Instead, I kept staring at the ceiling.

My wife was in denial, just as part of me was. She didn't think I would ever kill myself. If you had asked if I was capable of that a year ago, I would have laughed in your face and said nothing could make me even contemplate it.

How the mighty fall.

I had to admit that I was glad that Will was here to talk to her. I didn't have words to explain anything to her.

Finally, I felt the urge to drift off, and Will was standing over me. "You doing alright?"

"Yeah, I think I want to sleep for a little while. I'm feeling better physically."

"Alright, but I'm going to wake you up in a little while."

I slipped down to my side and closed my eyes. The room kept moving, but not as bad as it had earlier. I heard him walk away and the soft voice of my wife as I drifted off.

Will woke me up once with a shake on the shoulder and told me I needed to drink a glass of water. My back screamed, and I mentioned that it was time for my medication.

Will retrieved two pills off the table and handed them to me. "You can take these, but nothing else."

I nodded, swallowed the pills, and lay back down.

The next time I woke up, I found Drew leaning over me, kissing my brow. "Bye, Daddy."

"Bye?"

He grinned. "Yeah, I gotta go to school. Mom told us to kiss you and say goodbye."

I stared at my son, wanting to break down into tears. I glanced at the table, a towel was laid over the pills to cover them, but I could tell by the little bumps that they were still right where I'd dumped them. What if I had taken all of those? I would have missed this moment.

I sat up and hugged Drew tightly. Dane hugged me, too, but he was starting to get to that age where embracing his father wasn't that cool.

By the door to the hallway, Gracelyn stood. She was dressed, but not for work. She waited for the boys, studied me for a moment, and then walked out behind them.

Will was seated in a chair near me. "You want a cup of coffee? Nate is going to be here soon. You might want to take a shower and brush those pearly whites before he arrives."

"Why? Is he going to be offended?"

He laughed. "No, but you'll feel a little more human." He added, "I had a long talk with your wife. She's a good woman. She's going to stand by your side through this. You're lucky, a lot of women wouldn't."

"She is a good woman, better than I deserve."

"Cut that shit out," Will growled. "It might be true, but not for the reasons you are thinking."

I laughed slightly. "Yeah, I guess."

"Go take a shower. I don't need to worry about you slitting your wrist or anything in there, do I? It wouldn't be the first time I had to stand outside the shower and watch a guy clean himself up, but I'd sure prefer not to."

I laughed again. "I think I'll be okay."

"Yeah, well, no locking the door, and no girl showers either. In, out, under three."

"Yes, sir," I said as I got to my feet slowly. He was on his feet, too, probably to make sure I didn't fall over, but I managed to do it on my own. My lower back screamed, and I had a headache, but it was tolerable.

I collected my clothes and hit the shower. Three minutes after I turned on the water, there was a rap at the door. "Time's up, Vanover!"

I laughed. "Damn, give me one more minute. It takes a while for the water to warm up."

I heard him laugh, and then I finished rinsing off. A few minutes later, I found him in the kitchen, a fresh pot of coffee brewing and eggs cooking on the stove.

"I hope those eggs are for you."

"Nope, you are going to suck them down, along with the orange juice, toast, and sausage."

"I'm not hungry."

"I don't care," he said as he gave me a stern look.

Well, it looked like I was going to be eating.

Will put the plate in front of me when the garage door opened and Gracelyn stepped in. She stood by the door, unsure of what to do.

"You eat?" I asked.

"I'm not hungry."

Will snorted. "Yeah, well, that didn't work for him, so it's not going to work for you. Have a seat, and I'll get you a plate."

She smiled at him, and I realized that I had missed her smiling at me. When was the last time she had done that?

Will had made enough for all of us, and as we ate, Will and Gracelyn talked about the boys. Will shared about his two kids who were grown now. I listened to them, choking down the food because I wasn't sure what would happen today, and my anxiety was returning.

Will picked up his phone after it beeped. "Nate will be here in about twenty minutes."

"What is going to happen when he arrives?" I asked.

"Well, I'm going to be able to go home and get some sleep," he commented with a chuckle but then grew serious. "You guys will talk, and you'll make some tough decisions about your future. I suggest you take whatever he offers seriously and do it."

"Okay, I will."

We finished breakfast, and I went back to the living room and stared at the towel. Gracelyn spoke behind me, "I wanted to clean them up, but Will told me that you had to do that."

"I'm glad you covered them, not something that the boys should see," I told her.

She shook her head and stepped forward, wringing her hands in front of her. "Brady, were you seriously thinking about killing yourself?"

I couldn't look her in the eye. I didn't want to see the disappointment there. I stared at the floor instead. "I don't know how to explain it to you, Gracey. I just know that I'm in a bad place. I don't know how to fix that."

"Brady." She stepped forward and took my face in her hands. Her eyes glittered with unshed tears. "Why didn't you say anything to me?"

"Because I didn't want you to see the loser I was."

"Oh, Brady"—the tears spilled over—"you are not a loser. You are an incredible man. I love you more than you know."

"I don't deserve it."

"If you don't deserve it, then I don't deserve your love either," she said earnestly. Her words broke my heart. She had no idea how much I loved her or how it tore at my gut to hurt her.

I pulled her into my arms and held her. For a long moment, it was just the two of us, and we both cried a little bit. I looked up to see Will standing in the hallway, his arms crossed as he leaned against the wall. There was a knock on the door, and then he nodded at me and went to answer it.

I stepped back from Gracelyn, and she wiped her eyes, staring up at me. "I love you, Brady Lance Vanover. Don't you ever forget that."

I cupped her cheek and kissed her once tenderly as two new voices came down the hallway. Gracelyn went to step away, but I put my arm around her shoulders and pulled her close. I needed her strength.

Will walked into the room, and behind him a man and a woman followed. "Brady and Gracelyn Vanover, this is Nate Hardy and Lauren Logan from Rise Again Warrior."

Nate had light brown skin and dark brown hair cut short, and he stared at me hard with light green eyes as if he were digging straight into my soul, looking for something. I wasn't sure what he saw, but what I saw was a kindred spirit, someone I could trust—someone who would help me. He glanced at Gracelyn and nodded, and then he stepped toward me. I held my hand out to him, and I could see it was shaking.

Nate looked at my hand and then back to my face as he stepped into my personal space and put his arms around me. "Handshakes are not how I say hello to my brothers in need."

Suddenly, it was hard to breathe with the knot stuck in my throat. I tried to swallow it three times before I finally got it down.

"I got you, man. Let go. I got *you*," he said softly beside my ear.

The fear and anger that I had been holding back since I'd woken up in the hospital began to crash over me. For the first time in my adult life, I clung to a virtual stranger and bawled like a baby.

CHAPTER TWENTY

GRACELYN

*T*he scene in front of me was so powerful that there was no way not to be touched by it. I'd seen my husband misty-eyed. I'd even seen him cry a few tears, but I had never seen him fall to pieces.

I covered my mouth with my hand as I stepped back to give them room. Brady wasn't just crying, he was sobbing, and it broke my heart. An arm wrapped around me, and I glanced up to see Will smiling at me. He led me out of the room, and the woman followed us.

Will led me to the front door and out onto the porch. I was wiping my eyes as the woman closed the door.

"I'm surprised you didn't stay in there, Lauren."

Lauren smiled sweetly at him. "I think Brady needs a moment to connect further with Nate. I'll go check on them in a minute." She stepped forward and brushed her dark brown hair over her shoulder. I looked into her beautiful face, noting her bright hazel eyes. She carried grace, poise, strength, and determination, but most of all, empathy radiated from her eyes.

"Gracelyn, I'm Lauren Logan. I'm the head of the mental

health division at Rise Again Warrior. My husband, Shane, is the one who started this organization."

"Don't lie, Lauren. You helped him start it."

She grinned at Will. "I'm not lying. Shane had the vision. I only helped him bring it to life."

"And I am thankful every day that you two were able to." Will turned to me. "Lauren was a tremendous help to me when I first arrived at RAW. I was bitter, angry, and wanted to hate the world."

"You also wanted help," Lauren added, touching his arm for a moment. "If you hadn't wanted help, nothing we would have done would have assisted you."

"That's true."

Lauren turned to me. "Which is why we are here. Brady reached out for help, and I know it is terrifying to you. I'm sure you have a thousand things going through your mind, and you probably think that this is partly your fault."

"I do!" I said quickly.

"It's not your fault, Gracelyn. It's nobody's fault. Brady was injured. He lost people close to him. He has suffered a lot. Now that he is losing all that he knows, it's messing with his mind. Add in the confusion of having a traumatic brain injury to the mix, and he's a wreck. There is nothing that you could have done to help him. What he needs are other people like him that are learning to deal with this. That is what is going to help him heal and move forward."

"Did I make him worse? I was letting him do his own thing. Should I have pushed him?"

"No, pushing him in the wrong way might have been detrimental to him."

"So what happens now? You guys talk to him and figure out if you can help him? What if you can't?"

Lauren took my hand and led me to the two porch chairs that had seen better days. After she sat down, she kept hold of my hand. "Gracelyn, we are going to do everything that we can to help him. I already know that we can—if Brady wants the help. We have a state-of-the-art facility that can deal with his psychological issues and his physical ones. We can teach him how to deal with his pain and find a purpose for his life again."

"What do you mean to 'find a purpose'?"

"He lost his friends; he's dealing with a world of pain; and now he has lost his career. I do not doubt that he is trying to figure out how to move on, how to support his family. He's trying to figure out what he can do with the injuries that he has. We have programs that can teach him skills, help him get certifications and degrees, and help him find a job."

I had to admit that I was slightly awestruck. "Will I be able to see him?"

"Yes, but not right away. Were you two together when Brady went through basic training?"

"Yes, we were newlyweds."

She grinned. "Then this is going to be kind of like that. He's going to have to work toward it. He can email you after the first week; he can call you after the second week. If he is doing well, he can start doing video chats with you and your children after week three, but we need to make sure he is making progress."

"Won't communicating with his family make it better for him?"

She shook her head and glanced at Will. "No, not if it's his family that is causing the stress. I'm pretty sure that the fact that Brady doesn't think he can support his family anymore weighs heavily on his shoulders."

"But he doesn't need to support us. I am capable of working."

She squeezed my hand. "Gracelyn, I believe that, but think about this. If the shoe was on the other foot, and you were the one that couldn't work and couldn't care for your family, what would be going through your mind? If you weren't able to cook and clean or take the kids to school or sports, how would you feel? Would you feel like a burden? Would it put stress on you not to help?" She paused and, after a moment, continued. "Men are wired very differently than we are. We tend to fix, to nurture. Men need to provide, protect, oversee. If they lose that ability, they lose their identity, their purpose. Brady needs to find his purpose again."

I shifted back slightly as my jaw dropped. Of course, that is precisely how both of us would feel. My parents had taught me to be a lady, but also an independent one. Even though my husband was head of the family, I should be doing everything I could to keep our family going from his side. "Yes, it would. I had no idea that was what was going on with Brady."

"I'm sure you didn't, and Brady wouldn't know how to express that to you. Right now, he feels like less than a man because he can't support you and do what he once promised to do for you."

I shook my head and pulled my hand back from hers, wiping it over my face for a moment.

"So what now?" I asked as I leaned back in the seat.

"Now, I'm going to go in and talk to Brady, and then we are all going to sit down and discuss what happens next. If Brady agrees, we'd like to take him back with us today. I already have the paperwork in the works to get him medically transferred to us."

"Lauren—" I glanced up at Will— "and you, too, Will, thank you. I don't know what I would have done if Brady had hurt himself."

"Well, he's not the only one who needs our assistance. It would help if you received support too. I encourage you to go through classes to learn to recognize the signs and learn how to communicate with him. Men and women who have TBIs go through some very drastic mental and personality changes. Learning to understand them is important."

"Alright, where do I do that? Is it on base?"

Lauren dug around in the large shoulder bag sitting beside her. She withdrew a packet of information and handed it to me. "This is the spouse support program. You'll start it immediately. I'll get you hooked up with a therapist and a group. They will meet with you formally every week, but they are there if you need them at other times. Your sessions with them will be done via video and around your work schedule.

"The therapist will also give you some updates on Brady's progress. They won't tell you much, but if a family issue comes up in his therapy, they will discuss it with you, so all of you are on the same page. Once Brady transitions to the next phase of the program, you can visit him at the facility on Family Day. We do those every three months.

"This packet has a lot of information. I was hoping you could read it over while I'm talking to Brady. Then we can answer any questions you might have."

"How much is this going to cost? Does our insurance cover this?"

"There is no charge to you or him. Medical covers what he will need, and what it doesn't will be covered by our organization."

Lauren excused herself after that and returned inside to speak with Brady.

"This is slightly overwhelming."

Will chuckled. "My wife thought so, too, at first, but she figured it all out quickly. I'll give you her number. She's only a few minutes away if you want to sit down and have coffee with her and talk. She can fill you in on all the inside information."

"I would appreciate that."

I started to flip through the folder, looking at the brochure. "Does this place really look like this?"

"Yep, only nicer. I would have stayed there forever if I could have, but my wife wanted me back here. She has her own business, and her parents live here. I decided to come back, open my bar, and watch for people to help."

"If you wanted to help, why name your bar Purgatory?"

"Because these men and women that need help see that word and feel like it is the place they belong. It calls to them, and if it calls strongly enough, they wander in."

He grinned, and I no longer saw the scars along his face. Instead, I saw angel wings over his shoulders. "How many people have you helped?"

His expression saddened. "Four. I tried to help a fifth one, but I was too late."

"Well, Will, I was angry when I saw Brady drunk last night and wanted to punch the person in the nose who sold him the beer, but I have to admit that I'd rather hug you now. I don't know what I would have done if Brady hadn't walked into Purgatory yesterday."

"I will never say no to a hug."

I got to my feet and threw my arms around him. "Thank you for everything, Will."

"You're welcome, Gracelyn. I hope that you and Brady can heal what is broken, and he finds his place. You make sure to stay in touch."

"I promise we will."

Will left shortly after that, but not before we exchanged numbers, and he went inside to say goodbye to Brady.

After he left, I checked my phone. It had vibrated in my pocket a few minutes ago.

Doug had sent me a text message, asking if things were alright. I had sent him one earlier saying I needed the day off but hadn't given him an explanation. Typically, I would have called him, but it didn't feel right to share this with him. This was too personal and not mine to share. I responded with a message about one of the kids not feeling well and told him I'd talk to him later.

I slipped my phone into my pocket and set about reading all the information in the packet.

I was almost done when Nate came outside to speak with me. I went to stand, but he held his hand up and took the seat beside me. "Sorry that we didn't get to speak earlier. I felt it was more important to connect with Brady than you."

"That's okay. I have to agree, given the way Brady reacted to you. I had no idea that he was suffering like that." I paused. "Do you think that you can help him?"

"The more important question in this, Gracelyn, is: Do I think Brady wants to be helped? The answer to that is yes, he does. He made the call. He opened up to me a little bit, and he's talking to Lauren right now. He has a long road ahead, but we can give him the tools to overcome this. It won't be fixed overnight or with a few therapy sessions. He needs deep therapy and to be immersed into a program that will help him."

"And you guys can give him that?"

He nodded.

I wanted my husband back, but more importantly, I wanted my husband to *want* to be back and be happy and healthy. "When do you leave?"

He smiled. "After lunch."

"Will it be before three-thirty?"

"Why?"

"That is what time the boys get home. I'd like the boys to say goodbye to their father if that's possible."

"Then we will leave at four-thirty. I'll let our pilot know to start the flight plan."

"You have a personal pilot?"

He chuckled. "One of the perks of having a best friend who is uber-rich. We have two private planes available for us. It helps us get to people faster."

"Wow."

The front door opened, and Lauren stuck her head out.

173

"Do you guys want to come in and join us?" she asked.

We did, and the first thing I noticed was that all the pills were off the table, and the four bottles were sitting in the center of it. I sat next to Brady on the couch, and he held my hand tightly, but he didn't look at me. I wasn't sure if the quiver came from him or me, but I held on to him just as tightly.

Lauren explained a little more about what would happen and what Brady would go through. Most of what she told me I'd already learned in the packet she had given me. She answered a few questions for me and then asked me to take her to the medical complex on base so she could turn in the proper paperwork to get him transferred. While we were out, Brady would pack under Nate's supervision, and we could pick up lunch on our way back.

As I gathered my purse and keys, I looked back at Brady. He looked scared but hopeful. I smiled at him, trying to ease that. He wasn't the only one to feel that way.

CHAPTER TWENTY-ONE

BRADY

*I*t took me a little while to calm down and stop sniveling like a baby, and when I did finally get myself together, I looked around and found that Nate and I were alone.

He cupped the back of my neck. "It's okay, man. You're going to be okay."

I blew my nose with a leftover paper towel from my barfing episode. "No offense, Hardy, but how is it going to be okay just because *you're* here?"

He cocked his head slightly and then lifted his chin, his green eyes intense as if he knew something that I didn't. "Because you aren't alone anymore, Brady."

I glanced around, slightly confused, and Nate took my arm and led me to the couch. "Have a seat. I didn't mean alone in this room. I meant alone in life." He put his hand up when I went to speak. "And I know you're married, and you have kids and probably parents and siblings too. That's not what I'm talking about. I'm talking about brothers and sisters who have different parents but share one common strand of DNA—the DNA that belongs to Uncle Sam. We all have it. All of us that served and gave our all to a country that doesn't quite understand us, a country with bureaucrats that don't know how to help us and are, quite frankly, afraid of us."

I studied him as the words sank in, and he continued, "There are many of us that physically struggle every damn day to put one foot in front of the other. Others have so much guilt on their shoulders that they can't even crawl across a room. Thousands of us have lost pieces of our bodies, minds, souls for what we did while we served, what we did when we were under oath following orders. Those are the people you are with now, Brady." He put his hand on my shoulder and squeezed. "Those are the people who are going to teach you how to survive, and then one day, you're going to help someone else survive."

I barked out a twisted laugh. "Yeah, I don't see *that* happening."

"Not right now, you don't. I never imagined it either when I was sitting on the side of the road, crying like a kid who had just lost his favorite toy. I couldn't imagine living another day, and I never expected to be sitting here in front of you, telling you that you're going to be okay."

"How are you so sure I will be?"

"Because, Brady, you want to be okay. If you didn't, you wouldn't have called. You're a fighter, Vanover. I saw some of your service record. I know who you were, what you accomplished. I've even seen the video of the explosion."

"What?" I stared back at him in shock. "They have video?"

He dropped his hand and leaned back slightly. "You haven't seen it? Man, it's in your file. Lauren got access to it. She's registered with the VA as a psychologist and has access to all records in that department. She pulled your jacket. I'm probably not supposed to admit that I saw your stuff, HIPAA and all that crap, but I did. I wanted to know as much about you as I could when I stepped through your front door. The docs probably didn't think you were at the right spot in your recovery to show you the video."

"Can I see it?"

"When Lauren determines that you can, absolutely."

"Don't I have the right to see it now?" I started to get angry.

"Whoa, calm down. Tell me something, Brady: If you saw your buddies blown to pieces right now, would that help your mindset or throw you into a spiral where you couldn't get those pills down your throat fast enough? I'm betting on the second one. When the time is right, and Lauren thinks you are ready and can deal with it in a healthy way, she'll show you."

Begrudgingly, I had to admit that he was right. "Fine."

"So what led up to your call last night? Have you been drinking this whole time you've been taking your meds?"

"No. Last week I learned I was being released. Gracelyn found out yesterday when she came to see Dr. Felcroft with me." I hesitated.

"Spill it, Brady. There ain't nothing you can say that I haven't heard."

"I got upset because now she's going to see what a loser I am." I stopped as all my thoughts jumbled in my head. Sometimes they did that, and I had to try to sort them out. "I should have died in that blast so she wouldn't have to deal with me." I stared at the pills, suddenly wanting to snatch them up and pack them all down my throat. Why had I made that phone call?

"That's what you think? Well, that sucks to be you. I wonder if Lauren wishes Shane Logan hadn't come home after he lost both his legs." I stared at him and frowned, not understanding. "I mean, they weren't together then, but if he hadn't come home after that? He wouldn't have met Lauren, and they wouldn't have started Rise Again. Damn, I might not even be around anymore, and, God knows, Will wouldn't be. He was in a very bad place."

I just kept staring at him, not sure what to say.

"The point I'm trying to get across here is that if they hadn't gone through what they did. If *we* hadn't struggled, fought to hold on, and found like-minded people, where would we be? Where would the other organizations that help be? We'd all be gone, and that twenty-two-a-day statistic would be more like thirty-two, and none of this would exist. We wouldn't be helping veterans get back on their feet with counseling, education, job training, prosthetics, or two dozen other things that we offer, but we survived for a reason. We have a purpose, and now you, Technical Sgt. Brady Vanover, you have one too."

I nodded slowly, understanding what he was saying, but at the same time, not sure I believed in it for me—maybe for them, but not me. I was a mechanic; there was nothing special about that.

"I have a task for you," Nate said as he picked up the towel carefully and removed it from the table, exposing the pills.

"What? Swallow as many as I can at once?"

For a second, I thought he was going to swat me upside the head, but he didn't. He laughed instead. "No, doofus. Where are the bottles?"

I collected them off the side table and handed them to him. He opened them and set each one with the label facing me on the table.

He pointed at the table. "Pick up a pill."

"Okay," I said, stretching the word as I leaned forward. I grabbed the nearest one and lifted it. "You want me to put it into the vial?"

He nodded. "I do, but before you drop it in, I want you to think of one reason why you shouldn't be dead and tell me."

"What?" What the hell was he talking about?

He shrugged and leaned back, throwing an arm over the back of the couch as if we were just two guys hanging out on a day off. "What would you miss if you killed yourself? What do you love? What are the reasons to be alive?"

"Man, I don't know." I dropped the pill back on the table and went to get up, but his hand snapped around my bicep so fast I never saw it coming.

"Pick up that pill, Vanover."

I glared at him.

"Pick up that pill and tell me one reason why you shouldn't be dead. It could be because of your wife or your kids. It could be because you'd miss the taste of tacos or football games. I don't care what the hell it is, but you are going to pick up every single pill on that table and think of a reason *not* to kill yourself. You got that?"

"You're seriously going to make me do that?"

"It's an order, Vanover. You gonna disobey an order?"

I swallowed. My immediate reaction was to shake my head and say, "No, sir," but I held my tongue, and I turned back to the table. I reached out to pick one up.

"No, pick up the one you just threw down."

"Why? You're going to make me do it to every single one of them so it will eventually get picked up."

"Because it was the first one you chose." He leaned forward and put his finger on a pill, sliding it over the surface until it was right in front of me. "This one."

"Are you for real?"

"Do I look like an optical illusion?"

"Whatever, man. This is stupid."

"Stupid is easy, so this should be too. Let's go."

I shook my head and picked up the pill that he had dragged in front of me. "I don't want to die because it would hurt my wife."

"Good, put it away and pick up another one."

I rolled my eyes but did what he said.

"Because of my boys," I said and dropped the pill into another vial.

He reached out and tipped the vial over, spilling it back to the table.

"What the hell now?"

"You have to say, 'I don't want to die because,' and then add why. Not just 'because of them,' but *why* because of them."

"This is ridiculous."

"So are thoughts of dying. Keep going."

I growled but picked it up again and glared at him. "I don't want to die because I would miss watching my boys grow up."

He grinned at me. I dropped it into its vial and picked up another one. "I don't want to die because I'd miss my wife's enchiladas."

He chuckled softly as the pill clicked inside the plastic container. I was glad I could entertain him.

"I don't want to die because I'd never get to throw a ball with Dane."

Nate remained quiet as I picked one up after the other and came up with a reason for not dying. Most of them were stupid like I'd miss my favorite television shows or t-shirts, but a few were serious, and as I went on, they became a bit more serious. I thought it would be hard and that I'd run out of ideas, but I didn't. It grew easier and easier as I went.

I got choked up on one near the end. "I don't want to die— but I'm afraid of what comes next." I thought maybe Nate would say something since I didn't use "because" in there, but he remained quiet.

The last pill I picked up, I stared at for a long moment, and then I began to blink as tears filled my eyes. "I don't want to die —because I don't want to die."

I dropped it into the container and turned to see Nate brush his cheek, his eyes glassy, and Lauren a few feet away, just as emotional.

"You did good, man. You did good." Nate slapped me on my back gently.

For a while, we talked, and Lauren explained about the facility and what it had to offer. How had I been so lucky to find them? Had it really been because I stepped into Purgatory? Someday, I would pay Will back for his kindness.

A little while later, Gracelyn came to sit with me, and while I couldn't face her, I wanted her close. I hoped that she understood. I appreciated the questions that she asked since I was rather overwhelmed and not thinking clearly.

I knew that Gracelyn was strong enough to make it through this. I just hoped that she would wait for me to do so too.

After she and Lauren left to go to the medical center, Nate helped me get packed. He told me more about the facility and what would be expected of me. I had to admit that for someone who didn't think they would ever be going back to work in the military, it was a relief to know that the program was structured in a more militaristic way. At least for newcomers it was. He said that, as I progressed, they would help me transition to a more civilian mindset and way of doing things. That was the whole purpose: to teach me how to survive in the civilian world.

I had all my things together, and I lay on the couch and dozed for a little while after being allowed to take a couple of pills. Not once did Nate move them away from me, and I wondered if it was a test.

Gracelyn and Lauren returned, and we ate lunch with casual chitchat among the three of them. My nerves were ramping up and so was my anxiety, despite my medication. Suddenly, I wasn't so sure that I wanted to do this.

"You alright, Brady?" Nate asked as if he were right inside my head and knew the moment I started to second-guess all of this.

I looked him in the eyes. "No."

"It's okay to be nervous. This is going to be a big change, but you're going to be safe and with people that understand you and can help."

I turned to Gracelyn, expecting to see the disappointment in her eyes, but instead, I saw love and hope. "Gracey, what should I do?" I fought not to break down like a child again, and she got up from her chair and came to me.

"Brady, baby, you go. You get better. You get the help that you need. We will be here waiting for you when you come home, and we will come to visit and write and video chat."

"But I'm leaving you again."

She cupped my cheeks, tears streaming down her face. "But you are going to get better. I'd rather you leave me this way," she paused and swallowed hard before she continued, "than in a casket."

I started to cry as I pulled her onto my lap and held her. "I'm sorry, baby. I'm sorry I'm not well."

She leaned back. "You'll get better, and I'll be waiting for you."

"You promise?"

She nodded. "Cross my heart, Brady. I will always wait for you."

I held her for a few more minutes, and then we finished lunch. It was almost time for the boys to be home when Will returned, a pretty brunette at his side that he introduced as his wife, Nora.

He came to me shortly before the boys got home. "I figured your wife could use a friend today."

"Thanks, Will. I don't know how I can thank you."

"You don't worry about Gracelyn or the kids. We have their six, and Nate has yours."

"One day, I will repay the favor."

"Pay it forward, Brady. Just pay it forward."

Saying goodbye to my sons was hard. I had done it a ton of times, but this seemed so much more drastic. They were more solemn than usual, and I thought that was because they were picking up on the nervous vibe with all the people around. They stuck close to Gracelyn until it was my turn to say goodbye to her.

She threw her arms around my neck, crying quietly and trying to keep herself together. "I love you, Brady. Get well. Get better and come home. I will be here."

I took her face in my hands and asked, "Do you promise me you will wait?"

"Till death do us part," she said, "but please don't lose hope. I don't want to live without you."

I kissed her goodbye and realized that I hadn't kissed her enough these last few months. One day I would fix that—one day when I was in a better frame of mine.

"I love you, Gracelyn."

"And I love you, Brady."

She stood on the front lawn as I climbed into the van with Nate and Lauren. Will stood on her one side, Nora on her other, and the boys in front of her. My wife was protected until I could return and do it myself.

CHAPTER TWENTY-TWO

GRACELYN

I felt like I was floating on a wave, just going with the flow, but the wave seemed to crash into a wall when Lauren and I returned to the car after getting Lauren what she needed. I stared out the window. "I don't understand any of this."

"What part are you having trouble understanding?"

I turned to look at her. "How can he want to kill himself when he has a family that loves him? I know he thinks I'm having an affair with my boss, which I'm not by the way, but that can't be the reason."

"It's not one thing, Gracelyn. Remember I told you that Brady looks at himself as the provider and protector, and he doesn't know how to do that now, especially when he hasn't grieved for the ones he lost or for himself."

"Why would he grieve for himself?"

She gave me a tender smile. "He has ultimately lost a large piece of himself. The brain injury alone will play many games with his identity, and to know he lost his job, his career, too, because of a mistake is overwhelming."

"A mistake? He thinks the RPG attack was a mistake?"

She shook her head. "No, I'm talking about his back injury. Had they diagnosed it in Germany and treated it, he probably would have made a full recovery. Because they didn't, his spinal cord is damaged. We might be able to help him some, but he's going to have to learn to deal with a significant level of pain for the rest of his life."

"Are you saying that they didn't treat him properly?"

"Well, I can't tell you much, but from my first look, I'd have to say they never did an X-ray or MRI on his back. If they had, they would have seen the damage."

"Does he know this?"

"I'm pretty sure he does."

I rubbed my face. "This is so overwhelming."

"It will get better. Once Brady is there, the tension at home will ease and make it easier for all of you. You can rest easy knowing that Brady is in a safe environment. He will be treated with respect and honor and love, and he'll be with people who understand exactly what he is going through."

I reached over and put my hand on her arm. "Lauren, thank you. I don't know how to thank all of you for this and for what you do."

She patted my hand. "It is an honor to be there for our military, to help them find purpose and life again."

We stopped and picked up hoagies from Brady's favorite place and then headed back to the house. When I stepped in, I felt the tension in the air. It wasn't the kind of anxiety where you thought something horrible was going to happen. It was as if the inevitable was about to rain down, and the unknown was looming over us.

Brady had emotionally cracked during lunch, shedding tears that were very unlike him, and I wanted to crumple at his feet and tell him to stay here and that I could make him better. Lauren's words came back to me, though, and I knew that I could not heal Brady, but maybe they could.

I couldn't comprehend how someone could *want* to end their life. It made no sense to me, but I didn't need to understand it. I just had to accept it.

To me, life was so precious and to be cherished at every moment. I had grown up in a Christ-loving home, and attending church had given me insight into being thankful for everything. Even bad things had silver linings, although sometimes that silver blackened with tarnish. Eventually, the tarnish would polish off, and the silver would shine through and reflect the true purpose of why we had to travel that challenging path in the first place.

Brady hadn't grown up in a home where they worshipped, but I think he believed. He attended church with the boys and me when he was able, and I knew he prayed once in a while on his own. How deep his understanding and relationship were, I didn't know. That was between him and God.

While he was recovering, I planned to seek solace and understanding in my prayers. Maybe one day, I would know the right thing to say to someone to help him or her. Perhaps one day, I could look back on today and see how this weary road had polished the silver.

After the vehicle disappeared around the corner, I could hold it back no longer, and I began to sob—not just silent, hard tears, but wailing and heartbreaking cries that buckled my knees. I hated myself for doing that in front of the boys, but I couldn't hold it in anymore. I had been strong for Brady, and I would be strong for my boys, but right in that moment, I needed to be weak.

Strong arms caught me, and I heard Nora saying something to the boys as those powerful arms wrapped around me and followed me to the ground. I sat there in the front yard of the house, sobbing as if I'd lost Brady for good.

Maybe part of me thought I had, or perhaps I was crying for

the fact that I hadn't. There were a thousand ways I could have lost Brady.

Brady could have died a hundred times while he was deployed—but he didn't. He could have been killed coming and going from the base—but that hadn't happened. He might have remained in the hangar and been reduced to ash—but he had been spared.

Instead, I had almost lost my husband to his own hand because evil thoughts had filled his mind, and his self-esteem, which had once been his shining glory, had been beaten up and shoved into a corner to quiver in fear.

Will held me on the front lawn for I don't know how long. He rocked me, ran his hand down my hair, cooed in my ear to let it out, and I did. I cried until I couldn't cry anymore, and then I found a few tears left.

When I finished, I sat back, and Will handed me a handkerchief. I stared at it and then looked at him. "Who carries one of those nowadays?"

He grinned, and his angel wings spread over his shoulders and danced in the breeze. "I never go anywhere without one. You never know when you're going to have to console an incredibly strong woman."

I snorted a laugh and then blew my nose into the soft, worn cotton.

"You a little better now?"

"Yes," I said as I shifted a little away from him and scanned the neighborhood. "Wow. I can't believe I just did that out here in the front yard. Our neighbors must think I'm nuts."

He chuckled. "Who cares what they think? Besides, I'm pretty sure a lot of them were crying with you. Those were tears from a woman who loves a man, and her heart is breaking."

I gave him a sad smile and sighed as I wiped the tears from my face. "My boys are probably totally freaking out."

"They are in good hands with Nora, but I'm sure they would like to know that you are okay. You ready to go in?"

"Yeah."

He stood slowly, like he was in pain, and then reached down to help me off the ground.

"How did you get hurt, Will—if you don't mind my asking?"

He shook his head. "I made peace with it a long time ago. I don't mind talking about it. I was in the airborne, and we were landing in hostile territory. The wind shifted, and several of us were going in off target. We ended up landing almost smack-dab in the middle of a village under attack. Virtually the same time that I made my landing, the building beside me exploded, and the blast hit me and threw me back, kind of like it did to Brady, but I was closer, close enough to feel my skin burning away."

He sighed. "I didn't think I'd make it. Brady said that he remembered thinking that same thing as he closed his eyes after landing on the ground. I begged many times for the medics and docs to let me die, but no one would listen to me. I should have died. I had internal injuries and a host of other issues, but I survived.

"For years, I was in excruciating pain, mentally and physically. I thought about killing myself at least once a day, but something stopped me. Sometimes it was one of my children, sometimes my wife. Sometimes it was something I saw on television or another veteran struggling. Once in a while, it was hearing about another veteran losing the fight to his demons.

"I came to be thankful for all those excuses not to do it, but once my kids were out of the house, and it was just Nora and me, I wondered why I was still holding on. That's when things got the darkest for me. I started drinking, abusing my pills, even trying harder drugs to just lose myself or hope that I'd overdose by accident.

"Then one day, a buddy gave me a serious heart-to-heart and

told me about a support group. I joined it. I told myself it was only the one time to get him off my back, but once I got online and met Lauren and listened to a few of these other guys, I wanted to come back. Lauren put me in touch with Nate, and the rest is history. I spent nine months behind the wire at RAW and came out with a whole new purpose and outlook on life."

I touched his scarred face. "I am so thankful for you, Will, not only for helping Brady and me, but for your sacrifice, for your love and honor."

He seemed to blush as he dropped his head. "Thank you, ma'am."

"You're welcome," I told him, and then the two of us went inside. Nora was in the living room playing video games with the boys, but as soon as I walked in, Dane paused the game.

"Mom, are you okay?"

I went to my boys, and Nora moved so I could sit on the coffee table in front of them. "I am okay. I'm sorry about that. I know it was pretty scary to see."

Drew shrugged. "Ms. Nora said that you had to let the sad out so that you could be happy again."

I glanced at Nora as I smiled. "I did have to let the sad out."

"Were you sad because Dad left?"

"I was," I told him and collected a hand from each of them as I took a deep breath and released it. "I know you guys are aware that your father hasn't been himself lately."

"Yeah," Dane said as Drew nodded sadly.

"Well, this trip will hopefully change that. Your dad is going someplace where they help sad people to be happy again."

Drew looked distressed and squeezed my hand. "You aren't going to go, too, are you?"

"Oh, no, honey. I'm okay. My sadness might have seemed like a lot, but your daddy can't see past his sadness, whereas I can. He needs help doing that."

"He's going to come back though, right? He's not going to die in another explosion."

"He's not going to war or to a base someplace far away." I turned to Will. "Can you get the folder for RAW for me?"

He nodded and retrieved it from the kitchen. I moved to sit between the boys. "Here, this is where he is going to be. It's in Tennessee, only about four hours from Grandma and Grandpa."

I paged through the colorful brochure that had lots of pictures of the facility. The boys oohed and ahhed over the things that they saw. By the time we finished looking through it, we all felt better—especially when the boys learned that we would get to visit it in a few months.

The boys returned to their game, and I sat in the kitchen with Nora and Will for a few minutes. "I can't thank you two enough for being here for us. After the incident, I seemed to have lost touch with all my friends. Most of them lost someone in that explosion, and it felt wrong to talk about Brady with them."

"You guys were all on one path, but the tracks branched off. Now, your way is different. When you start going to your support group, you are going to make new friends. These friends will understand everything that you are going through, and they will be there for you in ways that your other friends never were."

Nora grinned. "I used to be jealous of Will and how close he was with the people he worked with, but then I joined my group, and I found that same kind of kinship. Now I have sisters, and a few brothers, that are as close to me, if not closer, than any blood relative that I have. One word or tear or look, and they know what I need. You're going to find that too."

I hoped so.

They left a little while later, and I found something simple to cook for dinner, and then I went to watch a movie with the boys. By bedtime, we were all exhausted, and I was about to lie down when my cellphone rang.

"Hello?"

"Gracelyn, it's Nate Hardy."

"Nate, is there a problem?"

"No, not at all. Brady got here, and we gave him a tour and got him settled. He's going to be busy the next couple of days with tests and meeting with different people. He's scared, but he's trying to be positive. I just wanted you to know that he's in good hands, and he's resting now."

I released a heavy sigh. "I'm so glad to hear that, Nate. Thank you for letting me know."

"If there are any problems, one of our team will reach out to you. Brady will be able to reach out next week. In the meantime, you rest and take care of yourself. We have him now."

I hung up and lay down, and for the first time since Brady was injured, I fell asleep and didn't wake up for a full eight hours.

CHAPTER TWENTY-THREE

BRADY

J had never been in a private plane, and I was admittedly impressed. The chairs were very comfortable, and after the emotional goodbye with my family, I needed some downtime. Once we were in the air, I put my seat back and closed my eyes. Within moments I drifted off to sleep.

Nate woke me with a hand on my arm. "We're landing in a couple of minutes."

"Did I sleep the whole way?"

Lauren grinned at me. "Yes, you did. Amazing what happens when you know you're safe."

"I guess." Or maybe because I had been through the wringer the last twenty-four hours. I had to think that was more of the reason than feeling safe.

We landed, and a large SUV was waiting for us on the tarmac. A tall, fit man with a beard hugged Nate and said a friendly hello to Lauren. The design on his t-shirt said something about overcoming the odds.

"Do you always travel this way?" I asked.

"Most of the time," Nate said with a grin. "Although there are times when the planes are in use, so we fly commercial."

Before I stepped in, the guy driving turned to me. There was a harshness about him as if he had been to hell and back. The light-green color of his eyes softened his appearance only slightly. I could imagine those eyes staring into hell and challenging it to come get him. "Brady, it's nice to meet you. I'm Derek Stall. We spoke on the phone last night."

I shook his hand. "I think I remember speaking with you."

He chuckled. "Yeah, I hear that. Don't worry, by the time you leave, you'll be sick of listening to me."

I laughed as he turned away, taking note of his broad shoulders and a wide back that tapered down into a trim waist. It was apparent that he spent a lot of time in the gym, and I envied the hell out of him. I had a feeling that I'd never be able to do that again, not with my back pain. That sucked because lifting weights had always been my place to seek solace. I could block out the world with each repetition, each curl of a dumbbell. It was just another thing that I had lost in my life, another thing to be pissed about.

Nate sat up front with Derek, while Lauren and I were in the second row. Nate and Derek talked about a few people, and then Lauren asked how Dana was doing.

"She's a maniac," he said it in exasperation as he shook his head, but he was also grinning like a kid. "This wedding is going to be a gigantic event. I told her I wanted only a few friends and family, but there are over two hundred people on the guestlist—for her side!"

Lauren laughed and turned to me. "If you didn't figure it out, Dana is his fiancée. She works at RAW. You'll meet her as she works with new residents, although she works real closely with the homeless vets we bring in."

They bring homeless here? I nodded and remained quiet as they continued to talk about the wedding and make jokes that had Derek rolling his eyes. The camaraderie reminded me of hanging with my flight, and I rubbed my hand over my heart as it ached.

A few minutes later, we rolled up to a guard shack and fence, and after a few friendly words, the gate opened, and we were inside. My stomach rolled, and I wanted to burst from the vehicle and run, but I forced myself to stay still as I looked around.

It looked a lot like a base, especially with the fence all around it. While many people wore similar clothes, cargos with polos or t-shirts, they weren't all the same.

"Is there a uniform?" I asked as the car came to a stop in a parking space.

"Sort of," Nate said. "In Phase One or Two, you wear beige cargos, shorts or pants, your choice. You'll wear a red shirt in One, and a gray shirt in Two. In Phase Three, you go to navy polos, and when you hit the final stage, you wear whatever you want. The staff will have it written on their chest. If you need anything, ask them."

We climbed out, and Derek came around to the back of the truck. He removed my bags, and I reached for them, but he said, "I got this today. Until you get medically cleared to lift more than ten pounds, we got you. Once you get cleared for that, then you can start carrying some things around."

I was going to argue, but several women walked slowly by, grinning at Nate and checking me out. That was the last thing I needed. Nate laughed. "He's married, ladies, and his wife will fight you for him, so keep your distance."

One groaned playfully and rolled her eyes, but everyone laughed, and they walked away. I thanked Nate quietly for that.

Lauren stepped in front of me. "Brady, I am going to leave you in their capable hands. I will speak with you one-on-one probably tomorrow to set up your therapy schedule. In the meantime, get squared away and get some rest. If you thought coming here was hard, well, tomorrow is when it will start to get really difficult."

"Thank you, Lauren."

"I'll see you tomorrow. I hope you are able to get some rest."

Nate and Derek led me to a sidewalk. "Over there is the food. You can't bring anything into the barracks. We had an issue with a guy hiding food, and then we had mice, but it's open for three squares. There are some à la carte choices to grab if you miss a meal or get extra hungry in between meals."

"I can barely get one meal down now," I said.

"Yeah, well, we are going to change that," Nate said dryly.

"Another order?" I asked him.

He laughed while Derek chuckled beside him.

"You learn fast, Vanover," Nate said. "Let's stop in the office first, and I'll get your welcome folder."

He turned when someone in a wheelchair called his name. The man rolled toward us, the side of his face heavily scarred and both of his lower extremities missing. Nate spoke as he came to a stop a few feet away, "Lauren just went up to the front office."

"Alright, I'll catch her there. You must be Technical Sgt. Brady Vanover." He stuck his hand out. "I'm Shane Logan."

Nate turned to me. "You have Shane to thank for all of this. All of this was his vision."

I scanned around us for a moment. "Pretty impressive, sir."

"I couldn't have done it without every single person here. Let me know if you need anything." I told him I would, and then he turned to Nate. "Nate, can I grab you for a minute?"

"Yeah, sure. Derek can get him through intake."

"Absolutely," Derek said. "We'll catch you later." Derek and I walked away and went into a small building on the left. "This is the housing office. If you have any problems with anything, pop your head in here, and someone can help you out."

A blond with beautiful blue eyes turned to us and threw a

brilliant smile at Derek as she got to her feet. "You're back, and you have Brady." She stepped forward and thrust out her hand. "Hi, I'm Dana Donahue, soon to be Mrs. Derek Stall. Welcome, Brady. We are so glad to have you here."

"It's nice to meet you," I told her. I would reserve the part about being glad to be here until after I settled in. There was the possibility that I might end up despising this place, but I had a feeling that I would actually come to like it.

"You have everything set up for him?" Derek asked.

She stepped forward and lifted her face to his. "Do I ever fail to have things ready?"

The look that passed between them was something that Gracelyn and I used to share. Would we ever look at each other that way again?

He touched her cheek. "No, you never do, Ocean Eyes."

She popped up on her toes and put a peck on his lips before turning back to me. "Sorry, I just can't help myself when he's around."

I laughed good-naturedly, but then my smile faded. "It's actually nice to see. I remember when my wife and I were like that."

Derek put his arm around Dana. "You'll get back there. If that's what you want, you'll find it."

"I don't know about that."

Dana grinned at Derek. "Sounds like it's time for a story, but you can tell him later." She stepped forward, handing me a folder from her desk. "This is more about your stay here. For the first few weeks, you are on a very strict schedule. Make sure you are where you need to be when you need to be there. You lose points if you aren't."

"Points?"

"Yeah, to earn extra privileges."

I laughed. "This place sounds like a prison."

Derek's eyes grew serious. "I'm pretty sure the only prison

you're stuck in is the one that's inside your mind. You'll get it figured out quickly, Vanover. I have no doubt."

"If you say so."

We stared at one another for a long moment, and then I looked away. His confidence made me nervous.

"Cut it out," she said to Derek before she stepped closer to me and gave me one of her incredible smiles. "You are in Phase One, building three. You're in the bunk room, but we had a special mattress brought in for your cot."

I raised a brow. "Why?"

"We are aware of your back issues, and the mattress should make it easier to rest. Normally, those beds are reserved for Phase Two residents, but we do bring them in for people with back and spine issues."

"You don't have to treat me differently than anyone else."

Dana's gaze softened. "Brady, every person here is different and gets treated differently. In general, everyone gets the same things, but it is all tailored to you and your recovery."

"Okay, I guess that makes sense."

The phone began to ring, and she smiled at me. "Derek will show you to your quarters, and I'll see you later. Come to me with any issues that you might have. Either Ron or I are in the office to help during the day."

Derek pointed toward the door behind me after that, and we went back outside and stood on the sidewalk where he pointed out the buildings. "Those are Phase One barracks. Those over there are Phase Two. In the back corner, you have Phase Three, and that tall building that looks like an apartment building is Phase Four. You might or might not get in there. Usually, guys with families check out after Phase Three as long as they feel ready. A few have transitioned into the fourth phase and stayed a little longer to get more education and job placement before heading out."

"Okay," I said softly. Way off on the far side, four people

were running toward the back. "Do they have a weight room here?"

He grinned. "Oh, man, do they. You will get plenty of time in there."

"Not sure I'll ever be lifting again," I said as we started to head toward the barracks.

"You will, Brady. I didn't think I'd ever get back to it either. I was a shell of a man when I got here. I'd been living on the streets, and I was a bag of bones compared to what I had been and what I am now. I've had two surgeries on my knee, and I've done a lot of rehab for the abuse I've done to my body. The gym is more than just a place to work out. It's where you'll do your therapy." He eyed me up and down. "It's obvious that you enjoy lifting. You might never do what you did before, but that doesn't mean you can't still rebuild some body mass and strength. This place is going to help you find the best possible you for the future. It's not just about mental; it's about the physical too."

Derek led me into the third building, and I stood in the front room. There were a few seating areas and a pool table off to the side, along with a large television and two comfy-looking couches.

"This is where you will do your group therapy. You will have group every day; I think they have it at three here."

"Do you have to attend?"

"Yep, you do. You don't always have to talk, but you do have to attend. You will have group every day, and one-on-one therapy three times a week. Although, if you need to talk to someone in between that, all you have to do is speak up. There are a dozen of us that will sit down with you and listen."

I nodded, not all that thrilled with all the therapy, but what had I expected?

Derek chuckled. "The first time I was in group therapy, I wasn't really *in* the group—just going through the motions— and a red flag was waved at me. I was taunted to speak, and I about cracked to a million pieces as I opened my mouth, and it all spewed out. I sure hadn't wanted to talk, but I did. That day was the first day of my healing."

"Wait! You were here as a patient?"

"Well, that's part of the long story, but yes. I went through the program, and I'm still going through it."

"What's your story?" I asked.

"You'll get to hear it tomorrow. I'm in here for group. Staff switches around groups so we are always around different people."

"You run it?"

He laughed. "No, man. I'm still healing, and I'm not certified to lead therapy. Part of my healing is telling my story, so you'll hear it tomorrow."

"Alright."

"Okay, so down here is the shower room. I don't have to tell you to keep it clean. We aren't your mother. We aren't going to clean up after you. All of you are responsible for cleaning up and keeping it that way. Back here is the bunk room." He glanced around. "You're in bed eight. I can tell by the mattress."

He went over to it and set my bag down on top as I looked around.

"It's like being in Afghanistan all over again," I commented.

"Yep." He turned to me. "Is that going to be a problem?"

I shook my head, but I wasn't so sure about that. It was then that I realized that my back was starting to flare up, and my anxiety was kicking in big time. "I need to get some of my pain pills."

"Yeah, speaking of those. Get them out of your bag."

I pulled them out, and he took them from me. "I'll show you where they are stored."

"You mean I don't get to keep them with me?" Panic began to creep in.

Derek turned and looked at me seriously. "Vanover, you're

here because you were contemplating taking all of these at one time. Do you honestly think that we are going to let you keep your pills here? If you need meds, you walk your ass out to get them. You aren't the only person in here with thoughts of going to sleep and never waking up, especially in this barrack."

"Why especially here?"

He glanced around. "See the orange pull tabs on the wall?"

"Yeah," I said as I glanced around. They were in all four corners of the room.

"Those are suicide alarms. This building is monitored closely; staff members are always in this building. They work shifts so there is someone always available for a crisis. If anyone gets into a major crisis, those alarms are pulled, and the reaction team is alerted to come."

I stared at the pull bar and then glanced over the beds. All of them appeared to be in use.

"You ever have anyone actually succeed here?" I asked.

"Yeah, one, but that was before we had a designated barracks for critical watches."

"Do I have to stay here the whole time?"

"Once the docs here feel you are off the critical list, you'll get moved to a different barracks. This unit changes over quickly. Most guys are only in here a couple weeks to a month before they are moved." He grinned at me. "Something to work toward."

As he turned, I glanced around again. All of these guys were fighting to live too. Maybe Nate was right, and I really wasn't alone after all.

CHAPTER TWENTY-FOUR

GRACELYN

*T*he next morning, I woke up rested, and I smiled slightly as I stretched after turning off my alarm. I glanced to the other side of the bed, then rolled to my side, brushing my hand over the spot where Brady's head should have been.

What had his night been like? Was he alright? Was he suffering? Upset that he had gone? Was he angry that I had told him to go? Anxiety rippled through me, and I threw back the covers and got out of bed to get ready for work.

The boys got ready without me having to hassle them, and while they smiled and looked rested, they were quieter than normal. I guess all of us were worried about Brady in our own way. I was pouring my coffee into my to-go cup when I got a text message from Nate.

I won't text you every day, but I wanted you to know that he had a good night.

A moment later a picture downloaded to my phone, and tears flooded my eyes as I covered my mouth to hold back the sob. Brady was sitting at a table with several other men, all of them wearing red shirts, except for one who had broad shoulders and was wearing a white polo. Brady was lifting his coffee cup to his mouth and he was actually smiling—smiling!

"Drew, Dane, come look at this. Nate just sent me a picture of your father."

They rushed to my side, and both of them grinned as they looked at him. "He's eating pancakes!" Drew exclaimed. "I want pancakes!"

"Well, how about we have pancakes for dinner tonight?" I asked Drew.

He thought that was a great idea.

"Okay, guys, get your backpacks and let's get going. We might actually be early today."

They ran off, both a little lighter on their feet than they had been just a few minutes ago. I stared at the picture, feeling so much hope as I typed a message to Nate.

You have no idea how much the boys and I needed this today. Just to know he is there, safe, and SMILING! OMG! He's smiling. Thank you, Nate. I feel hope for his future—for our future.

You're welcome, Gracelyn. We will be in touch soon.

I thanked him again and then met the boys at the front door. On the way to school, they talked about all the possibilities that we could do to the pancakes, and Drew ended up saying that he wanted to make peanut butter and jelly pancakes. Dane thought he was gross but admitted he would try a bite. I felt confident that he would love it.

I dropped the boys off and was walking into the office when I received another text message. This one was from Will asking how the boys and I were today. I told him that we were doing really well and even sent him the picture of Brady that Nate had sent me. He was glad to see it and told me to reach out if I needed anything.

I was at my desk a little while later when I heard someone enter the room, and then a hand landed on my shoulder and squeezed for a moment. "How are you this morning, Gracelyn? Everything alright at home now?"

"Morning, Doug. It was an eventful day yesterday, but things are better."

"Well, I'm glad to hear that. Maybe you can tell me about it over lunch."

"Yeah, maybe," I told him as the phone rang. I wasn't sure if I should be telling him about what happened, but I could decide that later.

I ended up having lunch with Doug after a busy morning, and we went to our favorite bistro around the corner from the office. I had just shoved a large bite of my salad into my mouth when Doug spoke.

"What happened yesterday?"

I chewed and deliberated on what I should say. In the end, I spoke the truth because that was who I was. "Brady had a rough night Wednesday night. Remember I told you that he normally has therapy on Thursdays?" He nodded. "Well, it was different this week. I took Wednesday off so that I could attend a therapy session with him and speak with his therapist. Brady walked out of the session in the middle of it because he got upset that the doctor told me something."

Doug frowned. "What would have upset him enough to leave?"

"It's because he's being medically discharged from the military. Remember I told you that they already started the paperwork, and Brady hadn't told me yet. I was taken by surprise and I questioned him on why he didn't tell me. He got angry and walked out, and I looked for him for a long time, but I couldn't find him. I ran a few errands and then went home to find him passed out on the couch."

"Wore himself out walking home, huh?" He chuckled as he took a bite of his burger.

I shook my head. "No, he'd been drinking."

He chewed slowly and thoughtfully. "Isn't he on medication?"

"Yes, and I guess the mixture knocked him out. He woke up in the middle of the night and started drinking again." I gnawed on my bottom lip. "I woke up when I heard someone else's voice in the living room."

"One of the boys find him?"

"No, a man named Will was there. He's a veteran who owns a bar called Purgatory. He was trying to help Brady."

"Help Brady do what? Drink more?" he scoffed.

I paused. "Not kill himself."

Doug's eyes went wide. "Wait, are you trying to tell me that Brady was mixing booze and pills to kill himself?"

I nodded.

"Damn, Gracelyn." He put his hand across the table and rested it over mine. His touch was familiar, but not the one that should be comforting me, and I pulled my hand back after a moment, smiling gently at him as I picked up my fork and took another bite of my salad.

"Wow, Gracelyn, I'm not sure what to say. Where is he now?"

"In Tennessee."

Surprised, he asked, "Tennessee? What's in Tennessee?"

I explained to him how Brady had walked into Purgatory and met Will, and what happened after that. I ended with showing him the photo that Nate had sent me this morning.

"You are okay? The boys are alright?"

"Yeah, seeing this photo this morning, and seeing that smile on his face." I sighed happily. "Doug, I can't remember the last time I saw Brady smile. I know he has a long way to go, a very long way to go, but he is on the right track now."

"Are you sure? I mean, that is great and all, but people that are suicidal are slightly off their rocker. You really want your boys around him when he's like that?"

I startled back slightly. "Are you saying that Brady is crazy because he wanted to hurt himself?"

"Well, no—"

"That's sure what it sounded like, Doug."

"I'm not saying he is crazy, Gracelyn. I guess I was trying to say that someone who is willing to kill himself is rather unstable. It's not unusual for them to take people with them when they go."

I shifted all the way back in my seat, shocked. "Doug! Brady would never do anything to hurt me or the boys."

"Did you think he would do something to hurt himself?" He paused, then leaned forward. "I know you love Brady, and you are an incredible woman for putting up with everything that you have these last few months. I'm just saying that maybe you should be careful with him around the boys for a while."

"Well, that's not going to be a problem. Brady will be in Tennessee for at least six months, if not a year."

"They are keeping him for a year?" He looked doubtful. "I've never heard of a recovery program being that long."

"It's not just a recovery program, Doug." I spent the rest of lunch explaining to him what the place had to offer, at least what I could remember from the brochure. I hadn't had time to check out their website or to watch any of the videos yet, but I hoped to do that this weekend.

After lunch, we returned to the office, and before we got out of the car, Doug turned to me. He reached over the console and took my hand. "Gracelyn, I know you love Brady, and you are doing everything that you can for him. I'm not trying to cross any lines here, but if you need me for anything while he's gone, just let me know."

The look in his eye told me that his anything might include things that I shouldn't be thinking about. I slipped my hand from his after a quick squeeze. "Thank you, Doug. I really appreciate that, but we are alright."

"Just know that you can call me anytime, and I'll be there."

"Thank you," I repeated, but I doubted I would ever do that. After lunch today, and the couple times that he had touched me, I was thinking that maybe I needed to put a bit more distance between us. Maybe Brady was right, and Doug did want more from me. Doug and I never had finished that conversation about what was going on between us, and it was probably better to just let it go at that.

My heart belonged to Brady, and my heart would always belong to Brady.

That evening, the boys helped me cook dinner, and true to his word, Drew spread peanut butter and jelly on his pancakes and made them a sandwich. Dane ended up trying it and saying it was pretty good and told me I had to try it too. By the time dinner was over, it was a universal decision that peanut butter and jelly sandwiches were awesome made with pancakes.

We watched a movie, and then after I tucked them in bed, I walked back to the living room and stared at the coffee table. Had it been just yesterday that all that had gone down?

I poured myself a glass of wine and picked up the phone, curling in a chair in the living room and checking my text messages. Nora checked on us and invited us to a picnic next weekend at their house. I told them that the boys had games, but we could come by after, and she gave me the address.

It wasn't the first picnic we had attended without Brady; we had gone to a lot while he traveled. Yet, this one seemed different. I sighed as I thought about Brady and where he was. I remembered the look on his face when he had said he didn't know what to do. The pain had been so evident, as was the fear. Brady was never afraid, but he had been then. I was sure he still was—as was I.

I sighed and lifted my phone, staring at the picture Nate had sent me. I had to believe there was hope that he would get through this.

I shifted my screen from the picture gallery to the phone and pulled up my mother's phone number. She knew nothing of what was happening. The last thing I had told her was that Brady had walked out of the session. What was she going to say about this?

The phone rang a couple times, and then she answered, "Hi, Gracelyn, is everything alright? You don't usually call this late."

"I'm sorry, were you in bed?"

"No, sitting on the porch listening to the night critters. Are you okay?"

"Yeah, I'm fine. We're fine. A lot has happened over the last two days. I didn't get a chance to call you last night, and today has been a whirlwind with the boys. This is the first chance I've had to sit down and think about calling you."

"What has kept you so busy?"

"Brady. Hey, Mom, have you ever heard of a place called Rise Again Warrior? It's near Knoxville."

"Rise Again Warrior. I don't think so, why?"

"Well, that's where Brady is right now."

"Why is he there? Was he transferred there for work or is that a medical facility?"

"Well, it's kind of a medical facility, but it's not through the military. It's for veterans, or those getting out of the military."

"Okay, well, that sounds good, but what do they do?"

I took in a long breath, and then released it. "Mom, Brady was suicidal. He was contemplating taking all his pills, and when I got home yesterday, he was drunk and passed out."

"What? Gracelyn, you must be wrong. Brady would never do anything to hurt himself."

"Mom, you don't know what Brady's been going through. I barely know what's been inside his mind. My husband needed help because he was thinking about killing himself."

She scoffed, "I can't believe that he would do such a thing. You must be imagining things."

"Mom!" I blurted to get her attention. "I'm not joking, and this is serious. My husband wanted to take his life because he was losing his career, and he lives in chronic pain. This is not a joke, and I am not imagining things. Did you know that on average twenty-two men and women, active duty and veterans, commit suicide every day? Did you know that? Brady was about to become a statistic."

"Gracelyn, you two need to calm down a little bit. I'm sure Brady will be fine once he calms down."

I laughed. "You don't get it, Mom. If Brady hadn't met Will yesterday at the bar, this call might be me notifying you that he was dead."

I heard my mom huff on the other end of the line. "Okay, well, so what is he doing? Is he in an institution? You aren't going to tell anyone about this, are you?"

"No, he's not in an institution! He's at Rise Again Warrior, and he's going through treatment there."

"Oh, okay, well, I would keep that information to yourself and not tell people that he's not well in the head."

I laughed. "Mom, he's not crazy! Why do people immediately think that someone who is suicidal is crazy?"

"How could they not be, dear? Life is precious. Anyone who would want to end it can't be of sound mind."

I was getting angry, and I knew that I needed to hang up before I said something that I would regret. "Okay, well, I just wanted you to know where he is. I need to go. I'll talk to you later, Mom."

I didn't wait for her to respond. I hung up and growled at the phone, feeling so frustrated, and my gaze landed on the packet from RAW. I snagged it and dug through the paperwork in there to find the list of dates and times. I glanced at my watch. There was a session starting in ten minutes.

I needed to call Brady's parents and let them know what was

going on, but at the moment, I did not have the energy for that. I could wait a little longer.

I added more wine to my glass and then collected my laptop and got comfortable. My fingers trembled as I typed in the address, and a few moments later, I connected to a room with seven other people—six women, one man.

A woman at the top right corner was smiling at everyone. "Glad you all made it tonight. For those who don't know me, I'm Remy. I work at RAW, and I was in the army for six years. I'm working on my psychology degree for family therapy and addictions, along with suicide prevention. I've met many of you, but there are a couple new faces here tonight. Let's just get started by everyone telling us your name and what phase your loved one is in. Taylor, can you start?"

A woman spoke up. "I'm Taylor. My husband, John, is in Phase Two."

Another woman held up her hand as she spoke. "I'm Susan. My son, Brett, is in Phase One. We just had our first phone call last night." Her eyes misted, and I smiled at her obvious joy.

The guy went next. "Tim here. James, my son, was about to go into Phase Three, but had a setback that I'd like to talk about tonight."

Remy spoke, "Tim, absolutely. Let's finish the introductions and then you can speak."

Another woman smiled nervously and said, "Jessica. It's good to see you all today. My husband Carl is in Phase Two."

The next woman smiled. "I'm Lex, um, this is my first time here. My twin brother, Alan, has been there two weeks. I think that's still Phase One."

Remy nodded. "Yep, that would be Phase One."

"Barb, here," an older woman said. "My husband is in Phase Four and coming home soon!"

There were smiles and claps from a few of the people. I had not expected her to say her husband with her age.

I gnawed on my bottom lip for a moment as I realized it was my turn to go. "Good evening, everyone. I'm Gracelyn. My husband Brady just arrived last night. I have no clue what a phase even is."

CHAPTER TWENTY-FIVE

BRADY

*D*erek showed me where the dispensary was, and I wasn't too keen on the fact that I was going to have to get out of my bunk and trudge all the way over there in the middle of the night when I needed my medication. He did tell me that if it became too difficult, then they could have a dose locked up in my building, and the staff on duty could get it for me if walking to the dispensary was too much.

I wasn't very happy that I had to ask permission to take my pills. I felt as if they were putting a challenge out there to man up and deal with the pain without the meds. I was not ready to go without them. I *couldn't* go without them. "I don't see why I can't keep them with me."

Derek slowly turned his head my way, his eyes holding a glint that was like a smack upside the head with a you're-kidding-me comment attached to it. I had to admit that he intimidated me just a little bit, although I wasn't going to admit that anytime soon. "You want to keep whining about it or go get chow?"

"I'm not hungry."

Derek laughed. "Yeah, Hardy was right. You have a long way

to go. Let's go eat. You might not be hungry, but I am, and the rest of your barrack will be finishing dinner. I'll introduce you."

"My head is starting to throb. I'd rather go lie down before I get a migraine."

Derek looked at me closely. "Stop whining like a little kid, Vanover. The headache is probably because you haven't eaten. Let's put something into your gut. After you eat, then you can go lie down if you feel like you need to. I'm sure today has been taxing, but you're going to fuel your body. You're a lifter, and you're starving your muscles. You know the importance of good health and feeding your body."

I wasn't going to win this fight, and I knew it. I fell into step with him. As we walked, I checked out the property. I saw people off in the distance playing football, and a few in another area doing exercises on an obstacle course. A few people passed us, and they said hello to Derek and nodded to me.

Inside the food hall, I paused. It was a lot bigger than I had anticipated, and there were at least seventy people in here of all ages and color. I saw the tables off to the far side where most of the guys were wearing red shirts, although there were a few gray mixed in.

I followed Derek to the food line, and he handed me a black tray. "The food is really good here, and if you have anything special that you'd like, just let Clay know." He pointed his chin at a tall, burly black man behind the counter. "He is a god in the kitchen. Loves to do special orders for guys who are missing certain things from home."

"Seriously? He'll make you whatever you want?"

"Yeah, he will." He grinned at me and then turned to Clay. "This is Brady Vanover; he just arrived."

"Welcome, Brady." He gave me a good once-over. "You let me know if there is something special that you want. Just give me like a day or two lead, and I'll have it for you."

"Thanks, appreciate that," I told him and then scanned the

food under the glass. Holy smokes, it looked good, even to me, who had a hard time choking down food these days.

Derek got a plate filled with pasta, fish with a cream sauce, and a large side salad. I decided to take it easy tonight and just have one of the large salads, but then Derek told Clay to toss over a serving of grilled chicken to add protein to my meal. I almost glared at him, but I had a feeling that would go over about as well as if I'd glared at my commanding officer.

I took the tray with my food over to the drink station and stopped in my tracks when I saw the beer dispenser off to the side.

Derek knocked my shoulder. "Don't even think about that. It's for parties and special occasions, and you have to earn the right to have one."

"Is that one of the things I can get with my points?"

"Yep, but first you have to be off all narcs. We both know that's going to take a while," he said over his shoulder, and I glanced around to see who might have heard him. A few people were looking in my direction, but it was with casual interest of wondering who the new guy was, and have our paths ever crossed before?

After I got myself a bottle of water, I scanned the room and found Derek moving toward the other red shirts. I followed him, suddenly feeling nervous. What were these guys going to think of me? What would they think when they found out I was in the suicide watch barracks?

Derek was laughing at something that someone said as I joined him, and he glanced at me and nodded, so I slipped into the seat next to him.

"Guys, we have a new Phase One. This is Technical Sgt. Brady Vanover; he just got here a little while ago from Denver. He's in building three, so give him a hand to get settled." Most of the guys smiled and nodded. He looked at me. "I'm not going to introduce you to everyone because you'll just forget their names anyway, but there are a few you are going to want to know."

Did he have to mention that I was in building three? I glanced nervously around the table and didn't see one person giving me an odd look or one of pity. Instead, they smiled, said a kind word, or nodded.

"This is Jersey." He pointed to a guy two down. "He's with you in building three, and so is Alan beside him. Jersey's close to shifting to another barracks, and Alan just got here last week." He pointed to another guy a few more down. "That's Brett, he's also in three with you. Those guys can answer your questions about what happens there."

After that introduction, the group went back to their conversation, and Derek joined them. I ate in silence, the pain in my spine making it hard to focus, and my head began to throb. Within a couple minutes, the level of noise and movement in the room, along with my anxiety, had a migraine crashing over me before I could even do anything.

I put my head into my hands, blocking the light, and putting my thumbs into my ears to tone down the noise as my stomach pitched. An arm went around my back, and I groaned as I felt hands on each side, but the pain of the headache became too intense for me to do anything other than be lifted and moved.

I was aware that I was breathing fresh air, and I heard voices talking softly around me, but my head was banging so hard that I couldn't comprehend anything. I heard someone say something about meds, and I prayed that they were going to get some for me. I assumed that we were going to the barracks, but I was laid down on a gurney, and I slit my lids enough to see medical equipment around me.

I felt someone poking me with a needle in one arm, and then another one in the other arm. Soft voices continued, but the words were just out of my reach as the pain of the migraine banged against the inside of my skull. I began to feel sleepy almost instantly, and a second later, I was gone.

When I woke up, my headache was a dull ache, no longer a migraine, but now just a regular ol' annoying headache. I glanced around to see someone sitting in the corner, his head back against the wall. I remembered him from the food hall but couldn't remember his name.

I shifted, and he opened his eyes.

"How you feeling?" he asked.

"Not as bad as I was."

He glanced to the side and nodded at the IV bag. "They gave you two bags of fluid. You were dehydrated; that's probably why the headache was so intense and hit you so quickly."

"I get migraines all the time."

"Yeah, they are probably worse because you don't drink enough fluids. I had that problem. I heard them mention you have a TBI. I do too. I'm going through therapy for it; I'm pretty sure they will put you through it too. It's pretty extensive therapy. I've been here for almost two months, and I'm starting to feel like I might recover."

"What was your name again?"

"Jersey Righter."

"Jersey, that's right. How did you get a head injury?"

"Explosion. I was out of the danger zone, but the blast did a number on my head. It busted my eardrums, and the percussion of the blast slammed my head back and forth like I was a bobblehead doll. I couldn't stand up straight, kept falling over. Lights and sound made me want to puke; occasionally they still do. Sometimes if I tried to look at words on a page, they all jumbled in my mind."

What he said was very similar to how I frequently felt. "You ever feel like you forget words?"

He laughed softly. "All the freaking time, and not hard words, easy ones."

I grinned. "Yeah, I feel like that too. I stopped talking sometimes because I was having that issue. I'd open my mouth, know what I wanted to say, but the words wouldn't be there. It got frustrating, so I just stopped trying."

"They will help you with that."

"How do you help with something like that?"

"It's called concussion therapy. I went through three different kinds. They all work different parts of your brain and help it start healing right."

"They seriously have therapy for concussions?"

"They do." He grinned. "Sounds kind of stupid to say you have physical therapy for a concussion, but they work you hard. You'll see progress if that's what you want."

"If that's what I want?"

"You're in building three, so that means you're thinking of what comes after this life, or more specifically how you can end this one—and the pain."

I stared at him for a long time, not sure what to say.

He continued after a moment, "If you are here, something in you wants to push past the pain and keep on living. Don't let that go, but I'm going to warn you, if you're already thinking of putting a bullet in your head, once you start therapy, I mean the mental kind, not the brain kind, you're going to think about it more, but if you hold on and fight through, they will start showing you what you have to live for, the reasons that you don't want to give up. Keep fighting, and you'll make it through."

"How did you get here?"

"My best friend found me with my gun inside my mouth and talked me down. Got me in here through a friend."

"You still active duty?"

"No. My enlistment was up about four months ago. I was supposed to do twenty. I had plans on being a lifer, but that didn't happen. When my enlistment came up, I walked."

"You didn't go out medically?"

"No. I just wanted away from it all. It was stupid. I should have pushed for a medical discharge, but I couldn't deal with the red tape in the mindset I was in."

"Makes sense."

"You out yet?"

"They just started the process, hence the reason I thought about taking all my pills. I didn't know how I was going to take care of my family now with all my issues. I had wanted to join the air force since I was in middle school. I have no idea what the hell I'm going to do now."

"I hear you, and so will every guy here. I didn't want to be here. I fought it, but my friend begged me to come. I'm not ready to tell him this, but I'm glad he did. Coming here has been the hardest thing I have ever had to do, but it's the best. You'll see that. Just be open, and don't care what anyone thinks of you or what you say. There is not a guy or girl here who hasn't struggled with similar things, and what you say will not surprise them or upset them, so be honest. It took me a few weeks to do that, and I wasted a lot of time. Since I opened up, I have started to feel the change already."

"I'll take the advice," I told him as a nurse stepped into the room.

She had a kind smile and bright-brown eyes. "Brady, nice to see you awake. I'm Amy. How is the headache?"

"Better, just a dull ache now."

"That's good. We gave you something to calm your mind, so you weren't stressing, and then we filled you with fluids and vitamins." She looked at the bag. "As soon as I take your vitals, I can let Jersey take you back to your barracks."

I shifted and was surprised that my back didn't hurt as badly as it usually did when I lay still for too long.

A few minutes later, Jersey was helping me to my feet and then out of the building. By the time we got out there, I was able to walk on my own. We chatted on the way, or he chatted, telling me more about the place. I could see a few small bonfires toward the back, and the smoke drifted through the night air.

"Those are Phase Three and Fours. They hang out back there at night."

"Phase One and Two aren't allowed?"

He shrugged. "I don't know if we are or aren't. No one has ever told me I could go back, so I don't try. It's like that uncrossed line of enlisted and officer."

I chuckled. "Yeah, I get it."

We entered the building, and there were a few people in the common room. Jersey introduced me and made a comment on how I'd never remember their names so not to try, and then we headed back to the sleeping area. My bag was still on my bed as it had been when I'd arrived, and four more guys were lying on their bunks, reading, typing on their computers, or listening to music with their eyes closed.

Jersey let me get myself unpacked, using the footlocker at the end of my bunk, and then I went to take a shower. When I got back, I found seven red shirts on my bunk, along with three pairs of beige cargo pants, and two pairs of shorts. I folded them neatly and put them into the footlocker, too, then I lay down on my bunk and sighed as I stared at the ceiling.

I was far away from my family, and I missed them. I hoped that Gracelyn and the boys were doing alright and that Gracey would forgive me for this. I glanced around at the other guys here and found a sense of normalcy slip over me. I wasn't just with a bunch of guys who had issues. I was with guys who were struggling just like me because of what they had been through. These guys might be from other branches of service, but they were still my brothers. I realized then that walking out of the session with Dr. Felcroft and my wife and finding myself on the barstool in Purgatory might have just saved my life.

CHAPTER TWENTY-SIX

GRACELYN

$\mathcal{I}$t had been almost a week since Brady had left. I'd received a few updates on him from both Nate and Lauren, all saying that things were positive and that he was settling in as expected. He'd already undergone a battery of tests and started therapy. I knew that sometime in the next couple of days, the boys and I would finally be able to speak with him.

As I drove to work, I thought back on all the times he had been gone before. I had easily been able to put him out of my mind, not that I'd been trying to forget about him or that I hadn't wanted to think about my husband. It had always been easier to slip Brady to the back of my mind so that I didn't constantly worry the entire time he was gone.

I knew other women who did nothing but complain about their husbands being deployed. They whined about what they had to do to take care of the house or that they had to do everything for their kids and they just needed a break. Well, I could use a break, too, but I didn't complain about it.

Others were continually stressing over what might happen to their spouses and stalking news reports. Personally, I avoided the news—all of it. I didn't want to hear what was happening a world away. What good would it do to be reminded that my husband was in a war zone and might not return home?

If the news wasn't about that, it was about the unrest in our country, the political backstabbing, and the fight to defund police. I was a patriot, but I was not a fan of the politicians that ran our country, and I was taught that you always respected those who protected you. How could people think to defund the very people who were protecting them here on home soil? It made no sense to me, and it raised my blood pressure to think about, so I avoided it.

I had known going into this marriage that there would be many times that I would have to be both the mother and father. I knew that I would have to be strong enough to make those tough decisions and to keep the drama on the home front to a minimum so that Brady didn't get stressed over what was happening here. God knew he had enough to worry about when he was in another country working for the freedom of Americans and others around the world.

Even though I didn't pay attention to the news, I wasn't blind to what was happening around the world. I'd have to be locked inside my house not to hear the turmoil in the world around me. I also saw and recognized the trauma that our service members endured. I'd read the articles, seen videos, even heard people talking about their spouses or someone they knew struggling. Many times, those stories had broken my heart and I had thanked God that my husband hadn't endured that particular trauma—except now he had. Now Brady was in a precarious position. I never would have guessed that my husband could ever be suicidal. He was always so helpful, so engaged with others, and always willing to help other people out. It was one of the things that I loved most about him, his willingness to stop doing anything to help someone else.

I gnawed on my lip as I thought about some of the signs that I had missed. Here I had thought leaving him alone to recover was a good thing, when it had been the opposite. Maybe if I had tried to talk to him more often, he might have opened up to me. What if I had not let him hide in the bedroom when he had first gotten home? What if I'd pushed him harder? Would that have made him better or worse?

The guilt was almost overwhelming, and I thought back on the discussion we'd had in my therapy session just last night.

Lex had been in this session again and had talked at length about how she felt she failed her brother, Alan. She said she felt incredibly guilty that she hadn't sensed his pain because she'd been so wrapped up in her wedding plans. She felt so much guilt that she put her wedding on hold until her brother was better.

I felt every ounce of her pain as she spoke, and I realized that she had treated his deployments as I had Brady's. She had put it out of her mind so that she didn't worry about him constantly and was happy when he returned stateside. She had been waiting for him to come back so he could help with the wedding plans.

She said that even though he was a little withdrawn, he had pretended to be alright. He had gone out with friends, hung out with her. He had even suggested a family dinner, something he had never done before. It should have tipped her off because he hated the family drama that occurred when everyone was together. During the dinner, he had been reserved, and now looking back she realized he hadn't been part of it, but merely a bystander. Now she wondered if that dinner had been his way of saying goodbye, or if it had been the last straw.

Two days later, she had woken early knowing in the pit of her stomach that something was wrong. She jumped in her car in her pajamas and drove two hours to her brother's small house after he didn't answer his phone. She said she felt it in her bones that he needed her, and she had to break a window to get into his place. She found Alan lying on the floor, six empty pill bottles around him, and foam seeping out of his mouth.

Of course, we knew he survived, but the doctors told her that if she had been twenty or thirty minutes later, he would have died. Alan refused to speak to her when he woke up. He was angry at her for saving him and even screamed at her once that she didn't know the pain that was in his head or his heart. If she did, she would have let him die. He had told her to go away and not come back. He even said the dreaded words that every single one of us felt to our souls. His final words to her as she'd left his room sobbing had been, "I hate you for saving me! Why couldn't you just let me die, Lex! I will never forgive you!"

I had sat there silently crying through her entire story. I knew in my heart that story could have been Brady's. I could have woken up to find Brady foaming at the mouth or maybe already dead. What if the boys had found him that way? What kind of trauma would that have caused them?

I pictured Brady storming from Dr. Felcroft's office where I had seen the pain and anger in his eyes. At the time, I thought it was only because I had accused him of not telling me something. I hadn't even been able to fathom the depth of his despair.

Lex explained that she had sat in the lobby for hours, staring out the window and watching people come and go. One of the people that had walked past wore a t-shirt about stopping veteran suicide, and she had picked up her phone and started to do some research. She found information on Rise Again Warrior and called them. She spoke to someone named Derek for over an hour, and then thirteen hours later, Nate and Lauren showed up at the hospital and spoke with her and then her brother.

She had seen the fury in her brother's gaze when she had brought them in to see him, but three days later, when her brother checked out, he hugged her goodbye, one of those hugs like someone is trying to keep from being sucked into an abyss, the type of hug that you never forgot. He didn't speak to her, and hadn't spoken to her since his outburst, but she knew that he was taking the program seriously as she received reports from his therapist.

Lex had found a way to help her brother, yet the guilt still weighed heavily on her shoulders. Remy told her that it wasn't her fault. She also said that what was going on inside of her brother wasn't her problem to fix. It wasn't any of our problems. Our loved ones needed help, help that they could not get from their families. They needed the assistance of their other family, the ones who knew what they had gone through, who had lived through the hell and survived.

I took some solace in that, although it was hard to remove all the guilt from my shoulders. Remy said that our love and support were vital to their recovery, as was learning about the process of their healing and learning to recognize the signs when they needed to be pushed or given room to breathe.

It made sense, and I looked forward to learning more once I moved on to the next phase. As Brady was going through phases, so was I. The first phase for me was accepting that I could not control Brady's behavior, nor could I have stopped him from trying to hurt himself on my own. It was a phase that required us to bare our souls and put all our fears out there for all to see.

When I got to the next phase, I would learn to recognize signs, phrases, behaviors that could alert me in the future that something was wrong. It would also teach me ways to deal with it, and how best to respond to distress signals.

Plus, I was learning how to accept and strengthen myself, with a support group behind me and a dozen phone numbers I could call at any time to help me find sanity or vent my stress and pain.

When we got to the third phase, Brady and I would receive couples counseling, and I knew that part of Brady's recovery was talking to me about what he'd been through. He might not want to tell me about the explosion, but he was supposed to talk to me about some of what was causing his pain, both mentally and physically.

I both looked forward to and feared that conversation.

As I parked in the lot at my office, I stared out the window for a moment and sighed. I didn't know how long it would take Brady to get to that point, and I would have to keep marching forward until then.

I turned to the door just as someone rapped on the glass. I smiled up at Doug and climbed out. "Morning," I said to him as I closed my door.

"You alright? You looked deep in thought."

I waved his concern away as we started toward the building, "Oh, I'm fine. I was thinking about Brady."

If I hadn't been glancing his way, I wouldn't have seen the slight frown that passed over his face momentarily.

"Are things okay with him?" he asked politely.

"As far as I know. We should get to talk to him this weekend," I said as we reached the door. Doug held it for me as I stepped in, and the two of us headed to the bank of elevators.

"It will do you all good to hear his voice. I know all of you are worried about him."

"We are." I smiled up at him. For a moment, the two of us stared at one another, and I briefly thought, had I not been with Brady, I might have dated a man like Doug. He was kind and responsive, and he was a good boss. He pushed you but didn't get all bent out of shape if you didn't get something finished.

We stepped into the elevator, and we ended up near the back corner, with six other people in the metal box with us. The elevator was big enough to fit us all without feeling like sardines, and as was the norm inside the elevator, silence fell over the occupants. When the doors opened on the next floor up, four more people got on, and I shifted back to make room.

I came up against Doug's arm which must have been resting on the railing behind us. The two of us glanced at one another, and I anticipated that he would move his arm from behind me, but he didn't. I had no choice but to lean against it—or on the stranger in front of me.

I wasn't sure why I was so aware of his arm, but I felt the muscle in his forearm shift as he twisted his hand. A shiver went up my back as his palm landed on my lower back and stayed there. Two more floors, and the doors opened and people stepped out, but they were from the other side of the car, and the people in front of me didn't move much.

The heat of Doug's hand was branding my lower back, and I was tempted to ask him to remove it, but I didn't want to make a scene in the elevator. When we finally arrived at our floor, I almost shoved the man in front of me to the side as I said, "Excuse me."

In the hallway, I was a few steps in front of Doug and didn't wait for him to open the door for me. I went straight to my desk and set my purse down, slipping into my chair as Doug passed by on the way to his office without a word.

It wasn't a big deal. It really wasn't, but it had felt like a big deal. It almost felt as if I had been cheating on Brady, but it had only been a touch, just a hand on my lower back, a touch that had been all too familiar and—dare I say—enjoyable.

CHAPTER TWENTY-SEVEN

BRADY

The week had been a whirlwind, and my emotions had been up and down a hundred times. My pain levels had also been on a rollercoaster ride, and by the following Thursday morning I was exhausted as I thought about the last week.

Friday, Saturday, and Monday, I'd gone through extensive physicals and a battery of tests that included X-rays and MRIs of my leg and spine. I'd even done some nerve testing on my spinal column and the nerves in the affected area. Plus, I'd taken another CT scan of my brain to confirm that I had no brain bleeds or other abnormalities going on up there. They put me through hearing and vision tests, and I learned that I had a slight hearing loss in my left ear.

After those tests were completed, on Tuesday and Wednesday, I'd met with the doctors to go over the reports. I saw an orthopedic, an ear, nose, and throat doctor, and two different neurologists—one who specialized in spinal injuries, the other one brain injuries. I was slightly overwhelmed by it all, and they had explained how I could go back and read over my chart anytime I wanted through one of the guest health terminals in the med center.

Despite all I'd done, I'd also had a lot of downtime. They had allowed me to rest in one of the back rooms during the day so that I wouldn't be disturbed as easily, and I didn't even care that those rooms had cameras to watch me. With all the testing, the movement, the bright lights, the sounds, and the people talking and talking and freaking talking, I was always on the verge of a migraine, but they helped me avoid having another bad one.

It was now Thursday, and I was going to finally get my first peek at the gym. The docs told me that since they now knew what was going on inside my body, it was time to start the therapy and treatments.

I pulled back the door and stepped in, my jaw dropping slightly as I scanned the ginormous room. If I had walked in here six months ago, I would have thought I had died and gone to heaven. The place had every conceivable piece of training equipment, and there were multiple stations and several rooms on the other side where they could do specialized training and workouts. As I took a tour, I found that they even had two endless pools, and I hoped that I'd get some time in one of them.

As I watched other therapists working with some of the guys, my anxiety increased, and the machines and equipment began to look more like torture devices. I'd never been one to run from pain; in fact, when it came to lifting weights, I relished it, but I wasn't the same man now. I didn't know if I was going to be able to handle this or not. The last thing I wanted was to look like a fool among my peers.

I didn't have anything to worry about on the first day though. Donovan, my trainer/therapist, brought me into a private room after my tour, and he ran me through some very-light-range-of-motion exercises. He also asked a ton of questions about what my previous lifting experience was.

For the first time since I'd arrived, I talked openly. This

wasn't about the pain I had endured or the guilt that weighed me down. It had nothing to do with my career ending. This was about something I had once loved to do and hoped that, eventually, I could one day do again. Ever since Derek had mentioned the gym, I'd been dying to see it, and my palms itched to lift a few dumbbells.

If they had told me that I'd never be able to work out again or lift heavily, I might have felt as if I'd lost another piece of my identity, but as I finished up, Donovan slapped me lightly on the shoulder and grinned.

"Brady, before you know it, you're going to be back in here. Your weights aren't going to be as high—at least not for a while. Your spinal injury will cause some issues, but we're going to work together to figure out how to get around that and adapt to your circumstances. I bet, in a couple of months, you're going to be helping some of these guys with their workouts. You've got a lot of experience, and a lot of guys that come through here are clueless and don't want to ask us for help. I bet you anything, within two months, guys are asking you for tips."

I laughed at him and shook my head. I doubted that, but it was nice of him to give me something to possibly look forward to. He told me that I'd have therapy every other day to start out, and then we'd see how it went. Once I finished with Donovan, he brought me to a woman named Emma in another part of the building.

"Brady, it's nice to meet you. Come on in, and let's get started with your concussion assessment."

I frowned as I sat down. "How are you going to assess a head injury?"

"Well, there are lots of things that we are going to do, and I have quite a few questions before we start doing tests. Because we don't have a baseline for you on record, we are going to have to play it by ear, and I'm going to depend on you to tell me what is going on inside your head and how you are feeling. If something doesn't feel right, or if you are struggling with something, you let me know. I'm only one part of the process; there are two other therapists that you will have. I do the vestibular side of concussion therapy."

"What does that mean?"

"Let me ask you this. Do you ever get dizzy? I mean since your injury. We all get dizzy sometimes, but let's talk about after your TBI. Do you get dizzy?"

I shrugged a shoulder. "Yeah, all the time."

She nodded. "Okay, what about nauseous? Do you get sick to your stomach if you move a certain way or if you're in a vehicle moving?"

I shook my head. "I don't think so, at least not that I've noticed." I frowned. "Well, maybe that's not true. I wasn't driving before I came here, but when my wife was driving or I was in the back of an Uber, I'd close my eyes sometimes because it was easier than trying to look at everything around me."

"Okay, that's pretty normal. What about your balance? Do you seem to lose you balance more often?"

"Maybe a little."

"Do you find yourself reaching out to touch the wall or a piece of furniture as you walk around more often?"

My forehead furrowed as I considered that. "Yeah, I guess I do." I laughed slightly. "Back at the barracks, I run my hand down the wall as I walk, and I did that at our house too. When I took the stairs, I'd hold the banister, and also put my palm on the other wall to keep me straight as I went down."

"When you look down, do you get vertigo?"

"Yeah."

"What about up?"

I glanced up at the ceiling because I wasn't sure what the answer was to that, and my mind twirled slightly. Emma reached out a hand and put it on my arm to steady me as I had shifted sideways slightly.

"Looks like you get it when you look up too."

I smirked at her. "Yeah, I guess so. It was kind of like the world was on spin-cycle all of a sudden."

"Yep, exactly." She picked up a pen and made a few notes. "Alright, so all those things I just talked to you about, those are vestibular things. I am going to help you with movement and balance. A lot of it has to do with your eyes moving and sending signals to your brain. We have a lot of little games that are going to work your brain to train it back to where it needs to go."

"Games? Like tricks of the trade?"

She grinned, her brown eyes twinkling mischievously. "No, like games. We are going to play games."

I chuckled softly. "Okay, if you say it works. Jersey said his therapy was really helpful, so I'm going to hope it works for me too."

"Jersey has made great strides since he started here. I'm glad that he says it's working for him. After you finish here with me, if you don't have a crazy headache, you'll go to Sally, and she's going to test your speech and see what needs to be done with that."

"But I talk just fine."

She cocked her head to the side. "You ever have trouble remembering words, simple ones?"

"Um—" I paused.

"Let's do this. Tell me the first eight things that come to your mind that begin with the letter R."

I laughed. "That's easy: Red, raccoon, race." I hesitated as my mind seemed to go blank. "Um, rabbit."

She grinned at me. "It's not as easy as you remember it being, huh? Sally is going to help your brain start working the right way again with all kinds of drills like that. Over time, it will become easier."

"If you say so." I shook my head, feeling slightly embarrassed that I couldn't come up with more words. I blurted out two more. "Rare, rent."

"Good. After you see Sally, you're going to work with Cal. He is an occupational therapist. They work on your cognitive processes. A lot of that goes hand in hand with what Sally and I will be doing, but they will also address how the concussion affects your sleep, your mental status, and how it all goes back together so you can get back to working and dealing with life without getting mentally and physically fatigued."

"Wow, okay. It seems like a lot."

"It is a lot, Brady, but you're struggling right now. I bet a lot of what you are feeling is because of your TBI. You have a serious injury in your brain, and when people look at you, they see you standing upright. You might be in some physical pain, but they can't see the real damage. The fact that you can't drive, that you rely on all these medications to keep you going each day, and now you've lost your career, most of that comes down to your TBI, although they are discharging you because of the spinal injury. Either way, you have a hidden injury. People don't see the TBI, and they sure don't understand it. They think you get hit on the head, you recover quickly, and then you get back to doing what you were doing."

"How long does it take to recover from a concussion?"

"Well, don't let this freak you out, but for most people that have your level of TBI, or that I think you do, it can take them eighteen months to find their new normal."

"Eighteen months?" I felt myself becoming agitated. "What the hell is a new normal? I won't go back to being what I was?"

She smiled, although not as widely as before. "You might, but you might not. I can't tell you that until after we complete these tests and start you on therapy. The brain is a funny place, and it has its own timeline."

"Okay, so now what?" I muttered, feeling frustrated.

"Well, now we get to the fun part. We are going to start

testing you so that we know what your baseline is. I want you to be honest with me. No matter what the answer is, you tell me what it is, and if your head starts hurting too much, you let me know. Let's start with your pain level. Right now, what would you say your pain level is in your head?"

"I don't know. I have a slight headache, so maybe a three."

"Okay, while we do these tests, if you hit a seven, you let me know."

"Alright."

After that, we started on the testing. She gave me a piece of paper and asked me to read the paragraphs. She timed me as I read the page. When I finished, I shook my head. "I didn't realize that I read that slowly."

"It's a difficult task to view the words, process them into your brain, then send the signals to your mouth to speak those words. That is a lot of steps. You did well for your first time. Let's try this now. I want you to count by sevens to one hundred."

I blinked, confused for a moment, and then thought, Well, that's easy. I was glad I hadn't said that out loud because it took me much longer than it should have. A few times, I paused and had to use my fingers pressing on my leg to get to the next number. She timed me on that too.

The next thing we did was stand in front of a big board with a bunch of clear buttons on it. I stood a foot away and she started the machine. There were sixty buttons in front of me in circular rows. As I stared at the board, I felt like I was being sucked into a black hole. The goal was to push the clear buttons when they lit up. A few times, I got dizzy and had to look away, missing the button and getting frustrated, but she told me to do my best.

Once we were done with that, she had me walk in a straight line, heel to toe, once with my eyes open, once with my eyes closed. That was a huge mess as I felt like I was on a tightrope and going to fall to my death. A few times, her hand touched my arm to help me stay balanced.

She also had me climb up on a stability ball, and I couldn't stand upright for more than three seconds before I was grabbing for something to steady me.

The more the tests went on, the more I saw just how bad off I was. These tasks were simple tasks, but I was failing every single one of them. What did she think of that? I didn't have the courage to ask.

When she finished, we sat down, and she asked what my pain level was. It was definitely higher now. "I guess a six, maybe seven now."

She nodded. "That's probably going to go higher. Usually, it does a few hours after we work your brain. I'm going to tell Sally and Cal that they can do your evaluation tomorrow."

"I can do it now."

"We never want to tax your brain when you are in pain. You can do more damage."

I couldn't bear not knowing what she thought. "How did I do?"

She smiled warmly. "Well, I can tell you that you have a concussion, but I can also tell you that within a few weeks, you are going to start seeing progress, and that alone is going to help your mental state of mind."

"Can concussions really affect your state of mind?"

"Oh, yeah. They can turn you into a totally different person. Brady, with all that you have going on right now, be glad that you made that phone call. I can't imagine someone trying to tackle all these issues at once on their own. Your team of doctors and therapists is going to discuss your treatment status and set up a schedule for you. We all work together so that we are on board and not working against each other. While you will do some physical PT, you won't do much until we get your balance under control. I'll make sure Donovan knows to stick to ground or low-impact exercises."

She stood. "Brady before you know it, you're going to be back to a very similar side of yourself, not the man you used to be, a different one, but one that is better. Just believe that you can do it."

That was the problem. Because while I was here and everyone was telling me that I got this and I could accomplish anything, I hadn't drunk the Kool-Aid yet, and I wasn't one hundred percent on board. As I left, my head was banging, and Emma told me to return to barracks and rest until group therapy.

I made sure to stop by the dispensary and pick up my pain meds, and then I dragged my butt back to the barracks and collapsed in a heap, feeling as if I'd been working my butt off for days—and not just a couple of hours.

CHAPTER TWENTY-EIGHT

GRACELYN

*S*aturday morning, the boys and I were eating breakfast when my cellphone rang. All of us turned from our meal to stare at the counter where it was resting. I jumped up and lunged for the phone, only to see it was my mother.

"It's Grandma," I said to the boys who immediately looked as crestfallen as I felt. I answered the phone as I slipped back into my seat. "Hey, Mom, how are you?" I hadn't spoken to her since I had told her about Brady going to RAW.

I was so glad that the conversation that I'd had with his parents had gone over better. They had been very concerned, and his mother had asked me to send updates as I heard them. His brother had even texted me to say he was thinking about us and hoped that Brady came through this and recovered fully. They had been total opposites of my mother.

"Oh, we are doing well. Your father's back is acting up, and he doesn't want to admit he's getting old—especially not in front of his golf buddies."

"Oh, yeah, of course not," I said absently as I pushed my eggs around on my plate.

"And Esther, you remember Esther, right?" She didn't wait

for me to respond. Of course, I knew who Esther was. She was my mother's best friend and had been since they were in high school together. "Well, she has been seeing this doctor for a foot problem, and now she's seeing a chiropractor. She's trying to help me talk your father into going to the chiropractor, but you know how he is." She sighed. "He thinks they are quacks, but he really needs to do something. He's too young to be having so many back issues."

My father was fifty-one. He was young, but a lot of people had back problems, and now he had them too. I was pretty sure that Brady's issues were more intense than my father's occasional aches.

"What are you doing? How are the boys?" She changed tack almost immediately, as if she remembered that talking about the back might remind me of Brady.

"We are eating breakfast. They are fine," I said as I glanced at the two of them, both chewing their cereal and looking glum.

"Just fine?"

"Yes, Mom. They are fine. School is fine. Sports are fine. Health is fine."

"Oh, well, that's good." She sounded irritated. "What's new with you? Work going well?"

"Work is great. I'm great."

She huffed into my ear. "What is up with you? All you can say is fine and great."

"Mom, aren't you going to ask about Brady?"

"Well, of course I was going to ask about him, but I figured you wouldn't want to talk about his little problem in front of the boys."

"His little problem? You mean the fact that he wanted to kill himself. Is that what you are suggesting is his little problem?"

"Gracelyn, don't say such things in front of your children."

"Why not?"

"Because you don't want them to think their father isn't right in the head."

"He's not, Mom! Brady is depressed and suicidal and dealing with a major brain trauma and nerve issues. Plus, he's losing his career. How could he be right in the head with all that going on?"

I glanced at the boys; they watched me closely. Maybe she was right and I shouldn't be talking about this in front of them, but I wanted them to know that it was okay to have issues and not be afraid to talk about them.

"Gracelyn, seriously. You make more out of this than there actually is. Concussions are no big deal."

I burst from my seat. "Are you serious? You think concussions are no big deal? I got a report from Brady's doctors yesterday that he is undergoing not one, not two, but three different kinds of therapies just for his concussion. Plus, he's undergoing therapy for his back and nerve issues, and rebuilding his leg muscle—and he's seeing other therapists to help him deal with the trauma of the explosion."

She sighed, and I could just imagine her shaking her head as she sat in her favorite porch chair and sipped her morning tea. "If he has that many issues, Gracelyn, then maybe you need to file for divorce. You don't want your children around a sick man."

"Oh, my God! Mom! Do you hear yourself? You just told me to divorce the man I love, the father of my children, because he has a mental health issue? I would never do that! How can you even suggest that?"

"If he needs all the help that you are suggesting, then maybe he is too damaged to be fixed. That's all I'm saying."

"Yeah, well—" I fisted my hand by my side and squeezed the phone so hard that I thought I might crush it. "I don't care how damaged my husband might be. I am going to stand beside him and help him every step of the way. I love him and so do his sons. We are not leaving him when he needs us the most."

"Gracelyn—"

"No, do not 'Gracelyn' me! I'm done with your narrow-minded ways, Mom. I don't want to talk to you right now, and don't bother calling me until you can be civil and accept that I will put my husband and his mental health as my top priority along with my children and myself."

I yanked the phone away from my ear and pushed the end button so hard I thought I might stick my finger through the glass. I growled as I tossed the phone to the counter and spun on my kids.

"Your grandmother drives me nuts sometimes."

Dane grinned, but Drew looked worried. "Mom, do you think Dad is going to get better?"

I squatted down in front of him. "Drew, I know your father is going to work as hard as he can to get better."

"What is mental health?" he asked.

I pondered that for a moment, wondering how best to explain it to my six-year-old son. "I guess the best way to explain that is your father is trying to be happy again. He lost his ability to be happy and feel safe when he got hurt and his friends got hurt. Now he needs to find that again."

"So when he finds his happy, he will have mental health again?"

"Well, he will be happier; that's for sure," I told him as I brushed the hair off his brow and stood, kissing his forehead. "Now finish your breakfast. We have a busy day."

"Do you think Dad will call?" Dane asked.

"I think if he can, he will," I told him. I collected my plate and put it into the sink, taking a moment to calm myself down all the way. I was still fuming at my mother, and I knew that blowing up at her wasn't very nice, but I just couldn't handle her blasé attitude. How dare she suggest that I leave Brady because he was having problems. Never!

I pushed her from my mind and went to get ready. Dane had two baseball games today, and Drew had a soccer game across town. I wasn't sure how I was going to manage it, but I would figure it out. After that, we were supposed to go to Nora and Will's house for a barbeque, and I hadn't even thought to ask if they needed me to bring anything. I had a feeling that they would understand.

The morning was a whirlwind, and I got Dane to his game. Drew and I watched them play, but in the seventh inning, I had to get Drew over to his soccer game. I asked one of the other moms to keep an eye on Dane for me while I was there since Dane's game was twenty minutes away. Dane would have a break for about an hour, so I left a little money with Clara so Dane could get a snack before his next game.

I barely got Drew to his game before it started and took a seat in the grass off to the side, feeling winded and cranky. As I sat there, I looked around and saw several women walking on the trail around the park. What if I started walking? What if I got up right now and took a walk while Drew played? Would he miss me? Probably not. He was so focused on his game that he barely even looked my way while he was playing.

I pushed myself off the ground and approached one of the other parents. "Do you mind just keeping an eye on Drew? I'm going take a lap around the park."

Lisa smiled. "No, go right ahead. I'd go with you, but I twisted my knee the other day. If Drew is looking for you, we'll let him know you'll be right back."

"Great, thank you!" I slipped my car keys into my pocket and hit the trail. What I didn't realize was that the trail was nearly a mile long, and when I hit half a mile, I started to feel it. Man, was I out of shape! This was ridiculous. I thought about cutting through the parking lot, but I was determined to at least make it one time around.

I had just passed the six-tenths of a mile mark when my cell-phone rang, and I saw Clara's name on my screen. "Hey, Clara. Did they win?"

"Gracelyn, Dane was rushed to the hospital."

I stopped dead in my tracks. "What?"

"He got stung by bees and started wheezing, so they called an ambulance and they just rushed him to Mercy."

"Oh, my God!"

"I'm so sorry, Gracelyn. Are you gonna be okay?"

"I'll be fine," I said as I started to walk again and blinked back tears. My son couldn't breathe, and he was rushed to the hospital. What if he died? I started to pick up speed, and before I knew it, I was running toward the soccer field. I huffed and I puffed as I ran, and my legs screamed as I kept moving as quickly as I could.

I didn't even want to imagine what I looked like as I came around the final corner and could see the soccer fields in the distance. Why had I gone on a walk? Why had I left my son alone? Why had I stopped exercising? My lungs burned, and I thought I would pass out as I approached the soccer field and had to slow down. I searched the little players on the field and saw Drew. I made a beeline right onto the field, huffing as if I'd just run a marathon and not a half mile. Whistles started going off, and one of the refs yelled at me, but I ignored him as I rushed toward Drew.

"Mom, what are you doing? We're playing a game!"

"Drew, we have to go," I said as I grabbed his arm, but he pulled back.

"No! I want to play my game!"

"Drew, we have to go!" I yelled at him, losing my composure and realizing that a lot of people were watching me now.

"Mrs. Vanover, is everything okay?" the coach asked from behind me.

"No, I have to go. Drew has to come with me now."

"Mom, I don't wanna go!" Drew wailed.

"Gracelyn," a deep voice spoke behind me and I spun around to see Doug. "What's going on?"

Seeing him there, seeing his strength, his concern, I wanted to fall into his arms. "I have to get to the hospital. Dane was hurt."

Half a dozen people were standing there staring at me.

"What's wrong with Dane?" Doug asked.

"He got stung by bees and couldn't breathe. They rushed him to Mercy." I turned around and looked at Drew. "Let's go, now!"

Drew looked a little crestfallen, but he began to follow me.

I started rushing toward my car, my entire body shaking as I forced back the tears again, and just as I reached my car, I heard Doug call my name again.

"Gracelyn, you can't drive in your state. Get in the passenger seat; I'll take you."

I stared at him. "Why are you here, Doug?"

He stopped in front of me. "My daughter is the referee. I came to watch her. She's been bugging me to. I had no idea this was your son's game. Now get in. Let's get you two to the hospital."

As I buckled my seatbelt, Drew asked from the back seat, "Is Dane going to have bad mental health now, Mom?"

I laughed nervously. "Oh, I'm sure he's not going to be very happy," I said as Doug started the minivan and pulled out of the parking space.

"How far are we from the hospital?" I asked Doug as I tried to process what was happening.

"Ten minutes."

I nodded, and as I sat there, I felt my legs shaking. Was that from the adrenaline and fear, or the running? Probably a little of both.

I glanced at Doug as he turned onto the main road. "Thank you. You have no idea how much I appreciate this."

He glanced my way and smiled. "You don't need to thank me, Gracelyn. You know I would do anything for you and the boys."

I nodded. "I know, but thank you. My legs are shaking so badly that I'm not sure I could have driven my car."

He glanced at me before he made another turn. We were quiet for the rest of the ride, and when we arrived at the hospital, I could barely walk. How could I be that out of shape?

Inside the hospital, I asked for Dane, and they said I could come right back. Drew stayed in the waiting room with Doug, and I was led back to his room where he was sitting wide-eyed, watching television.

I somehow held myself together as I stepped into his room. It wouldn't have gone over very well if I had dropped to my knees and sobbed.

"Baby, how are you?"

"Hey, Mom. I got to ride in an ambulance!"

I chuckled. "Yeah, I heard about that."

He grinned. "I got stung by six bees at once."

"How did that happen?"

"I took a shortcut through the bushes on the way to the snack booth, and I guess I walked through a nest or something."

"Oh, Dane! I'm so sorry I wasn't there."

"It's okay."

The doctor came in a few minutes later and told me that Dane would need to take it easy for a few days to make sure he didn't have a secondary reaction and that he would need to be prescribed an Epi-Pen for the future. One sting could cause him to have a major reaction now.

After the doctor left, the nurse brought Dane ice cream, and

I went to fill out the paperwork. I returned to the waiting room to check on Drew, and I found Drew and Doug watching something on his phone. As I approached, Doug handed off his phone to Drew and stood.

"How is he?"

"He's going to be okay," I said, and then the waterworks that I had been holding back began. Doug wrapped his arms around me and held me as I quietly fell apart.

CHAPTER TWENTY-NINE

BRADY

Saturday was another busy day, and it wasn't until Sunday that I finally got a chance to call home. I was both excited to make the call and very apprehensive. I hadn't had any contact with Gracelyn since I'd left, and I wondered what she thought of all this. For all I knew, she was already visiting the attorney's office and filing for divorce. She deserved better than me anyway, or at least that's what I thought sometimes.

I took a deep breath and released it before I dialed the phone. There was a phone in the barracks that we were allowed to use when it was our turn to call home. Next week, I could use the computer on the desk to do a video chat, and then in another two weeks, I could possibly get my phone back. I heard that a lot of the guys didn't ask for their phones back because it was disruptive to their therapy. They stuck to calling or video chatting once or twice a week. I wasn't sure what I would do when my time came.

The phone rang twice, and then I was grinning as I heard my youngest answer the phone. "Hello?"

"Hey, Drew, it's Dad."

"Dad!" he yelled excitedly into the phone. "Are your mental healths better now? Are you gonna come home now?"

I chuckled. "No, I'm not coming home yet. I'm afraid it's going to be a little while before that happens. How are you?"

"Okay, I guess. I didn't get to finish my soccer game yesterday."

"Why not?"

"Because Dane got bit by bees and went to the hospital."

"What?" I asked, sitting up straight. "Is Dane okay? Where is he?"

"Yeah, he's okay. He's sleeping. Mom gave him medicine so he won't itch. He got bit by like *ten* of them, and he couldn't breathe. He even got to ride in an ambulance. He said they had the lights and sirens on too."

"Really?" I nodded, listening to his story and wondering just how many bees stung Dane. "Where is your Mom?"

"She's crying in the shower."

"What?"

"Yeah, she started crying yesterday at the hospital, and Doug had to bring us home, and then she just kept crying, and I heard her crying last night, and now I can hear her crying again."

"What do you mean, Doug brought you home?"

"He works with Mommy. He was at my soccer game, and he drove Mommy's car to the hospital and then brought us home. He let me come with him to pick up pizza and then ate dinner with us."

For a long moment, I didn't know what to say. I clenched my jaw and unclenched it. I had been right. My wife was cheating on me, and she was bringing that son of a bitch around my kids.

"Dad, you still there?"

"Yeah, bud, I am, but I gotta go. Tell Dane I said hello, and I hope he feels better. I love you, buddy."

"I love you too."

"Okay, I gotta go. I'll talk to you later."

I heard Gracelyn's voice in the background asking whom he was talking to, and I quickly dropped the handset onto the base. The last thing I wanted to do right now was talk to Gracelyn. I spun and practically charged out of the room, heading to the front door. I burst out, my hands clenched at my sides, my eyes seeing only red.

I started walking, not sure where I was going, but knowing that I had to move. I had to do something. My wife was cheating on me. She was going to divorce me while I was here. Of course, she'd go for some guy who had his shit together. I was a wreck! What was my life possibly going to be like? What could I give her?

"Yo! Vanover!" A voice behind me grabbed my attention.

I spun as I snapped, "What?"

Derek raised a brow but didn't say anything as he jogged to my side and stopped. "What's got your panties in a wad?"

"None of your damn business," I growled as I turned around and began to walk away. A moment later, he was beside me. I glared at him. "What are you doing?"

"Walking."

"Go away. I don't want to talk to anyone."

"You don't have to talk. I'm just going to walk beside you."

"I want to be alone."

"No, you don't, not really."

I huffed but kept moving without responding. Whatever. He could do whatever he wanted. I didn't care.

We walked toward the back of the facility, and my mind turned in circles. Anger, pain, frustration, and fear all swirled around inside of me, and I wanted to explode. At one point, Derek removed his sunglasses and held them out to me.

"I don't need them."

"Shut up and put them on."

I sighed but took them from him. I realized after I put them on that they made a world of difference on my eyes. The sun had been bright and was causing a headache—or was that the stress?

When we got to the back side of the property, I was about to turn and walk back, but Derek pointed to a gate at the back, and I followed him. He pushed a few buttons on the gate lock and then opened the door, holding it for me. Once we were outside, he took out his phone and typed a message to someone, then slipped his phone back into his pocket and kept walking. A few times, he took it out and read something and then responded.

We walked to a trail in the woods and kept on going right into it. We must have walked three miles before I started to get tired and wondered if I'd have the energy to get back. Derek slowed his steps and led us toward a group of rocks.

"Let's rest for a couple minutes before we go back."

I wasn't going to say no, so I climbed up on the bigger rock and lay back to stare at the clouds.

"Why are you here?" I asked gruffly.

"You mean at RAW—or out here in the woods with you?" I saw him shrug from the corner of my eye. "Because I saw a brother in trouble, and I knew he needed some support."

"I told you I don't want to talk about it."

He turned and looked at me, his light-green eyes intimidating as hell. "Have I said anything about it?"

"No," I muttered. I watched a cloud float over the trees above. "I think my marriage is over."

"What makes you say that?"

"Because there is this guy that my wife works with, and he seems to always be there for her. He's probably better for her than I am anyway, but it pisses me off."

"Why does it piss you off?"

"Because she's my wife!" I sat up. "She took a vow to stick by my side, and now she's cheating on me."

"Do you know for sure that she's cheating on you? I mean, have you seen them together?"

"No, but I called home today and found out that he was with my family yesterday. I'm not there, so he's just stepping right on in."

"Did something happen? Why was he there, and who told you that he was there?"

"My son, Drew, told me. I guess my older boy got stung by bees and reacted, and he had to go to the hospital. Drew said that this guy, Doug, brought them to the hospital, and then home, and took my son out for pizza."

"Okay, so maybe it sounds suspicious, but what does Gracelyn say about it?"

"I don't know." I looked up into the distance. "I didn't talk to her. After I heard she was crying in his arms, I got so pissed I had to get off the phone before I lost it."

"Do you think you should have spoken to Gracelyn before you got angry?"

I glared at him. "You act like you're on her side."

"I'm not picking sides, but I'm telling you that you can't react to something if you don't know all the facts."

"Yeah," I muttered. "You don't know a damn thing about it."

He nodded and pulled out his phone and brought up a screen. I was too far away to see it, but I could tell it was an email and he started to read it out loud.

"Yesterday, our older son Dane was playing almost back-to-back baseball games and I left him with friends to get our younger son to his soccer game across town. While Drew was playing his soccer game, I received a call from another mother, Clara, at the baseball fields saying that Dane had been rushed to the hospital and was having trouble breathing. I started to panic. I literally walked right into the middle of Drew's soccer game and began to drag him off the field. Everyone was up in arms, but I wasn't thinking about anything but getting to my son and what a horrible mother I was for not being there for my son.

"My boss, Doug, whose daughter was the referee of the game, happened to be there and wouldn't let me drive because I was so upset and shaking. He brought us to the hospital and waited with Drew while I tended to Dane. After I knew Dane was going to be alright, I went back to the waiting room, and all the fear exploded out of me, and Doug, being the friend that he is, held me in the waiting room as I cried. When Dane was released, Doug brought us home, and then went out to pick up pizza for everyone after the long day. He stayed to eat, and after, he left.

"Brady thinks that I am being unfaithful to him with Doug, but that is not the case. Doug was there as a friend. I needed someone. I needed help, and he was there. I love Brady with every ounce of my heart, and I would never cheat on him. Please let him know the real truth of what happened and tell him that I promised him I would be there when he got well, and I have every intention of holding up my promise to him."

He slipped his phone back into his pocket and didn't say a word. I stared out through the trees as I thought over what she said. "How do you have that?"

"She emailed it to Lauren and Nate. When Nate heard I was with you walking, he sent it to me so that I knew what was up."

"You guys are sneaky."

Derek snickered. "Not trying to be. We are only trying to help. We are working on your mental health here. If we felt that your marriage was in jeopardy, we would want to do anything we could to either help fix it or help with the transition, so you didn't spiral."

I nodded as I stared off into the distance. "Do you think she's lying?"

"Do you? I mean, I don't know your wife. I've never met her. Does she routinely lie?"

"No, never. She's never lied to me—at least as far as I know."

"Then you have your answer."

"But what if she is lying?"

"Like I said, I don't know your wife, but from everything that I have heard about her, she's the real deal. She loves you, Brady, and she wants you to get better."

"Yeah, but what if she's lying so she doesn't feel guilty if I kill myself?"

"That's hard core, Brady. You said your old lady has never lied to you, so why would you even think she might be hiding it now so you don't hurt yourself?"

"I don't know!" I snapped. "My brain is messed up, Stall. You know that! I'm not thinking clearly."

"Then I think you need to make a phone call and talk to your wife."

"I thought I only got one call."

He rolled his eyes. "Man, you are a pain in my ass sometimes. I think this situation qualifies for a second call." He held out his phone.

I stared at it for a long moment, and then I took it. I was staring at it, wondering if I wanted to speak to her or not, when Derek growled, "Would you just dial the damn number already? Man, don't wuss out on me here."

I tossed him a look that held daggers, then dialed Gracelyn's number. The phone rang twice before she answered.

"Hello?"

I froze, unable to speak as I closed my eyes.

"Brady? Brady, is that you?" I loved the sound of my name when she spoke it. "Brady, talk to me, honey. It's not what you think it is. I swear."

"How do I know you aren't lying? You send this long email to strangers, and tell them this story, but how do I know it's true?"

"Because it is! Because I have never lied to you in all the years that we have been together. I am not going to start now."

I wanted to believe her, but that little devil was playing

255

havoc in the back of my mind and was telling me that I couldn't believe her. She would be better off without me. She could go on with her life. If I were dead, I wouldn't have to worry about this. She could move on, have Doug or whoever she wanted.

I pulled the phone away from my ear and tossed it to Derek as I began to walk slowly back to the facility, my demons laughing on my shoulder as I did.

CHAPTER THIRTY

GRACELYN

"*D*rew, who is on the phone?"

"It's Dad!" he squealed as he turned to me. I rushed to the phone as he held it out to me. "Brady? Hello, Brady?"

I looked at the phone and saw that the call had been disconnected. I quickly looked at the call information and found Drew had been talking to him for only three minutes. Why had he hung up?

"Drew, did your father have to go? He hung up."

He shrugged. "I don't know."

I squatted in front of him, my hair still dripping from my shower. Right after I turned off the water, I heard Drew talking, and I quickly dried myself so I could come out and check. I wasn't sure if Drew was bothering his brother who was supposed to be resting.

"Drew, what did your daddy say?"

"Um"— he twiddled his fingers together— "he asked where you were, and I told him you were in the shower crying and Dane was sleeping."

"You told him I was crying? I wasn't crying, Drew! What made you think I was crying?"

"I heard you moaning and making crying noises."

"Honey, that's because I'm sore from running yesterday, not because I was crying. Those were fake tears because Mommy is so out of shape."

"Oh, sorry."

"What else did you say to Daddy?"

"I told him about Dane and his trip to the hospital, and how Doug had brought us there and home and then bought us pizza."

I closed my eyes and hung my head. Brady was going to get the totally wrong idea. I knew that was why he had hung up when he heard my voice in the room. Dang it!

"Did I say something wrong?" Drew asked in a small voice.

I brushed my hand over his head as I stood. "No, honey, you didn't. I'm glad you got to speak with your daddy. Now, go watch TV for a little while. I need to make a few phone calls."

As he scampered away, I tried to call the number, but it rang a few times and went to a voicemail. I didn't leave a message. Instead, I pulled up Lauren's number and called her.

She answered after three rings. "This is Lauren."

"Lauren, it's Gracelyn Vanover, Brady's wife."

"Gracelyn, how are you?"

"I'm afraid that I'm not very good right now, but I think Brady might be worse."

"Oh, what's going on?"

"Brady called here for his weekly call, and Drew, our youngest, answered and told him a few things that I know Brady will take out of context."

"Oh, boy. Okay, tell me what you know, but first, let me just put eyes out on Brady."

"Okay, sure."

I heard her pick up a phone and start talking about someone

finding Brady and hanging out with him until she knew more. A moment later, Lauren was back on the phone with me. "Okay, so what happened?"

I explained what had happened, from the baseball game, to taking Drew to his soccer game, and then my walk, and what happened when Dane got hurt. I told her everything. I had nothing to hide. Yes, Doug had helped me, but it wasn't like he was at that game with me. His daughter had been working, and he'd been watching her. He hadn't known that I was going to be there. The soccer league had forty teams that played every weekend.

After I told her what happened yesterday, I explained how Brady had called and what Drew had told him about Doug.

"I swear, Lauren, nothing is going on with Doug. This is so frustrating. I'm just trying to keep my job because it's a good job, but if working for Doug is causing problems, then I'm going to have to quit."

"Well, don't do anything drastic right now."

"I can't afford to do anything drastic, Lauren. I need this job. When Brady is released, our monthly income is going to drop, and I have no idea where we are going to live or what we are going to do. We can't afford to live on just my salary."

"Like I said, don't do anything drastic. What do you do, by the way?"

"I'm an administrative assistant for a company that makes tactical equipment, some purchased by the military, a lot by police departments."

"Okay, well, is there another department you might be able to transfer to? Maybe to put a little distance between you and Doug?"

"No, I wish. He actually hired me after I quit working for his cousin, who was a ruthless rat bastard."

She chuckled. "Okay, well, let's just see what frame of mind Brady is in and what happens with this. How about this? How about you send me an email explaining exactly what happened, make it as short as possible. I'll get it over to whoever has Brady, and we'll get Brady to read it. Maybe it will calm the situation down if he hears what's going on."

"Okay, well, it can't hurt. I'll do that right now."

It didn't take me long to type up the email, and I made sure to let Brady know that I was serious about being here for him. I would quit my job if I had to. I could find something else, and if worst came to worst, I could take the boys and move back home to my parents' until Brady was out and we knew what our future held.

After I sent it, I did housework to keep myself busy. Otherwise, I would have been in the kitchen raiding the carb cabinet. After my little run yesterday, I realized just how out of shape I was, and I knew it was time to make a change.

One of the ladies in my support group said that she got into exercise to help relieve her stress and anxiety, and she lost twenty pounds doing it. After I cleaned the kitchen, I sat down with my laptop and did some research. Fifteen minutes later, I was seriously overwhelmed. I needed help. Maybe I could ask Jessica to help me out. She was close to my age and very friendly. I'd have to send her a message next time we were in group together.

I had just logged off the laptop when my phone rang, and I snatched it up and put it to my ear. "Hello?" There was silence, and I knew it was him. "Brady? Brady, is that you? Brady, talk to me, honey. It's not what you think it is. I swear."

His voice was tense as he finally spoke. "How do I know you aren't lying? You send this long email to strangers, and tell them this story, but how do I know it's true?"

I was so exasperated. I couldn't help but raise my voice. "Because it is! Because I have never lied to you in all the years that we have been together. I am not going to start now."

He was quiet for a moment, and then I heard shuffling. "Brady? Brady, please talk to me."

"Hi, Gracelyn," a deeper voice came on the line. "It's Derek Stall. He handed me the phone and walked away."

"Why?"

"He just doesn't want to listen right now. He's messed up. He had a good week, but it was tough."

"Is he trying?"

"I think it is more that he is adjusting to everything. We have thrown a lot at him, and he is still healing."

"What am I supposed to do now?"

"Give him space."

"Space?" I laughed. "I'm in Colorado, and he's in Tennessee. How much more space does he need?"

"I didn't mean literally. I mean figuratively." He paused and I knew he wasn't finished speaking, so I waited. "Gracelyn, you don't know me, but I have to ask you a question. Are you being honest with Brady?"

"Yes! Absolutely, yes! Doug is my boss. Yes, he was here to help me, and he kept me from falling to pieces in front of my kids, but he is just a friend. I love Brady with every ounce of my being. I cannot imagine a life without him, and I would never, *ever* cheat on him."

"Okay, then I'll take you at your word. I need to go catch up to him. Give him some time, and I'll have Lauren or Nate reach out to you soon and give you an update."

"Thank you, Derek."

"You're welcome, Gracelyn. We're going to help him. It's going to take time, but we will. In the meantime, just let him get situated and deal with what he has here."

"I will."

"And I hope your son is doing alright."

"He is, thank you."

A moment later he said goodbye, and I set the phone down

and rubbed my temples. I needed to do something, or I was going to crawl into that carb cabinet.

"Drew!" I called as I got up from the table. "Do you want to go kick your soccer ball?"

"Sure!" he called, and I heard him race down the hallway to get his ball. I changed shoes, and then the two of us went out front and started kicking his ball around.

It eased my tension, and I began to relax. I had to let go of my worries. Brady was either going to believe me, or he wasn't. In the meantime, I was going to remain focused on my boys and start focusing on myself. I deserved it.

Monday, Doug and I went out to lunch, my treat, because I wanted to thank him for his help. I also wanted to discuss some other things with him

We were seated at our favorite lunch spot when I wiped my mouth and thought carefully about what I was going to say. "Doug, I really appreciate everything that you did for me this weekend and all the other things that you have done for me."

"I'm just glad I was able to help. You don't need to thank me, Gracelyn. That's what friends are for."

"Yeah, I know"—I winced—"and that's kind of what I need to talk to you about. While I appreciate your assistance, I'm going to need to put a little distance between our work and personal relationship."

He looked confused. "You don't want to be friends? Is that what you're saying?"

"It's not that I don't want to be friends, Doug. I just think that it confuses the issue."

He leaned back. "What issue?"

I cocked my head and stared at him, as if to say, Come on, do I need to spell it out for you?

He glanced around. "Is Brady giving you a hard time because I helped you out?"

"Well, Drew mentioned it on the phone, and Brady got

upset. Brady didn't understand the entire situation, and he hung up before I could explain it. I just think that with all that Brady is going through, I have to make sure something like that doesn't happen again."

The tension in his shoulders relaxed, and he reached over the table and put his hand over mine. "Gracelyn, I'm sorry that what happened upset Brady. I really am. I just—"

"Gracelyn?" a woman's voice interrupted what he was about to say.

I turned to see Nora standing beside the table, a quizzical look on her face as she glanced pointedly at our hands.

"Nora!" I pulled my hand back immediately and stood. "How was your picnic? I'm so sorry that we didn't make it. Dane had an incident, and we were at the hospital."

"Oh, no!" I recounted what happened and then motioned toward Doug. "This is my boss, Doug. Doug, this is Nora, a friend of mine."

"Are you going to be home tonight?" Nora asked after she said a polite hello to Doug.

"Yeah, I should be. Why?"

"Will and I were going to come by and check on you guys. How about we bring dinner?"

"That would be wonderful."

"Excellent. Six-thirty, okay?"

"That will be perfect."

"Great." She hugged me and said goodbye to Doug. After I sat down, Doug seemed a bit distant. We both avoided the conversation we'd been having and focused on some work talk before we hurriedly finished our meals and went back to the office.

As I sat at my desk later, I wondered what Nora was going to say tonight. I had no doubt that she was going to say something. The look in her eye told me she was questioning a few things. I rubbed the bridge of my nose as I sighed.

At six-thirty-five, Nora and Will knocked on the door. Will carried the food to the kitchen as Nora pulled my arm and kept me near the door.

"What the hell was that?"

"What?" I played dumb, but she wasn't having it.

"I thought you said that you were not involved with your boss."

"I'm not. You are misinterpreting what you saw."

She crossed her arms over her chest and hiked a single manicured brow. "I am pretty sure I saw a man reach over the table and hold your hand, and you let him. I'm also pretty sure that man was not your husband. Are you telling me that I imagined all that?"

I rolled my eyes. "No, you didn't imagine it, but it's not what you think."

"Mom!" Dane called. "They brought your favorite breadsticks!"

"Okay, great! I'll be there in a minute."

Nora leaned forward and said softly, "As soon as dinner is over, you and I are having a very long and serious discussion. Got it?"

I nodded. I had a feeling that Nora's advice might be exactly what I needed, but I wasn't sure I wanted it.

CHAPTER THIRTY-ONE

BRADY

*S*unday was a rough day. Derek made sure that I was never alone. He didn't stick with me all day but assigned someone to be at my side. It was staff most of the time, but later in the day, as I calmed, a few of my barrack mates became my constant companions.

I should have minded that they thought I needed a babysitter, but I didn't. I knew that they were doing this for a reason. I was on the edge of that abyss and about to go spiraling deep and dark, and they knew it. After my fourth companion change happened, I welcomed it.

Jersey and Alan followed me out of the dining hall, laughing about a joke someone had told them. They flanked each side of me, and Jersey told us to follow him because he wanted to show us something. Having nothing else to do for the next hour, I did.

We wove through the buildings toward the back. Inside was a larger gymnasium area that I hadn't seen yet. "What's this place for?"

"They are putting in an indoor basketball court, and they will hold group meetings and such here. I think they also want to do some friendly competition between the phases or barrack houses," Jersey explained. "I got to check it out the other day."

"Pretty cool," I said as I looked around. I wasn't much for playing basketball, but I admired the facility.

"Come on. This isn't what I want to show you." He grinned over his shoulder and took off down a dark hallway as Alan and I followed. He pulled open another door, and we stepped in. My jaw dropped as I took in the massive rock wall. There were only a couple of emergency lights in the room, and they cast odd shadows over things. The wall must have been at least sixty feet long and thirty feet high.

I glanced at Alan. His mouth was hanging open, too, as he stared up into the rafters. "Damn."

"Damn is right! When are they going to open this up for us to use?" I asked.

"I think Nate said that it's going to be another two weeks before we can use it. Staff is going through instruction right now to make sure they know all the ins and outs of it for safety. They want to use it for trust exercises."

I walked closer to the wall, staring up, and then looked down quickly as the world started spinning out of control as I laughed. "Yeah, it's going to be a while before I can do this. My vertigo is way too out of control right now."

Jersey grinned. "Can't look up, can you?"

"Not without wanting to fall on my ass," I replied with a laugh.

Jersey turned to Alan. "What do you think? You going to do it when they open it up?"

He shrugged. "Yeah, of course. I've done them before." He glanced at Jersey but went back to staring at the ceiling.

Jersey stood next to him and looked up. I wished that I could see whatever held their attention. "What's so interesting up there?" I finally asked.

Alan shrugged, and Jersey frowned as he said, "There sure are a lot of ropes up there."

"Yeah, a lot of ropes," Alan repeated.

I looked between the two of them. "So there are a lot of ropes. I don't get it."

Jersey glanced at Alan and then me. "A lot of ropes where you could hang yourself."

Alan shifted his eyes to Jersey, then me, and then all three of us looked up. For a few seconds, the world didn't spin, and I could see everything clearly. There were at least two dozen different ropes up there. If you were at the top, you could tie one of those ropes and secure it, take a step off the ledge, and you'd be done.

I blinked, and the world started to spin again. As I tried to get it under control, I slapped Alan on the back. "Come on, guys. Let's get back to the barracks. I have a one-on-one with Lauren tonight."

The three of us left the building, each of us lost in our own thoughts. I wondered if the other guys were thinking about the ropes back there. Would I have the courage to kill myself that way? I wasn't sure. Would one of them? I didn't know them well enough to say.

When we returned to the barracks, Nate was waiting for me. "Lauren wants you to come up to her office. She's just finishing an online session."

"Alright." I climbed on the Gator with him, and he started driving up to the front office.

"Where were you guys?"

"Um, just walking around after dinner," I stated, not sure if we were allowed to be where we'd been.

"How are you feeling? I heard you had a rough morning."

I shrugged. "I guess I'm alright."

"You talk to your wife again?"

"No."

"You want to talk to your wife again?" he asked as he peeked my way.

"Not particularly right now."

He gave an abrupt nod. "Noted."

We were quiet for the rest of the ride up, and he opened the back door and held it for me. "You know your way up to her office, right?"

I glanced at the door and him. "What, you're not going to escort me to her couch?"

Nate smirked. "I think you can handle the two flights of stairs and hallway alone without getting into trouble—or am I wrong?"

"I can handle it."

"You sure?" he asked as I went to step past him. "I wouldn't want you to take a wrong turn and find a pair of scissors or something."

I turned and was eye to eye with him, noting the light color against his light-brown skin. "I'm not going to find something sharp and slit my wrists if that's what you're hinting at. I'm pissed, hurt, and confused, but I don't want to kill myself, not right now."

He nodded. "Good answer. I'll be back to give you a lift in an hour."

I was up the stairs when I heard the door click closed, and as I turned on the landing, I watched him get on the Gator.

I thought about how Nate was always around, and so were Derek and his fiancée Dana. They never seemed to leave this place unless they were heading out to bring someone else to the facility.

I pondered that as I found my way to Lauren's office. It was late, and there were only a few lights on up here. I heard a woman's voice down the way, and I followed it. A few steps away from the door, I paused as I listened to what she said.

"I will pass it along to him, Gracelyn." She paused. "Yep, you got it. Okay, good night."

Fury burst from my gut. What the hell was it with these people going behind my back and talking to others about me? I didn't remember permitting all that, although I had signed many papers when I had arrived.

I was tempted to turn and leave. I was outside the wire; I could hightail it down the stairs and out the front door. Instead, I took those last two steps toward the door and rapped on the wood harshly. I tried as hard as I could to remove the pissed-off feeling that I was pretty sure was reflected on my face. I wasn't sure I accomplished that as Lauren's head swiveled my way and her right brow twitched. She stared at me for a long moment, obviously waiting for me to speak.

"Why were you talking to my wife about me?"

"Because she's concerned about you. Why don't you come in and close the door so we can talk about it in private?"

I laughed. "There is nothing private about this place. Everyone knows your damn business whether you want them to or not."

"That's not true, Brady. People don't know all your business. They know what is important to know." She paused and studied me. "Do you think they judge you from what they know about you?"

"Of course they do."

"Why?"

"How can they not?"

She smiled and looked away, then she stood up, came around her desk, and approached me. "Brady, I'm going to ask you a question. If you can honestly say the answer is yes, you're free to leave right now, and we will skip this session. If the answer is no, then you close that door and come sit down."

"What is the question?"

"Do you judge everyone here by what you know about

them?" We stared at one another for a long time, and then she spun slowly around and went to sit down in a chair on the other side of the room.

I sighed as I closed the door. No, I did not judge the guys that I had met here because of what I knew. I didn't think the guys in my barracks were losers because they wanted to kill themselves. I thought they were broken and needed to be fixed, just like I did.

I sure didn't judge Derek for living on the streets or his need to make amends for what he'd done. I looked up to him for making it through and becoming this incredibly strong person who was fighting for other people.

Come to think of it, I looked up to Nate too. These guys had fallen to the bottom of the dark pit and had knocked on the door to the demon's den and had somehow found the strength to turn away and climb out. Now they did everything they could to show others how to make that journey.

Lauren didn't gloat when I took my seat. She merely gave me a small, caring smile before she spoke. "You don't judge these people because you see yourself in them, right?"

"Yeah."

"And I'm going to say that about ninety percent of them are going to see you in them, so they aren't going to judge either. Of course, there are always those people who will judge because they can't help themselves, but those are not the people you need to be concerned with."

"I was thinking about the fact that I actually look up to Derek and Nate," I told her.

She smiled brightly. "Two great men to look up to. I didn't know Nate when he was broken and finding his way, but I did know Derek. I saw him when he first arrived here. Spoke to him while he lay on the gurney in the med building after saving Dana's life. I knew those first minutes that I spoke with him that his soul was broken, and he would need to fight to fix it. We almost lost him to the streets again."

She glanced out the window toward the fenced-in area with all the buildings, looking thoughtful. The lights were coming on back there as the sun was setting. "But luckily, we didn't. He has been a tremendous help here at RAW. He and Dana are forces to be reckoned with."

I smiled, not sure what to say about that.

She was still staring out the window when she asked, "Brady, do you love your wife?"

I shifted in my seat at the abrupt change in topic as both anger and pain shot through my chest. "Yeah."

She turned to me and cocked her head slightly. "Do you think that Gracelyn loves you?"

Did I? "I guess she does."

"Has Gracelyn ever given you any indication that she has been unfaithful to you *before* your injury?"

I shook my head.

"Do you honestly believe that she could be unfaithful to you? I mean, deep inside your gut, what does it say?"

I stared at my hands in my lap as I picked at one of my nails. "I don't think that she would normally cheat, but I'm not the man she married anymore."

"Do you want her to cheat on you?"

"No!" I barked as my head snapped up. "Of course I don't."

"Are you sure you aren't looking for an excuse to end things? Maybe you are afraid that she won't want to deal with your head injury or won't like the man who comes out on the other side of this injury. Maybe you want her to be unfaithful in your mind because you're afraid to disappoint her, and you'd rather she do something to you than *you* hurt her."

I looked everywhere but at her as I thought about her words. Was that what I was doing?

"Do you think that might be it?"

"You're right. I don't want to disappoint her. I'm not the man I was, and I'll never be the man I was. She deserves better."

"What if she thinks you are the best she can ever have? What if, to her, your *new* normal is even *more* special than the old you? What if she loves this new normal more for all that you have lived and fought through?"

I snorted a laugh. "How could she love me if I can't give her what I promised?"

"What did you promise her, Brady? Did you promise her that you were going to do twenty and retire with a pension? Did you promise her you were going to get stationed on a base overseas and bring her with you?"

"No."

"Then what exactly did you promise her, Brady?"

"I promised to take care of her, provide for her, and protect her. I promised to be there for her when she needed me and love her forever."

"And if you kill yourself, won't you be breaking that promise?"

I stared at my lap again.

"If you took your life, your forever is over, and you could no longer provide for her and protect her. You wouldn't be there to help her through the hardest moments of her life—the moments that she would need you the most." She paused. "You see, Brady, when you kill yourself, when you take your precious life, and you end it on purpose, you punish those who love you. Those who have vowed to love and protect, to provide and be there when they are needed. You take that away, and what they are left with is guilt, a guilt that will last until their dying breath."

"What do they have to feel guilty for?"

"For not being enough," she stated immediately.

"What?"

"They will go to their grave knowing that they were not enough. They were not strong enough, didn't love you enough, weren't beautiful enough or loving enough. They would feel betrayed and angry and sad—so very, very sad that they could not be *enough*."

"It wouldn't be her fault."

"No, it wouldn't, but that won't stop her from thinking it is. It won't stop the nightmares or the constant wondering what she could have done differently. It won't stop the pain that not only your wife but your two kids will know for the rest of their lives. It wouldn't fill the hole left in their hearts. Is that what you want your family to feel?"

"No, of course not."

"Okay, then why don't you stop thinking about your wife leaving you and start finding a way to bring her closer?"

"Closer? I can't bring her closer right now."

"Not physically, but mentally you can. If your wife knows that you are focused on getting better and working toward your future, the one that you two have planned, then that will be enough for her right now"—she paused—"but you need to stop thinking that your wife is having an affair. I don't know her, but the professional side has seen everything, and I just cannot imagine Gracelyn doing something like that to you. She loves you too much, Brady."

I sighed as I clenched my eyes. "I guess I know Gracelyn does love me. It's like sometimes these dark creatures are just spewing things into my mind. They make me see the worst in people, the worst in situations."

Lauren smiled. "Then Brady, we need to have a few chats with those dark creatures and tell them to hit the road. You ready to do that?"

I stared at her and nodded slowly. "Yeah, I'm ready."

CHAPTER THIRTY-TWO

GRACELYN

"*O*kay, the floor is all yours."

I turned and gave Nora a curious look. "What floor?"

She chuckled. "The proverbial one that you are going to stand on and tell me what the hell is going on. You have said several times that you are not involved with your boss, but, girl, I saw how he was looking at you. I saw him holding your hand, and I saw you not fighting it. Did you lie to me? I don't care if you did, but now is the time to come clean."

I groaned. "I have not lied to you or Brady or to anyone else. I'm not involved with Doug. I was thanking him for what he did this weekend for us."

"What exactly did he do?"

I explained the whole situation to her and finished it by saying, "So I was telling him thank you today, nothing more. He's a touchy man. I can't help that. I'm a touchy woman too."

Nora didn't speak for a while. Instead, she scanned the houses and yards around us as we sat on my front porch. Will was inside playing video games with the kids.

"What did you feel when Doug was holding you at the hospital?" she asked the question but kept her face averted for which I was thankful because a momentary frown crossed my features.

"Honestly, I loved it." I put my hands over my face and groaned again. "Nora, all of this has been so difficult and emotional. I almost lost my husband a few months ago—forever —but in a way, I did kind of lose him. Since he came home, he hasn't held me or talked to me or kissed me." I glanced at her as she turned to me, her mouth open. "Except for when he said goodbye, and we've had sex exactly one time since he came home—one time. We used to have a great sex life, and I know he's in pain, but I feel like he doesn't even know I exist or doesn't notice me, and I'm sure he doesn't feel I'm desirable, not with all this extra weight that I packed on."

"Gracelyn, don't be silly. Brady is taking a lot of medication, and he had a concussion. His mind and body are so messed up right now that he probably can't have sex, even if he wanted to. I know Will couldn't for years. The medications he was on just took his libido and tanked it."

"I didn't even think about that."

"Yeah, I'm sure you didn't. I didn't either, and I tried everything to get Will's attention, but he'd just get up and walk away. Finally, once he was in therapy at RAW, he admitted that he couldn't get an erection. Even though he had the urges, it just didn't work. Once he was off some of the meds, the doctors told him that would change, and it did, but knowing that he wanted me but was embarrassed to tell me that he couldn't perform was eye-opening. We had lost that connection that we'd once had. We used to have sex two or three times a week. For a few years, we were lucky to have sex once every couple of months. Honestly, I thought it was me, and trust me, I understand what it feels like to want to be held and kissed and just desired."

I hung my head. "I didn't realize all that."

Nora waited until I looked up again. "I was unfaithful to Will." My eyes slammed to the door and back to her, and she waved a hand. "Yes, he knows. He forgave me, I forgave myself, and we talked about it in therapy. About four years after his injury, I needed someone to look at me and want me. I didn't care who it was. I just needed to feel like I could be loved again."

I could understand that, but I could not imagine making love to a man who was not my husband, no matter what I wanted or needed.

"I'm not proud of myself for what I did, and when I finally confessed, I found out that he was aware of my infidelity. He had let it continue. It broke my heart. He said that as much as he loved me, he knew he couldn't give me what I needed, but someone else could."

"Oh!" I gasped.

"Yeah, so that fed my guilt big-time. Then Will went to RAW, and when we finally got to the marriage counseling part, our relationship flourished back to what it had been when we'd started dating. He realized that I had stuck around all these years, not because he was my husband and I'd vowed to do it, but because he was the man that I loved with all my heart. I didn't care about the scars that covered his body or his mind. I loved the man inside. I fell back in love with the laugh, the silly jokes, the way he wanted to help other people, even when he was hurting, and he fell back in love with me once he was able to allow himself to. Now, there is nothing that can come between us."

"I'm glad to hear that, Nora."

"I see a lot of my relationship with Will in you and Brady. I get what you're feeling, Gracelyn, what your needs are, but I'm telling you right now, it's not worth it, not unless you want to ruin your marriage or want to use this as an excuse to get out. I think Brady would respect you a lot more if you told him that you wanted a divorce than if you went behind his back and cheated on him."

"I do *not* want a divorce!" I snapped quickly. "That is the last thing that I want. You know, I've told Doug that we needed to remain friends, that I love my husband, and I am going to stand by him."

"And yet, you tease the tiger," she said before she sipped from her wineglass.

"I'm not 'teasing the tiger'!"

"You go to lunch with him. You let him hold your hand. Has he tried to kiss you yet? Has he kissed you?"

"No! Absolutely not!"

"Okay, well, I'm pretty sure he wants to, and it will only be a matter of time before he does."

"Then what do I do?"

"Personally, I think there is only one thing you can do: Quit your job."

"Nora, I can't quit my job right now! I need this job, and until Brady figures out where we are going, I need to stay here."

"Why? Brady is being released from the air force. He's going to be in Tennessee for at least six months, if not longer. Where is your family? What if you moved closer to them?"

"But I like my job, and Doug is a good boss."

"You can find another job that you like and work for another good boss, one that doesn't try to flirt with you—unless you like that, and that's what you want."

"No, I do not want that," I growled, "but I don't want to quit my job either, not until I know what is going on. I don't want to upset Brady anymore. What would he think if I told him, 'Oh, hey, honey, I'm packing up the house and moving. Yep, someday when you get out, you can join us. Where? I have no idea, but I'm sure you'll like it.'?"

Nora laughed. "You do know that he's not in prison, right?"

"Yes, I know that," I said, exasperated. "You know what I meant."

"I do know what you meant, and I also know that you are walking a tightrope, but only you can make that decision."

"I know, I know." I took a long drink from my glass, finishing my wine. "I guess I need to figure out where we are going to move on to. Good thing we don't have all that much furniture right now. A lot of it got smoke damaged, and we got rid of it."

"Didn't the insurance company reimburse you for it?"

"Yeah, they did. We just didn't replace it yet because we didn't want to fill up this house until we knew what was going on."

"Well"—she grinned—"sounds like you can save it for your new house."

After they left, I received a phone call from Lauren, asking how things were and if there was anything else she needed to know before she met with Brady. I didn't think there was, but I asked her to tell him how much I loved him and that I was there for him always.

That night as I lay in bed, I thought over my conversation with Nora. Was I trying to find a way out of my marriage? No, I didn't think so. I did love Brady, and I wanted what we used to have. I knew that we wouldn't have exactly what we had, but I'd take anything I could get. It wasn't just me that needed him. It was our boys too.

What did I do about Doug then? Maybe I should just be firm with him about our relationship. He was my employer, and I was his employee, and that was it. I supposed I should avoid having lunch with him anymore, and that made me sad. I enjoyed our conversations, especially since I didn't have Brady to talk to. I frowned into the darkness.

Was I slowly replacing Brady with Doug? Now it was conversations, but later, would his hugs mean more? Would I want more because I wasn't getting anything from my husband?

Didn't I deserve more?

I rolled to my side as I realized how selfish those words were. Here Brady was fighting to find the will to live, and I was whining about not having someone to hold me and talk to me. I had my kids, and that was all I needed until Brady came back to me.

I needed to put my focus on myself and my kids and stop thinking about Doug. I need to trust that God would watch out for Brady and guide him to the help he needed. We would make it through this. We would. *Please, God, let us make it through this —together.*

CHAPTER THIRTY-THREE

BRADY

*I*t had been three weeks since my conversation with Lauren in her office. I hadn't spoken to my wife yet, despite everyone and their brother getting on my case about it. To appease them, I finally emailed her.

Dear Gracelyn,

I'm sorry that I have not been in touch in the last couple of weeks. I have had a lot going on. I also owe you another apology. I overreacted, but I seem to do that a lot these days. They say that my concussion is the cause and that my brain reacts with a fight or flight instinct more often than it should. We are working on that in my concussion therapy.

I am going through many different kinds of therapy right now, and it twists my head, body, and heart into knots, but I am working hard to get it all under control and working the way it should. They are also starting me on a new treatment for the nerve pain in my spine. We hope it will bring relief.

I know that you and the boys love me, and I am doing all I can to be worthy of that love. I do love you all, and you will never know how much it means to me that you are sticking close to me through this.

I'm sorry that I didn't say this over the phone to you, but some-

times putting words together with emotions triggers the flight response, and I didn't want to say something to hurt you again.

I don't feel like I have the right to ask you this, but please wait for me. I want you in my life—I need you in my life. Kiss the boys for me. I will talk to you soon—Brady

After I sent that email, I broke down in therapy later that day and shared with everyone what I had been going through and how scared I was that I might lose my wife—my family. The following day, I was allowed to check my email and found her short and sweet reply.

Brady, take all the time that you need. The boys and I are here for you when you are ready for us. We love you and have faith in you. Always yours, Gracelyn

I was surprised that it was so short, and I fretted over that until Nate asked me what was on my mind.

"I don't know," I replied and then continued quickly, "Gracelyn answered my email, but it was like only three sentences."

He laughed. "You expected more?"

I shrugged. "Well, yeah. I guess I expected her to tell me what was going on at home, but she only told me to take my time, and she'd be there when I was ready."

"Did you ask how things were at home?"

"No."

"Then why should she have given you that information? You probably told her that you needed space to get things together, so she's helping you do that by not giving you the stress of dealing with things you can't do anything about right now anyway."

"What are you talking about?" I barked at him.

Nate put his hand on my arm. "Look, don't worry about your wife. She and the boys are doing fine. I know for a fact that Gracelyn has been attending her therapy sessions, and she has a lot going on right now, but they are all good. Don't stress over things you don't have to stress over. She's a strong woman, and she's got your back on this, Brady."

"Have you spoken with her?"

He grinned. "Actually, I did speak with her recently."

"What did you do? Call her after I emailed her?"

"Nope." He laughed. "I just had the occasion to speak with her, and it honestly didn't have anything to do with you, so don't worry about it."

I glared at him, wondering what he wasn't telling me. I couldn't imagine him having a reason to come in contact with Gracelyn, especially since she was in Colorado, and I knew that Nate hadn't left the complex in a few days.

Nate's phone started alerting, and he pulled it out. His face grew serious, and he was turning as he said, "I gotta go." Before I could think to say anything, he was jogging away.

I was supposed to be heading toward the gym for therapy, but I stayed where I was and watched where Nate went. As he approached my building, two more staff members joined him, then another. My heart started beating fast as I realized what was happening. Someone had tripped the suicide alert alarm. I started back toward the building, but a hand on my shoulder stopped me in my tracks.

"Aren't you supposed to be going to therapy?" Derek asked gruffly.

"Yeah, but something is going on in the barracks."

"And they have it covered. You need to stay out of the way, Brady. I know you want to help, but let the trained people do it, alright?"

I turned and looked back at the building, where two more people were rushing up to the door—one of them a nurse from the med facility.

"Come on," he said, pulling me. "Let's get you to therapy."

"Don't you have to go?" I pointed over my shoulder.

"I think there are enough people there for now. I'll check in once I make sure you are doing alright."

"Do you know who it is?"

He looked pointedly at me. "Only thing I know is that it's not you."

I pursed my lips. That was kind of a sucky answer. How was I going to be able to focus on therapy knowing that someone was in trouble?

We arrived at the door, and Derek opened it. "Inside, Brady."

I stared back along the path we'd taken. I couldn't see the barracks from here, but something told me that I should go back. "Man, I can't, not until I know what is going on and who it is."

"Look, you go inside and start your therapy. I'll see what's what and come back and let you know. Okay?"

"For real?"

"Yes, for real."

I nodded and slipped past him into the gym. I was working with Donovan today, and he had me on the stationary bike for the first ten minutes to warm up slowly. My eyes were usually scanning the gym to watch everyone else, but today they were locked on the door. I had just finished the bike when Derek slipped through the door and made a beeline for me.

He gave me a comforting smile as he approached and put his hand on my shoulder. "It's all good, Brady. It was Melbourne. They are taking him over to the med center to calm him down a bit. Lauren is on her way down to talk to him. His anxiety tripped him up."

"He didn't hurt himself, did he?"

He shook his head. "Nope, he tripped the alarm himself."

The tension released from my shoulders in a massive wave as I released a deep breath. "Okay, thanks."

"You got it. Now focus. I'll see you later. I wanted to see if you could help me with something. What time are you done with therapy?"

"Um, I have four back-to-back sessions, so not until after four."

"How about you meet me back in here after chow? Say seven?"

"I can do that."

"Okay, I'll see you later," he called out as he took off. After that, I was able to focus and give more of myself to my therapy. As I did, I thought a little about Melbourne. He had been here for five weeks, and he was still in building three. He had two mandatory therapies a day, one in group, one as a one-on-one with Lauren. I had learned that Lauren only worked with critical patients, and after my last chat with her, I hadn't been with her again.

Now I had one-on-ones with a guy named Sean who was pretty cool and easy to talk to. He was retired navy and had a great sense of humor. The most important part of it was that he didn't make me feel uncomfortable, and I was pretty much able to tell him what was on my mind.

After I finished with Donovan, I worked with Emma and then Cal. Cal and I were looking at some different career options for me. Since I liked to fix things, and I had been a mechanic pretty much my whole life, he was looking into engineering careers. He was supposed to give me some information today to look over.

If I found something I was interested in, they would help me with the education once I was approved for it in Phase Two. Everyone in Phase One had to focus on themselves, and the same went with Phase Two. If they felt you could handle the additional workload, then you were allowed to start working on education and training, and as long as that didn't bring you down, then you usually moved up to Phase Three.

I wasn't sure if I would like anything that Cal found for me, but I was willing to check the information.

Over the last week, I had started to notice a difference in my head. I still got headaches and sometimes migraines, but they weren't daily, and I knew when I needed to rest and when I could push myself.

My leg was also a lot stronger, and since I wasn't as dizzy as I used to be, Donovan had started to up my workouts a little bit.

My back was the place that wasn't changing. It hurt—like, all the time. Sometimes it hurt so badly that I couldn't even sleep. Even with the great mattress that I had, I couldn't lie down. There were nights that I would drag my butt to the dispensary and then crawl into one of the lounge chairs in the main room and get a few hours of shut-eye.

If it weren't for my back, I'd say I was recovering by leaps and bounds, but the spine injury kept me from doing that. I'd spoken with the neurologist about it at length, and he said I was a candidate for an experimental treatment. He said that since my injury had occurred less than a year ago, I could undergo it, but it would require surgery. You would think that I'd be able to make the decision myself, but that wasn't an option. Nope. My entire team discussed it and weighed the options to make sure it would be worth the risks.

What were the risks? Well, failure, of course, and more damage to my spine which meant more harm to my mental status. The upside was that I might be able to live a semi-normal life and not be tied down with pain medications every single day. My career in the air force would still be over, but I could have an almost normal life doing something else.

After meeting with each of my therapists in the sports building, I headed back to my barracks for my group session. Everyone was present except Melbourne, and he became the topic of conversation. It wasn't that we talked about him, but we were talking about how the episode had affected us. Instead of just two staff members, we had four today.

Two days ago, Jersey had transferred over to another Phase One building, and I wondered if he knew. I hadn't said much to Melbourne, but I knew that Jersey talked to him a lot.

Alan was especially quiet during the session, but then I remembered that sometimes he was like that after a one-on-one session. He never said much in the group, and I wasn't sure what his trauma was that put him here. He didn't bring it up, and neither did anyone else.

After group was over, we had a little while before we could hit the food hall, and I lay on my cot, reading over the mechanical engineering information that Cal had given me.

Alan approached me and sat on his cot which was next to mine. He was tapping a book on his knee. "You said you wanted to read this sometime."

"Yeah."

"I'm done with it."

"I thought you had just started reading it."

He shook his head and glanced around. "I've read it like a dozen times."

"Okay," I replied. Alan turned to stare at me, and for a second, I wondered what was going on with him, but then he smiled and stood.

"Enjoy it," he said as he dropped it to the foot of my bunk.

"I'll get it back to you when I'm done," I called out to him as he started to walk away.

He put his hand up and waved to acknowledge me. "No hurry. I told you, I'm done with it."

He was gone before I could say anything else, and I returned my attention to the papers I had been reading. A few times, I glanced down at the book but told myself I needed to concentrate on this stuff in front of me.

When a few of the guys said they were heading to dinner, I joined them. I looked for Jersey when I got there, but he wasn't here yet, and while we ate, I realized that Alan wasn't either.

"Hey, any of you know why Jersey and Alan aren't here?" I asked the table. Several shrugged, and a few more looked around as if to check to make sure I hadn't missed them in the crowd.

No one seemed the least bit concerned. I began to have a feeling in my chest that something terrible was happening. No matter how much I told myself that everything was okay, I couldn't dispel the fear. Alan was always at chow with us.

I don't need it anymore.

The words echoed through my head, and I could picture the book lying on my cot.

I don't need it anymore.

Alan had told me that the book had helped him through some very dark times. I was on my feet and moving toward the door before I could have another thought. I heard one of the guys yell my name, but I just kept going. I moved as quickly as I could comfortably go back to my barrack and rushed to my cot.

The book still lay there, the paperback cover tattered and creased. I snagged it from the bed and fanned the pages and then stopped and went back a few pages where I had seen words written inside.

I'm sorry. I just can't do it anymore. There was a twisted line drawn next to it, and I stared at the drawing for a few seconds before I realized what it was.

I spun and raced from the room. I yanked the orange alarm handle as I rushed past. In the front room, one of the guys was lying on the couch reading a book.

He looked up at me as I ran around the corner, concerned at my fast approach and the alarm that was going off in the building. He sat up quickly. "What's wrong?"

"Tell them to come to the climbing wall!" I shouted as I burst out the front door.

I hadn't run in months. If I tried, the pain would be so bad that it took my breath away. I didn't feel the pain this time, not in my back. I ran as fast as I could go, and as I realized there were people behind me, I also realized that I was moving at a pretty fast clip.

I heard my name yelled, but I just kept going. At the building, I skidded to a stop at the door, slamming my shoulder against it before I was able to jerk it open. Feet continued to pound right behind me, and I bolted forward. Several sets of feet were behind me now, all moving as fast as I was. I skidded around the corner, used my hand to help me make it around the next one, and then I was yanking open the door to the rock wall.

The scene in front of me had me pausing for only a second before I was back in motion. I raced to the wall and jumped. I knew that you weren't supposed to do a climbing wall without safety equipment, but I had no choice.

I was hand over foot, climbing as fast as I could as I heard more voices below, and someone screamed. I looked to my left as a hand came into view beside me, and after I glanced again, I saw it was Derek. Side by side, we made the climb, neither of us wearing safety harnesses, and if either of us slipped, we'd be dead, but that didn't stop us.

Derek was faster than I was, and at the top, he threw down his hand and helped me the last two feet. The two of us ran along the top of the wall to where Alan was curled in a ball.

In his hands was a rope with a large circle tied off. He was sobbing and saying over and over again, "I couldn't do it. I couldn't do it. Oh, my God! I'm so sorry. I couldn't do it."

Derek and I looked at one another, and then together, we looked over the side of the wall. Alan hadn't been talking about himself. He hadn't been apologizing to us. He had been apologizing to the man who now hung lifeless by a rope six feet down, swinging just the tiniest bit back and forth. Alan had been apologizing to Jersey.

CHAPTER THIRTY-FOUR

GRACELYN

*I*t was almost a week after the misunderstanding with Brady, and I was at work. Doug had been traveling, and we hadn't had much of a chance to speak. To be honest, I was glad. I was able to go about my job and do it without the pressure of him being around, not that he was pressure, but it kept me from having to say anything.

He was getting back into the office this afternoon and said he had a project that would require my assistance. Quite honestly, I loved projects. I loved to be busy. There was nothing worse than sitting around twiddling my thumbs, but the thought of being in the office after hours with him put me slightly on edge.

When he arrived in the office and explained what he would need to do and how long it would take, I made a phone call and lined up a pickup of the boys from Clara. She was still feeling guilty for what had happened to Dane and had asked me a dozen times if there was something she could do to help. This would make her feel so much better, and I knew the boys would be in good hands.

After that was taken care of, I ran out to the local office supply store to acquire all the supplies we needed. When I returned to the office, Doug was working on the reports that would go with what I brought in his office, and I started working on the 243-page report for the forty-six people who would be in attendance at the presentation in two days in the conference room.

For the most part, Doug and I worked separately, but after he ordered dinner, he was done with his end of the work and came to join me where we ate and chatted as we had in the past. I no longer felt uncomfortable as we laughed and resumed working. It took us another hour to add the dividers and tabs to the binders' appropriate places. Tomorrow, I would pack all of these up and ship them overnight to the meeting that had been arranged.

I was exhausted but glad that I was able to get this done. It sounded like it was going to be an excellent sale for the company, and it was nice to be part of that, even if it was in a small way. I was cleaning up my space in the conference room when Doug joined me on my side of the table. I didn't think anything of it until his shoulder brushed mine, and then I shifted off to the side slightly to put a bit of distance between us.

His hand landed on my lower back, and I went rigid.

"Gracelyn, what's wrong?"

I rolled my shoulders back as I faced him, ready to tell him that I would appreciate it if he could keep his hands to himself—except as I looked up at him and saw the concern there, the confusion, I hesitated just the slightest bit.

"Um, Doug, I know we are friends or have been friends, but I think we need to shift our relationship back to being boss and employee."

He chuckled. "I thought that was what we were."

"We are."

He shuffled forward just the slightest bit as he placed his

body in front of mine. My backside was now against the conference table, and my hands gripped the sides.

"Then I don't see the problem, Gracelyn."

I wanted to stand as tall as I could, but I would almost be pressing against his body if I did that. I didn't want to have the thought, but the image of our bodies pressed against one another slipped over my mind. I shook my head to rid the image and lifted my face higher.

"Doug, I need you to take a step back, please."

He cocked his head. "Gracelyn, come on. Don't be like that." He ran his fingertips up my arm and then touched the side of my face. "You know I care about you. I've missed you these last few days."

"That's kind of you, but I still need you to step back."

Doug took hold of my face tenderly as he stared down at me. "Do you know how long I have wanted to show you how much I care about you? How long I have wanted to hold you like this and kiss you?"

I was tongue-tied, and my heart was pounding so hard in my chest that I almost felt dizzy. Doug leaned forward when I didn't respond and was almost to my lips when I realized what he was about to do—what *I* was about to do!

I shoved him back, and because he hadn't expected that, he stumbled slightly, and it gave me the room to dart past him, except his hand snaked out and grabbed my elbow. I squealed as he spun me around and pushed me roughly against the wall. His lips crashed over mine, and panic clawed through my chest.

If I didn't get away from him, he was going to rape me. I knew it. There was only one thing I could do. I stopped fighting his kiss and instead gave in to it. I led him to believe that I had been playing hard to get, and now he'd won. He groaned as I returned his kiss, and he ran his hands down my sides. I gagged down the vomit that wanted to explode from my mouth.

As his lips left my mouth, he started placing kisses on my

neck, his hands on my sides, his thumbs just under the swell of my breasts. This put a gap between our bodies, and I arched my back to create even more space. I gritted my teeth and clenched my eyes, and when I knew he was thoroughly distracted, I brought my knee up swiftly and right into his groin.

A long time ago, I had accidentally hit Brady there when we had been horsing around in bed, and I knew from the light tap I had given Brady then that the pain that Doug was feeling now was a thousandfold. He made a gurgling sound in his throat as he cupped himself and staggered back to his knees.

I was around him and running for the door in seconds. As I hit the threshold, I spun around. "Take that as my termination letter." I grabbed my purse, the two pictures that I kept on the corner of my desk, and my mug, and took off for the front door. I didn't care about anything else.

It wasn't until I was home and the boys were in bed that I second-guessed what I had done. I turned off all the lights in the house and was glad that this place had a garage. My car was inside, and no one would know if I was home. In my bedroom, behind closed drapes, I reached out to Remy and asked if she could talk.

A few minutes later, my phone rang, and I was surprised to find Lauren on the other line. "I didn't mean to trouble you, Lauren. I was hoping to speak to Remy."

"Remy took over one of my sessions tonight. She asked me to reach out since she couldn't. What's going on, Gracelyn? You sound very agitated."

"Oh, Lauren, I have no idea what I just did!" I rubbed my forehead and explained to her everything. Lauren listened to me for almost thirty minutes.

"You did the right thing, Gracelyn. It was obvious that he was not going to take no for an answer."

"Yeah, I guess, but Lauren, now I don't have a job, and Brady is going to lose his! I have no clue what I'm supposed to do now."

"You said you were an administrative assistant, right?"

"Yes."

She chuckled over the phone. "What are your thoughts on moving to Tennessee?"

"What?"

"Well, I'm not sure if you'd be qualified or even interested, but Shane's secretary, Sabrina, is about to take a new position. He's going to be looking for a new administrative assistant."

"Are you serious? You are offering me a job?"

"More like I'm offering you an opportunity to *interview* for the job."

"I'm not sure what Brady would think of that."

"Don't tell him, not right now. This is your life. He's focused on his. He's got a long time before he's ready to move on, so let's work on you first. Do you think there is any way that you can fly out here and do an interview, check out the company in person?"

"Would I get to see Brady?"

"No." She chuckled. "If you did, he'd wonder why, and then he would be worried about you."

I winced. "Yeah, I guess you are right."

"Well, what do you think? I can make flight arrangements for you. I'd send you a plane, but they are tied up right now."

"Oh, no! I couldn't accept a private plane anyway."

"Okay, well, you make arrangements for the boys, and I'll get your flight arrangements."

"Alright." I was grinning as we hung up the phone, and she said that she would talk to me the next day.

*T*hree days later, I was walking into the main building at Rise Again Warrior. I was also trying not to let my jaw hang open at the gorgeous lobby. Pictures lined the walls, and I took a few moments to admire them as I waited. I expected Lauren to come down, but instead, Nate Hardy showed up and welcomed me with open arms.

"It's great to see you. I couldn't believe it when I heard you were going to be here."

"Thank you. It's wonderful to see you, too, Nate. How is Brady?"

He put his hands on my shoulders, and while he was in my personal space, it didn't feel anything like it had with Doug. This felt safe. "Brady is good. He's progressing, just as he should be."

"He doesn't know I'm here, does he?"

"Nope, and we aren't going to tell him either. Let's see how things go. I'm going to take you up to Shane's office now."

"I was reading about Shane on the website. What an impressive man."

"He is impressive and slightly intimidating, even when he's in his wheelchair, but don't let that bother you. He's really as sweet as a teddy bear."

As we took the steps up, my curious eyes scampered around the work area visible below. So many people were working on such an important cause. My heart filled with love, pride, and thankfulness for what they were all doing.

When we arrived at Shane's office, Nate introduced me to Sabrina and explained that she'd just earned her therapy certifications and would soon be working behind the wire. I was glad that I knew that they called the facility out back the area behind the wire, but I was surprised that it was as impressive as it was.

I stood in Shane's office, Nate beside me, and looked out

over the entire complex. "Wow, and Brady is out there someplace."

Nate pulled out his phone and looked at something. Then he leaned closer and pointed. "See that two-story building on the left side?"

"Yeah."

"He's in there right now."

I stared at every inch of the building like I might be able to get just a peek of him. "How do you know where he is?"

"They are on strict schedules. I know that, right now, he is in one of his concussion therapies."

I turned to look at Nate. "You have his schedule memorized?"

He laughed. "No." He lifted his phone. "I can look to see where someone is supposed to be through the phone."

"Ah, okay."

A throat clearing behind us had me turning to see a handsome man with dark hair rolling toward us. He observed me, and I wondered if he was waiting to see if I would react to his scar. After being around Will, I didn't notice scars as much, and I had seen pictures of Mr. Logan online, so it wasn't a surprise.

I put my hand out. "Mr. Logan, it is such an honor to meet you."

"Gracelyn, the pleasure is all mine." He shook my hand in a very businesslike manner and then asked me to have a seat. Nate said he would see me later and closed the door on his way out.

I glanced toward the window. "I know I'm here for an interview, and I sincerely appreciate your time on that, but if I might, I wanted to touch on another subject quickly."

He looked puzzled but intrigued. "Sure, what is it that you wanted to talk about?"

I pointed to the window, and he followed my focus. "What

you have built—what you are doing—it's incredible. Thank you so very much for that and for being here for those men and women."

I saw pride in his features but also humility as he smiled slightly and lowered his head. "I can't take all the credit. A lot of people have been involved in the creation of Rise Again Warrior."

"Yes, I am aware. I have done a lot of research on your company, Mr. Logan."

"Shane, please."

"Shane." I tipped my head as I slipped to the edge of my seat and spoke excitedly to him. "I have gone over all the company's financials from the website and your lists of attributes. I pretty much combed your site from top to bottom. I read about fifteen other articles about your company, including several interviews with you, Lauren, and Nate, and a woman named Dana Donahue."

He cocked his head slightly. "You do your homework. I like that."

"I didn't want to come in here and have you think that I'm only here because of my husband being here. I wanted you to know that I'm a capable person who wants to work hard and enjoy my job. I want to work for someone who is fair and can acknowledge my hard work, not that I'm looking for special treatment. I believe that people should be rewarded with at least a thank you for a job done well."

Shane smiled at me and then proceeded to ask me two dozen questions. Most were about my abilities and work ethics, but at the end, he asked me more questions about the company to see just how much research I had done on the company.

"I'm impressed, Gracelyn. I think you would be a fantastic asset here"—his eyes slipped to the window, and mine followed —"but what do you think your husband would say once he learned that you were working here? I know that Brady had an issue with the fact that we were in contact with you about his treatment, so what is he going to think when he finds out you've been right here watching over him?"

"Shane, I'm not here to watch over my husband. That is your job or his team's job. I won't deny that it's nice to know that he is almost within reach, but I would never do anything or want to know anything that I shouldn't know."

"Would you be alright if we locked down his file so that you had no access?"

"Why would I even want access to his file?"

"Sometimes, my assistant needs to check certain things out, so they have access to some of the confidential records."

"Sir, if you want to block me from his records, by all means, block me from his records. I do not need to have access to his stuff. When and if I need to be made aware of something, someone on his team can let me know." I paused. "I will admit that since I started researching your company and learning more, I am excited at the prospect of being involved in something like this."

As Shane remained quiet, the two of us locked eyes, and the only muscles I moved were my eyelids as they blinked every once in a while.

"How long do you think you'd need to get moved out here? We can help with the moving expenses and assist you in finding suitable living arrangements nearby."

I swallowed, afraid that I had heard him wrong. "Are you offering me the job?"

"Yes, Gracelyn, I am. I think you would be a fantastic addition to the organization." He handed me a folder that had been sitting on the table in front of us and asked me to read it over. Inside was the salary and benefits package. It was quite a bit more than I had previously earned.

I wanted to burst to my feet and giggle with excitement, but instead, I closed the folder and glanced out the window. Then I stood and stepped around the table, putting my hand out. "Shane, I would like to accept your offer."

CHAPTER THIRTY-FIVE

BRADY

*D*erek called down below and told someone to get everyone else out of there, and then he instructed me to take care of Alan. I was on the ground, trying to get Alan up, when he wiggled into my lap and sobbed, clinging to me like I was rescuing him.

A few people had materialized at the top, and I realized there was a set of steps up the wall's back side. They tried to get Alan up, but he refused. I told them to leave him for a little while and attend to Jersey.

Alan stopped sobbing as Derek and someone else lowered Jersey's body to the ground. One of the doctors from the med center arrived and pronounced his time of death officially, and then I watched as they put his body into a black bag and lifted it to a stretcher.

I didn't realize until he was out of the room that I had been silently crying along with everyone else. Derek squatted in front of Alan. "We have to get up now, Alan. It's time to get out of here."

Derek and one of the nurses helped him get up, and then someone else took Derek's side, and they helped Alan to the back stairs. Derek looked at me, his eyes red-rimmed as I was sure mine were.

"How is your back?"

"It's not important," I responded.

Derek stepped closer to me. "It is important, Brady. Your well-being is fundamental, especially after something like this. I know you are shaken to the core, and you ran like a bat out of hell. Your back and leg must be killing you."

"I guess."

"Come on, let's get you down the stairs and get you checked out."

"I don't need to be checked out." He grunted, but as we started down the stairs, I stumbled slightly. My legs were like jelly, and the numbness that I had in my back was now gone. A million pinpricks poked my spine.

Derek put his arm around my shoulders for support. "Yeah, you don't need to get checked out, my ass."

I tried to laugh, but it came out as a groan. When we reached the bottom, I struggled to put one foot in front of the other. A wheelchair showed up out of nowhere, and behind the handle was Shane Logan.

"Have a seat, Brady. We'll get you to med to check you out."

"Thank you, sir."

I sat gingerly, and Derek said something to Mr. Logan as he wheeled me away, but my focus was on the rope that was lying on the floor at the base of the wall.

How could Jersey have done that? He had just gotten out of building three! He said he was better. He wasn't thinking about killing himself anymore! Why?

What had he told Alan?

"This was my fault," I said.

Derek slowed the chair. "Come again?"

"This was my fault. Alan told me they were going to do this —well, not in so many words."

Derek came to a stop and waved someone over, holding up a finger to me to wait. Mr. Logan joined us, along with Nate. "What are you talking about, Brady? Why do you think it is your fault?"

I looked into the faces of three strong men—men who in another time could have been my friends—or my commanders at the very least. I had a lot of respect for them and all they were doing here.

"Not that long ago, Jersey showed Alan and me the wall. The staff was just starting to go through training for it. Alan and Jersey both commented on how there were so many ropes and how it would be the perfect place to commit suicide."

"Just because you guys were there and that was said, that does not make it your fault," Derek said gruffly.

I shook my head. "No, not that. The other day I had asked Alan about the book that he always carried around with him. He said after he finished reading it, he'd loan it to me." My head hung, the image of Alan dropping the book onto my cot came to me and his words whispered through my mind. A tear fell into my lap, and I lifted my face to them again. "Tonight, Alan gave me that book, but he wasn't *loaning* it to me. He was *giving* it to me. He told me he was done with it."

"What exactly did he say?"

"He said, 'I don't need it anymore,' and he said that twice." I rubbed my hands over my face. "I should have realized what was going on! I didn't see the signs, not until we were at dinner and he and Jersey were missing. I ran back to the barracks, and I looked at the book. There was a note that said 'I'm sorry' and a small drawing of a rope about midway through it. I knew exactly where they were."

Mr. Logan's hands were fisted at his sides, but then he leaned forward and got into my face. "This is not your fault, Brady. You saved Alan. I'm sorry that you were not able to save Jersey, but you did save Alan."

I cried, "Did I? Did I save him, or is he just going to try again?"

"I don't know, Brady, but you saved him for now. You had his back; you figured it out before he found the courage to go through with it."

I felt sick. The image of Jersey hanging, the sound of Alan's wailing, the pain in my back, and the agony in my heart were making vicious waves of nausea race through me.

Mr. Logan stood and spoke softly. "Get him to med and do not leave his side."

The chair started to roll again, and before I knew it, we were in the med center, and I was being hoisted up onto a gurney, my back screaming in pain as a migraine crashed over me.

I woke up a while later, the room semi-dark, and two people were talking right outside the door. As I shifted, Derek stepped into the room, followed by his fiancée, Dana.

She rushed to my side, her bright-blue eyes filled with unshed tears as she took my hand. "Brady, how are you?"

"I'm okay. How is Alan?"

"He's resting," Derek said.

"How long was I out?"

"About three hours," Derek commented and then grinned. "You nap like an old man."

I laughed slightly. "How is everyone else?"

Derek sighed. "Well, the facility is kind of in lockdown mode. Everyone is confined to their barracks, and all the support staff is here working with them all." He paused. "We found out what happened, what caused Jersey to fall back."

"What?"

"His best friend was killed overseas. They were best friends in high school and all through the military. When Jersey got out, his buddy said he was going to do one more tour to rack up the hazard pay, and then he was going to get out."

"Damn," I muttered.

"Yeah, we didn't know about it," Dana added, "because he got a text from his buddy's brother earlier today. I guess when that happened, Jersey didn't just stumble. He fell." She winced at her words. "Sorry, bad choice of words."

I nodded. "Makes sense. They say it only takes one bad event to toss us back into the demon den."

"Yes," Derek said, "but that demon den has a lock and key. It's up to you if you want to unlock it and step in."

Derek and Dana shared a look, and then Derek looked earnestly at me. "Where is your head right now, Brady? Are you standing at the door to your demon den?"

I frowned as I pondered that. "I don't think so," I finally replied.

"You sure? Because this kind of thing can kick a lot of people back to that door."

"Yeah, I'm sure. That door is closed. Maybe it's strange, but seeing Jersey hanging there lifeless, or maybe it was seeing all the people staring up at him, upset, angry, hurt, but it shifted me somehow."

"What do you mean by that, Brady?" a woman's voice interrupted what Derek was going to say, and we all looked toward the door as Lauren stepped in.

"I mean, I've seen a lot of dead people, and I kind of got numb to that, but I wasn't numb to it today. I saw and felt *all* of it. I was angry at him for doing that, for not speaking out! I was sad because he hurt so damn much that he couldn't get past it, and no one knew!" Angry tears rolled down my cheeks. "I saw all those people standing there, upset and pissed off and broken —just shattered—and I realized that I never want to cause those emotions. I can't imagine doing that to my wife, to my children, to any of you."

Derek smiled sadly, and I saw moisture wavering in his eyes. Dana squeezed my hand and sniffed, and Lauren stepped to the foot of the bed and smiled.

She put her hand on my ankle and squeezed. "And welcome to the next phase of your recovery, Brady."

---

*T*he next day, I asked if I could reach out to my wife, and Derek said I could. I was sitting in the office, staring at the phone and getting up the courage to call her as I thought back over the last night.

Lauren had said I was stepping into the next phase. Tomorrow, I would leave building three and transition over to the other barracks. I had sworn that if I felt like I was ready to unlock that demon den door, then I would let someone know.

I hated what Jersey had done, and the facility's mood was pretty low today as everyone felt its effects. The volume was lower in the food hall than usual, as many people spoke about what they knew of him. I had quite a few people who I didn't know approach me and thank me for trying to save him. Every single one of them made me want to break down in sobs because I hadn't been able to. I tried to remember what Derek had said. Had I not put two and two together, Alan might also be dead.

Alan was still resting in the med center under sedation, and I wasn't sure what would happen to him now.

I picked up the phone and dialed Gracelyn's number. After two rings, she answered, and I almost dropped my head to the desk and sobbed. "Gracey," I finally managed to get out as the tears started rolling.

"Brady, oh, my Lord, Brady. I heard about Jersey and what you did for Alan. I am so sorry, honey. Are you okay?"

"I'm okay. I just needed to hear your voice." I tried to smile through the tears as I heard her sob. It didn't even faze me that she knew what had happened here. I was glad that she did because I didn't have to pretend I was okay or tell her what had happened.

"I'm so glad you needed to hear my voice, but are you really okay? That could not have been easy for you."

"No, it was hard, baby, but it made me realize something."

"What? What could something like that have made you realize?"

"That I don't want to die. That I don't want to hurt you or the kids like that, and that I can't live without you and the boys."

I heard her crying. "Brady, I love you so much. You know that I love you so much. I wish I could hold you right now. I wish I were there to wrap my arms around you and hold you, but I'm trying to right now. Imagine me there. Close your eyes and pretend."

"I'm so sorry, Gracelyn."

"Sorry? For what?"

"For putting you through this, for accusing you and leaving you. I shouldn't be upset that you were turning to someone else. I was jealous that I couldn't give you what you needed."

"Brady Vanover, let's just get one thing straight right now. You are all that I need. You are all that your boys need. We love you, and whatever you face, *we* face together. You got that?"

I laughed slightly. "Yeah, I got that."

"So I heard that family visitation is in three weeks. Do you want the boys and me to come? We will stay away if that's what you want."

"Are you kidding? I need to see you guys. I'm not going to run from you or these problems anymore, Gracelyn. I'm going to face them, but I need your help. I can't do it alone."

"Oh, Brady, you will never be alone again. Not only do you have me, but you have all of Rise Again Warrior on your side too."

"I love you so much, Gracelyn," I choked out as I fought not to break down. "I don't know what I would do without you."

"You don't have to worry about that, Brady. Before you know it, I'll be there. I'm here for you, honey—always."

I could not thank her enough for what she said. After we got off the phone, I took my mandatory therapy walk and thought over how lucky I was to have her in my life. She was such a strong woman, and I was determined to prove to her that I was worth it.

That night I lay down and stared at Alan's cot. In the center of it was his book. This time, a note that I had written to Alan was on the cover. "This belongs to you. Don't you ever give it away again."

I smiled as I rolled to my side and drifted off to sleep, thinking about my wife. I might be in pain, mentally and physically, but I would learn to deal with it and live a life to be proud of.

CHAPTER THIRTY-SIX

GRACELYN

I had spoken to Brady a couple of times over the last three weeks, but he still didn't know that I was working here at RAW. In fact, I had just finished my first official week, and while I was kept on my toes, I loved every minute of it. I also loved that I could look out the window of Shane's office and feel closer to Brady.

The boys hadn't been too happy about having to leave their friends or their sports teams, but luckily, Sabrina had helped out with that. She even found new teams for them to join. My new friends also helped me find a house that was only fifteen minutes away. It was bigger and more elaborate than what we had been living in, but the cost of living was much lower here. It also offered us a large fenced-in backyard that backed up to a big field. The boys loved it because it gave them lots of space to play their sports and just be boys.

I adored the kitchen and the fancy master bathroom. I couldn't wait for Brady to see it, and as we climbed into my minivan to head to family day, the butterflies burst forth in my belly.

Initially, I wasn't going to tell Brady that I had a job here, but the more I thought about it, the more I realized that I needed him to know. I wanted him to be aware that I was here, close by and waiting for him. I needed him to know that I was ready to build a new life with him and take his recovery seriously.

"I can't believe we finally get to see Dad!"

"You guys have been so good about keeping our surprise a secret," I said to them as I backed out of our driveway.

"Dad is going to be so surprised to find out we are living here in Tennessee now."

"Yes, he is." I grinned and hoped that it would be a good surprise.

As we drove to RAW, my cellphone rang, and I glanced at the screen. I sent the caller to voicemail. I didn't want my good mood ruined, and these days that was generally what happened when I spoke with my mother. She still didn't understand what the big deal was and why I would keep saying that Brady had been suicidal. If I even brought up his treatment, she hushed me and said that I shouldn't talk about such nonsense in front of the boys.

Her thought was that men were tough and should be able to handle the stress. If they couldn't, they weren't man enough. It irked me something awful. The last time I had spoken with her, I'd told her that it was alright for men to cry and hurt. It was okay for them to be weak with pain and heartbreak, and they did not have to be strong all the time.

The problem was that my mother was not the only person out there to have that opinion. So many people denied the fact that men could hurt. They refused to accept that a man could weep without being labeled a coward or weak.

It was the opposite. It took a strong man to admit he was hurting, to ask for help, to bare his soul to others, and to say, Please, I need assistance.

People with mental health issues should not be pushed aside or stereotyped as lost causes or people to be feared. Yes, some of them might be dangerous, but all humans were dangerous if need be.

I never would have thought I could do to Doug what I did, but when push came to shove, I resorted to physical pain to free myself. Didn't that make me dangerous?

For a moment, I thought of Doug. The day after that incident, I had emailed my resignation over to him. I never received a response from him, but a few days later, my final paycheck arrived, along with the rest of my things from my desk via messenger.

Then I had come here and met Shane and landed my new job. Within two weeks, we were packed and moved and put into a new house, and now I was going to see my husband whom I hadn't seen in about two months. It was almost like he was coming home from deployment today. That excitement of seeing him again, of holding him again, was almost overwhelming.

We drove to the facility and parked near the front, where I usually parked for work. The place was busy, and people were everywhere. Several waved and said hello to me as we walked the distance between the main building and the wire.

Today the gates were open, but we still needed to sign in. Instead of flashing my work badge, I marked myself as a guest of Brady. The boys and I were searching everywhere for him as we entered the grounds. I hadn't told Brady when we would be here, so he wasn't hanging around here waiting.

"Gracelyn." Dana waved her arm in the air. I had met her the other day, and I adored her. We had lunch, and she told me all about her wedding.

She hugged me when I reached her, and I introduced her to the boys as Derek joined us.

"Gracelyn, glad you made it." He winked at me. "So you must be Dane, and you're Drew, right?"

The boys shook his hand as Dane answered, "Yeah, how do you know who we are?"

"Your father has told me all about you. You want to go see him?"

"Yes!" Drew said excitedly as he jumped up and down.

"Come on, guys. I know exactly where he is."

As we walked, Derek asked the boys how they liked their new home, and I took the time to look around. I had purposefully not been given a tour of this area so that Brady wouldn't know I was working here yet. Now, I was sucking up all the details that I had been learning about all week long. I was so impressed by all of it and couldn't wait to take my formal tour finally.

Derek was a few feet in front of me as Dana pointed something out off to the side. Derek whistled and yelled for Brady. The butterflies in my belly went wild as I stepped around Derek to get my first look at Brady.

He was standing with two other guys, smiling and laughing about something, a red plastic cup in his hand, and I felt like I was seeing a man from the past. My eyes started to fill with tears as Drew took off for his father.

I was about to call Drew back, afraid that Drew would hurt Brady when he smashed into him, but Derek put his hand on my arm and stopped me.

Brady turned as he heard Drew's voice yelling for him and had just enough time to squat down and catch his son to his chest. Brady's eyes closed as he held him tightly, and tears eased down my cheeks. Dane was approaching a little more slowly, but as he got closer, he began to run, and Brady opened his arms wider for Dane to come into his embrace.

"He looks so good," I said on a soft sob.

"Yes, he does," Dana replied from my side, where she held my arm.

I heard her sniff as Brady lifted his face and opened his eyes, searching for me. For a moment, the world disappeared around us, and then Brady said something to the boys, kissing both of their heads before he stood.

I wanted to run to him as Drew had. I wanted to throw myself into his arms and hold him forever, but I stepped forward slowly on knees that shook. I met Brady in the middle.

He stood a foot away, staring into my face, and his voice cracked with emotion as he said, "Gracelyn."

I smiled nervously up at him, wanting him to hold me but afraid he wouldn't. "Brady."

Brady curled one hand around my neck and pulled me forward to bring my mouth to his. He kissed me in a way that I hadn't been kissed in over a year. I whimpered as I clung to my husband and returned it.

"This place is PG, guys," Derek said gently beside us, and Brady pulled back, resting his forehead on mine as he chuckled.

"Sorry, I couldn't help it," he said, but I wasn't sure if it was meant for Derek or me.

Brady pulled me close and held me tight, tucking his face into my neck for a few seconds before he finally stepped back and looked at me. "God, I missed you."

"I'm glad to hear that. I missed you too, Brady. You look great."

He wiped my tears away. "Me?" He stepped back and looked me up and down. "You look fantastic. What have you been doing?"

"Taking control of my life. I've lost about six pounds. I still have a long way to go, but I'm taking much better care of myself, and Jessica, she's in my therapy group, her husband is Carl in Phase Two, well, she's been mentoring me on nutrition and exercise."

"You look great, Gracelyn." He frowned and looked away. "You know you don't have to do this for me. I know I said some harsh things—"

I put my fingertips over his mouth. "Brady, I'm doing this for me. I was very unhappy with who I was, with my weight. It has nothing to do with you." I paused. "Okay, so maybe a little bit does because I want you to like how I look."

He took hold of my face. "I like the way you look, Gracelyn. No, I love the way you look, Gracelyn."

He kissed me again, not quite as passionately or as long as the first time, but it was still an intimate kiss. He laced his fingers with mine and said, "Come on, I want to introduce you to a few people. I see you met Derek and Dana."

"Oh, I love Dana. She's fantastic," I said.

He gave me an odd look. He couldn't know how I could have had the opportunity to talk to her at length. I smiled to myself as we went back to the kids and the men with whom he'd been talking.

"This is Brett and Alan," he said as we reached them. "This is my wife, Gracelyn."

Brett smiled and said hello, and Alan turned to me and then glanced at Brady. "If I hug your wife, will you mind?"

"Nah, man. Go for it." Brady slapped him on the back, and Alan stepped forward.

I expected a small hug and never imagined him wrapping his arms tightly around me and holding me for a few seconds. I looked at Brady over his shoulder, worried that he would be upset, but Brady was grinning and winked.

Alan finally let me go, his cheeks pink. "Sorry. I just wanted to thank you."

"Thank me?"

"For being there for my sister and for standing behind Brady." He turned and looked at Brady, something passing between them that I couldn't read. "He's a good man."

"Well, you're welcome."

Brady turned to our boys, who were talking to Derek and another boy about Dane's age.

"Can we?" Dane asked Brady.

"Yep, you can. Do not go into any building unless you are escorted, but you can run around out here all you want, and do not go outside the fence."

Dane nodded, and the three boys took off toward a field where a bunch of other kids played.

"Hey, Gracelyn." I turned to see Paul Grobski behind me. I waved. Paul was in charge of IT here at RAW, and I had talked to him the other day about how great the website was. Brady glanced at me and then Paul but didn't say anything.

Brady had his arm around my shoulders when Glen Carter came rolling by in his wheelchair. He also worked in the front office. "Gracelyn, it's good to see you again. Is this your husband, Brady?"

"Um, yes, it is. Brady, this is Glen. He works in the main building."

Brady shook his hand, and I saw him looking at me, but before I could say anything or answer the burning question in his eyes, Shane and Lauren approached us, a little girl with dark hair in Shane's arms.

"Brady, Gracelyn, how are you all doing today?" He shook Brady's hand and then directed his next set of words to me. "I bet it's a different view down here for you."

"It is," I replied before I gnawed on my bottom lip and smiled at the little girl he was holding. "Hello, Becca. How are you, sweetie?"

Brady frowned as he shifted away from me slightly. "How do you know all these people, and what did he mean by a different view?"

Shane chuckled. "Whoops, he doesn't know yet, does he?"

"Know what?"

I shook my head toward Shane as Lauren took Shane by the arm and said, "I think this is our cue to go."

"What's going on?" Brady asked after they walked away.

315

"Let's sit down."

"Gracelyn, I don't want to sit down."

"This is kind of a long story, Brady. You might not want to sit down, but I do."

"Fine." He led me to a picnic table over to the side. "What's going on?"

I took a moment to figure out how to say it and then decided to tell him the whole truth.

"So you were right, and Doug wanted more from me than me being an employee"—I put my hand up to stop him from talking—"but I put him in his place, and I quit."

"You quit your job?"

"Yes. He—" I stopped to gather my thoughts. "Let's just say that it ended very badly, but I did quit."

"When was this?"

"A few weeks ago."

"Why didn't you tell me, Gracelyn?"

"Because you had other things to worry about, Brady. Don't worry. I already have another job."

He leaned back, surprised. "You do?"

"Yes."

"Where?"

I grinned at him and then looked over his shoulder at the main building. "Right up there."

He looked back and seemed confused. "What are you talking about?"

I took his hand, hoping he couldn't feel the quivering in mine. "Brady, I work for Shane Logan now. I'm his new administrative assistant."

CHAPTER THIRTY-SEVEN

BRADY

Over the last few weeks, I had been putting one hundred percent into myself and my recovery. I took every therapy session seriously. In group therapy, I shared. I also listened and made sure to respond to those talking. In concussion therapy, I excelled by leaps and bounds and was about to test out of the speech side.

I still got headaches, and sometimes words were wonky, but for the most part, even my brain was finally recovering from the blast injury. My thigh was getting stronger every day, and my first surgery on my spine for the experimental procedure was scheduled for next week. If it went well, I would probably undergo at least two more.

I hadn't said anything to Gracelyn about it and wondered if I should tell her today or wait until after it was over. I didn't want to get her hopes up if it didn't work. Dealing with my frustration was going to be hard enough. I'd have to wait and see if it felt right to discuss it today.

As we prepared for Family Day, I found myself more excited than I had been in years. I couldn't wait to see my boys and hold my wife. I had only been gone a couple of months, but I already felt like a new man. I knew I had a ways to go, but I also knew I would get there.

Cal had also helped me decide to stick with mechanics, and I was going to learn more about other types of helicopters. I had always enjoyed tinkering with their mechanics, and there were jobs for mechanics out there. Maybe one day I could even learn to fly one. Now that would be cool.

I was talking to Alan and Brett when I heard Derek call my name, but it was another couple of seconds before I turned when I heard Drew's voice. I made it to my knee just in time to collect him against me, and I struggled to keep my composure. Then Dane was there, and I felt like a piece of me that had been dormant was coming to life. Now all I needed was my wife.

I searched her out. She was a breath of fresh air as I stared into her beautiful face. She was nervous, I could tell, but as I kissed my boys and told them I'd be right back, I knew she was just as excited as I was.

Holding her in my arms again was incredible, but so was kissing her. Man, I had missed her lips. I missed all of her. I felt like I could overcome any obstacle with her at my side, and I wanted to shout to everyone around me that this was my Gracelyn, my wife—except many people already seemed to know my wife, even people that I didn't know. "How do you know all these people, and what did he mean by a different view?"

A moment later, Shane and Lauren were gone, and Gracelyn and I were sitting down at a table off to the side. "What's going on?"

Gracelyn sat there nervously for a moment. "So you were right, and Doug wanted more from me than me being an employee."

I was going to say, See, I told you, but I held back as she gave me a look and held up her hand.

"But I put him in his place, and I quit."

"You quit your job?" I stared at her in surprise.

"Yes. He—" She hesitated. "Let's just say that it ended very badly, but I did quit."

"When was this?"

"A few weeks ago."

A few weeks ago? Damn! What were we going to do now? Stress began to blossom in my chest as the protector and provider in me sprang back to life. "Why didn't you tell me, Gracelyn?"

"Because you had other things to worry about, Brady. Don't worry. I already have another job."

Don't worry. Ha! Wait, she had a job? "You do?"

"Yes."

"Where?"

She was smiling at me, her eyes lighting up as she stared over my shoulder. "Right up there."

I looked at the administrative building, perplexed. "What are you talking about?"

Gracelyn held my hand. "Brady, I work for Shane Logan now. I'm his new administrative assistant."

"What?"

"After I quit, I put a message in to Remy—she's my group therapist—and she wasn't available, so Lauren called me back. I told her everything that had happened, and she mentioned that Shane needed a new assistant. I came out and interviewed."

"How long have you been here?"

"A week."

"You've been living in Tennessee for a week, and you didn't tell me?"

"I didn't want to add to your stress."

I laughed. "And this doesn't add to my stress? My wife is now hovering over my therapy, working for the man who runs this program."

"Brady, I'm not hovering over your therapy. This is the first

319

time I have been down here, and I have not been privileged to see any of your information. I asked Shane to lock it so that I couldn't access it. You have a team of therapists that are helping you. I have nothing to do with what is going on here."

"Then why did you take a job here?" I was angry, but I didn't want to be.

"Brady, honey, I took the job, first of all, because it's a fantastic job. The money and benefits are great, but the real reason I took it is that I love what they do here. I love what this organization is doing, trying to make a change, and I want to be a part of that, however small."

"Are you serious?" My anxiety began to subside.

"Yes. Since you have been here, I've seen so much and heard so many people talking about mental health, and I hate the stigma that goes with that about it being bad. I want to help change that and help other people who are struggling to find peace with themselves."

"And you think working for Shane does that?"

She laughed, holding her hand out. "Look around you, Brady. Who is doing this? It's not just Nate and Derek or any of your therapists. It's all the hard work that goes on up there in that building. That is what makes all this happen back here. I might not have my hand directly in helping, but I am helping. I love my job and working for Shane. He is such an amazing and inspirational man."

"Okay, but what about when I'm done here? What am I supposed to do?"

She tilted her head. "Did you have something back in Colorado that you wanted to do?"

"No, not really."

"Then why not start fresh here? You'd be close to friends, to our families, and you'd get a new start."

I glanced around. Maybe I'd be able to do volunteer work here if I was in the area. I did like it here, and Derek and I had become good friends. In fact, he had asked me to help him tailor a few workouts for a couple of the guys who wanted to get into bodybuilding. Maybe I'd be able to continue doing that. "I guess that would work."

"We have a world of opportunities, Brady. The boys love their new school, and thanks to everyone here, we found a great house only fifteen minutes away, and the boys are both already on sports teams."

I laughed, but a part of me felt left out. "You just started a whole new life without me."

She shook her head quickly. "Oh, no, not without you. I couldn't have done this without all of our friends. They are helping us. They are giving us a good place to start over. I took lots of pictures of the house so I can show you, and when you are allowed to leave the base, Nate said he'd bring you over for an afternoon."

"You have it all figured out, huh?"

She tucked her bottom lip under her teeth. "Are you upset? I know it's a lot of changes, and I don't want to stress you out with them."

I cupped her cheek. "No, I'm not upset. Surprised, a little jealous you did it all on your own, but I'm also proud of you."

She leaned back. "Proud of me? For what?"

"For being so damn strong, for not giving up on me, and for moving forward to make sure that our family was taken care of when I couldn't do it. I can't tell you how proud of you that I am for doing all of that. Not all women can do that."

"Any woman could do that if it were for the right man," she replied with a smile. "I love you, Brady, with every ounce of my heart, and I am sorry that I didn't see what Doug was up to earlier. It might have saved us both some heartache."

"Hey." I pulled her closer. "It's okay. He's in the past."

I glanced over her shoulder as I saw someone coming toward us. A grin split my lips as I got to my feet. Will and Nora paused a few feet away, and suddenly, I had a knot in my throat, and my eyes filled with tears.

Will came forward, and we embraced. I couldn't help but shed a few tears as I stood there. I cleared my throat, as did he when we separated. "You look good, Brady."

"I have my life to thank you for," I told him. "If I had not walked into Purgatory that day, I might have gotten lost in the demon's den and never found my way out."

"I'm glad you did, man. That's what my purpose is now, to make sure I find and try to help others like us."

"I will never forget you or what you did."

"You better not," he joked, and then I hugged Nora.

The afternoon was fantastic, and even though my back ached and my head was starting to hurt from all the noise and activity, I didn't want it to end.

Now that I knew my family was closer, I felt even better. Gracelyn was happy, my boys were happy, and I knew that I would find my true happiness eventually.

Rise Again Warrior hadn't just helped me get over my depression and anxiety. It had helped me repair many aspects of my life. From my soul to my body to my marriage, and I could never thank them enough.

As I walked Gracelyn and the boys to the fence to say goodbye, Shane Logan approached us. He was now in his wheelchair, and his daughter was tucked into his arm and looking utterly wiped out.

Seeing that precious child in the arms of her father made me want another child. Maybe Gracelyn would be up for that once I was back home.

"Did you guys have a good day?" Shane asked.

"We did," Gracelyn said. "I am so glad I finally got to see all of this down here."

"I am too." He turned to me and held out a card.

"What's this?"

"The name of a friend of mine. He owns a company that makes helicopters about twenty minutes from here."

I stared at the card and then looked at him. "Why are you giving me this?"

He grinned. "Because he knows about you, and he wants you to reach out to him when you are ready to start the work program. He's retired air force, and he's a big supporter."

"You're helping me get a job?"

He glanced at Gracelyn and grinned. "Yeah, I kind of have selfish reasons for that." I looked between him and my wife before he continued, "Your wife is an incredible assistant, and I don't want to lose her. It only makes sense to help you find a job locally so that she doesn't leave."

Gracelyn hugged my arm as I chuckled. "I appreciate this, Shane."

"And I appreciate how hard you are working, Brady. You still have a lot of work to do, but we'll get you there. Just have faith in yourself." He winked and then rolled off to speak to someone else.

Will and Nora pulled the boys off to the side after I said goodbye to them, and I laced my fingers with my wife's as I got closer. "I miss you already."

"And I miss you, but at least, you can look up at the building and know I'm there eight to five all week long."

"That is true, and you can look down here and know I am somewhere behind the fence."

She grinned. "It's called inside the wire, even I know that."

I laughed as I leaned forward to kiss her. "Yes, it is." I tilted back after we finished and stared into her eyes. "I love you, Gracelyn Vanover. You have no idea how much it means to me that you stuck around."

"Don't be silly, Brady. Waiting for you to come to me is what I do. I look forward to the day that I only have to wait a few hours, and not months and weeks."

"Soon, baby. Soon I'll be myself, and I'll be home."

"No, you'll be better than yourself. We'll be better than our old selves."

"Yeah, we will, baby. We will."

As I watched my wife walk away with my sons and Will and Nora, I knew that I did have a few more hurdles to get over, but I was one huge step closer to being back with my family.

As I turned and looked back over the grounds, I realized that Gracelyn wasn't the only one who wanted to make a difference. I wanted to make sure that I stayed involved and was able to help my brothers and sisters too. I wasn't sure if I could do that as a mechanic, but I'd find a way.

If this place could repair me, then I needed to use my mechanic abilities to help repair other people—and I would.

The End

THE RISE AGAIN WARRIOR SERIES

This series will be an intense and emotional journey through the lives of many service members, their families, and their friends. Focusing on the trials that they face after wartime is over, and they have returned home to a nation that sometimes seems to have forgotten what they were fighting for, and what all of these people sacrificed in the name of Honor & Duty.

My hope with this series is to let those servicemen and women know that they are not forgotten but also to help those who don't understand to do just that: To understand the sacrifices that were made for our Freedom.

It is an honor to write this series, and while I am always proud of the work that I accomplish as a writer, I am humbled by this story and the future of this series.

God Bless America and all those who have fought, are fighting and will continue to fight for our freedom.

Mission: Believe (Book 1)

Staff Sgt. Shane Logan is lucky to have come from a privileged family, and after losing both of his legs in the war, he now has the best prosthetics that money can buy. While he is trying to move forward with life, he struggles with the past and the way people react to him and his disability.

Dr. Lauren Falcone works tirelessly to help veterans deal with the trauma and pain of their deployments. Her unique virtual approach to therapy keeps her busy, and the assistance she provides to service members as they recover mentally helps her resolve her own anxieties.

When Shane meets Lauren at a fundraiser for his father's organization, he wonders if there just might be a chance for him to get his dream off the ground and maybe find a normal life with someone who can look past his flaws and see the man he is inside.

Shane and Lauren are drawn to each other by their hope to make life easier for veterans, both physically and emotionally. Their goal is to build Shane's dream organization, Rise Again Warrior, that will assist veterans to integrate more easily into society and have the opportunity to receive state-of-the-art technology and therapy.

Now, if they can only have faith in themselves, learn to deal with their own demons, and believe in each other, they might find a way to bring this dream to fruition.

Mission: Accept (Book 2)

Dana Donahue might be Shane Logan's cousin, but she's nothing like him—she's quite the opposite of him. Her thoughts focus on what money and people can do for her. She never approved of Shane joining the military and knows little about the world he has lived in for most of his life. All that will change when she has to ask him for a job after her father cuts her off.

Derek Stall lives on the streets by choice—not circumstance. Memories of what he did under order sometimes haunt him, other times give him the strength to move through one more day until he can finish the mission he started.

A chance meeting between Dana and Derek will lead to an unlikely friendship that might just save his life, but the drastic differences between them could be the dividing wedge that keeps them apart.

When Derek feels he has to leave Rise Again Warrior to complete his mission, he begins to realize that he could be leaving behind more than just a few friends. Could he be leaving behind the possibility of a healthy future before he finally accepts his past?

Mission: Repair, (Book 3)

Technical Sergeant Brady Vanover had a solid career in the United States Air Force, along with a loving wife, and two young children. Everything was his for the taking, but after a non-life-threatening injury on deployment, Brady is for the first time unsure of his future.

Brady continues to struggle with his pain, fight the system, and figure out where his life will go now. With anger issues growing and his need to self-medicate with alcohol and pain medication, Brady finds himself teetering on the edge of losing his himself and his family.

With the help of the Rise Again Warrior organization, Brady will have to work hard to repair what he has damaged, both mentally and physically.

Mission: Courage (Book 4)

After ten years in the Army, Gianna Roberts is detached and unsure what to do with herself. As a single mom, the stress of being home and raising children she barely knows weighs heavily on her heart. Before long, she finds herself on a dangerous road of self-destruction.

When Gianna Roberts arrives at Rise Again Warrior, she clashes with Nate Hardy upon arrival, but these two find that they have more in common than they initially thought.

With a fragile relationship growing, Nate will help Gianna find her courage to be the mother that she needs to be and leave behind the guilt and pain from her past.

ABOUT THE AUTHOR

Stacy Eaton is a USA Today Best Selling author and began her writing career in October of 2010. Stacy took an early retirement from law enforcement after over fifteen years of service in 2016, with her last three years in investigations and crime scene investigation to write full time.

Stacy resides in southeastern Pennsylvania with her husband, who works in law enforcement, and her teen daughter. She also has a son who is currently serving in the United States Navy and has two grandchildren.

Be sure to visit www.stacyeaton.com for updates and more information on her books.

Sign up for all the latest information on Stacy's Newsletter!

ALSO BY STACY EATON

Download a FREE Series Guide of books written by Stacy Eaton
ROMANCE TO GET YOUR BLOOD PUMPING
This guide includes a listing of all of her current books and upcoming releases. It includes genre's, heat levels, series links to other series, and the first chapter of almost all of the books.

Rise Again Warrior Series

Mission: Believe, Book 1 **

Mission: Accept, Book 2 **

Mission: Repair, Book 3 ***

Mission: Courage, Book 4

Loving a Young Series

Wesley, Book 1

Henley, Book 2

Huntley, Book 3

Riley, Book 4

Kayley, Book 5

Bradley, Book 6

The Unexpected Series

Unexpected Packages

Unexpected Arrivals

Unexpected Trouble

Unexpected Storms

Unexpected Desires

Unexpected Ties (coming soon)

Paranormal Romance:

My Blood Runs Blue Series

My Blood Runs Blue, Book 1 **

The Pulse of Blue Blood, Book 2 (Short Story) **

Blue Blood for Life, Book 3 **

Mixing the Blue Blood, Book 4 **

Blue Bloods Final Destiny, Book 5 **

My Blood Runs Blue Series, Books 1-4 **

The Return of Blue Blood Series:

Kristin: Blue Blood Returns, Book 1 **

Hugh: Blue Blood Compelled, Book 2 **

Zander: Blue Blood Reborn, Book 3 ***

Lena: Blue Blood Desired, Book 4

Garda ~ Welcome to the Realm

The Twisted Love Series

with Amy Manemann Co-Author

Love Lorn, Book 1 (Manemann)**

Love Torn, Book 2 (Eaton)**

Love Inked, Book 3

Love Drowned, Book 4

Love Carved, Book 5

Love Trapped, Book 6

Love Crossed, Book 7 (Coming Soon)

Love Twisted, Book 8 (Coming Soon)

Love Lies, Book 9 (Coming Soon)

Domestic Violence – Crime - Suspense:

Whether I'll Live or Die**

Barbara's Plea

You're Not Alone**

Romantic Suspense:

Liveon ~ No Evil **

Second Shield **

Distorted Loyalty**

Six Days of Memories **

Second Shield II: The Return **

Contemporary Romance:

Tempt Me Too**

Finding the Strength

Finding Love in Special Places:

Stacy's Short Story Series

Finding Love on Christmas Vacation

Finding Love on the Summer Surf

Finding Love with Dear Santa

Finding Love with a Champagne Toast

Heart of the Family Series

Mistletoe & Cocoa Kisses, Book 1 **

Roses & Champagne Kisses, Book 2 **

Orchids & Hurricane Kisses, Book 3 **

Carnations & Hot Toddy Kisses, Book 4 **

Heal Me Series

Cured, Book 1 **

Revived, Book 2

Mended, Book 3

Rescued, Book 4

The Heal Me Series, Books 1-4

The Celebration Series

Tangled in Tinsel, Book 1 **

Tears to Cheers, Book 2 **

Heathens to Hearts, Book 3 **

Rainbows Bring Riches, Book 4 ***

Sweet as Sugar, Book 5 ***

Making Mom Mad, Book 6 ***

Sparklers or Spankings, Book 7 ***

Raffles to Rattles, Book 8 ***

Flirting with Fireworks, Book 9 ***

Working under Wheels, Book 10 ***

Masquerading at Midnight, Book 11 ***

Blessings & Beans, Book 12 ***

Velvet & Vows, Book 13 ***

The Celebration Series Box Sets:

Part One: Books 1-5

Part Two: Books 6-9

Part Three: Books 10-13

The Sometimes Series:

Sometimes You Win, Book 1**

Sometimes You Lose, Book 2**

Sometimes You Play The Game, Book 3**

The Sometimes Series: Win, Lose & Play Set **

Pleasure Your Fantasies Series

Mistletoe Fantasies, Book 1 **

Whispered Fantasies, Book 2

Secret Fantasies, Book 3

** These books are also available on Audio

*** These books are coming to Audio soon

List Update 5-18-21

Made in the USA
Middletown, DE
09 July 2021